WIPE OUT

TERESA GODFREY

Teresa Godfrey (signature)

ROSWELL
PRESS

an imprint of Sunbury Press, Inc.
Mechanicsburg, PA USA

an imprint of Sunbury Press, Inc.
Mechanicsburg, PA USA

For information about special discounts for bulk purchases, please contact Sunbury Press Orders Dept. at (855) 338-8359 or orders@sunburypress.com.

To request one of our authors for speaking engagements or book signings, please contact Sunbury Press Publicity Dept. at publicity@sunburypress.com.

FIRST ROSWELL PRESS EDITION: January 2022

Set in Adobe Garamond Pro | Interior design by Crystal Devine | Cover by Tyler Handa | Edited by Abigail Henson.

Publisher's Cataloging-in-Publication Data
Names: Godfrey, Teresa, author.
Title: Wipe out / Teresa Godfrey.
Description: First trade paperback edition. | Mechanicsburg, PA : Roswell Press, 2022.
Summary: This is a conspiracy theorist's worst nightmare. After a pandemic known as the Wipe Out, family is outlawed, friendships are forbidden, and pro-creation is government-controlled. When Hazel, a military driver, is ordered to find a mother and son, she uncovers a dark core of manipulation and exploitation far beyond anything she could have imagined.
Identifiers: ISBN : 978-1-62006-577-8 (softcover).
Subjects: FICTION / Dystopian | FICTION / Feminist | FICTION / Science Fiction / General.

Product of the United States of America
0 1 1 2 3 5 8 13 21 34 55

Continue the Enlightenment!

For Monica

CHAPTER

1

I know the rules. And the rules state that an Earth History team must consist of an Arc, a driver, and a driver's assistant. No one can make me break the rules. Not even an Arc, though she tried.

"In two days, we can be at the changeover rendezvous," she said.

"That's two days driving without a look-out," I said.

"I can do look-out."

I was about to give her my answer to that when we both heard another loud moan.

"She needs more painkillers," I said.

The Arc sighed. She'd been doing a lot of sighing since my assistant, Op931, fell off the roof this morning. The Arc blamed me for driving too fast. I blamed Op931 for not paying attention to the terrain. Either way, Op931 was now lying up in the back of my ATU with a suspected broken pelvis.

"OK," said the Arc. "Give her more, and I'll contact Base. But I'm not missing the changeover."

I didn't want her to miss the changeover either. I get a different Arc every four months. They can't stick the bleakness out here, so they get shifted around between recce and lab work. I don't get any such privileges, and neither does my assistant.

I topped Op931 up with more analgesics and gave her a couple of tranquilizers as well, and waited to hear what Base had to say.

"They're sending out a MED team to take her to a hospital. They'll be here in three days. They'll bring a replacement for her," reported the Arc. "And they've agreed to postpone the changeover until after that."

I spent most of the three days sleeping so I'd be able to stay awake for the night watches. And so that I wouldn't have to listen to the Arc complaining. Op931 spent them doped to her eyeballs. It would be hard to say which of the three of us was most grateful when the medics finally arrived and stretchered Op931 into their truck. I'd thought my troubles were almost over. I knew when I saw her replacement, who'd been hovering in the background, that they were only just beginning. So did the Arc.

"Look at him," she said. "He's just a kid."

I looked and saw a pale, skinny boy looking nervously back at me.

"Where's your kit?" I asked him.

He didn't answer. I watched the slow realization dawn on him that he'd left it behind in the MED truck, which was now speeding off down the hillside. The Arc sighed and left me to it. At least he had a knife and a sidearm in his belt.

"Got any bush experience?"

He shook his head.

"OK. What's your ID?"

"Salt."

"I mean your numerical ID."

"Military Operative 5351438."

"OK. 438 will do. Age?"

"Nineteen."

Six years younger than me. That meant he was an Ex-Vivo. I didn't ask him who named him, probably some techie in his birth lab. It was a good name. I didn't tell him I got named Hazel. We're not supposed to have proper names, only numbers. That's the law. Suits me. If you give someone a name, you risk creating emotional attachments. The birth techies do it anyway.

"Did they brief you before you left?" I asked.

"They told me I was going to an Earth History Project. That's all."

"We'd better get you up to speed then."

I pointed to my Arc, who was checking her map and ignoring us.

"She's the Arc—Archaeologist—right? You stay out of her way. I drive the All-Terrain Utility vehicle. Your job is to do what I say. Got that?"

The Arc called to me.

"Can we get going now?"

I ordered Op438 to get on the roof and hold on tight and told him, "If you see a crater, a boulder, a fallen tree in my path, you yell. OK?"

He nodded.

"And if you see anything that looks like a building, or any sort of human-made construction, you yell even louder because that's what we're looking for."

✦

We set off in the direction of the Arc changeover rendezvous through an overgrown mess of bramble, bushes, and trees with no path and nothing to guide us, except a couple of Pre-Wipe Out maps and Op438 on look-out. By the time we parked up that night, Op438 was barely able to stand. I took the first watch on the ATU roof to let him get some sleep down below in the bunk behind the driving seat, while the Arc settled into her bunk in the rear. I anticipated at least another day's driving before we made it to the changeover.

Most nights are hazy and humid in the bush, but that one was one of those calm, clear nights when the sky fills with stars, and you start to feel lonesome for something, but you don't know what. I have to be careful when I start thinking like that. You can go into a downward spiral, and before you know it, you want to give up, do nothing, wallow in your nothingness. I can't let anything distract me from my job, and right now, my job is to protect us from any predators who might be brave enough to get close.

I couldn't have been on look-out more than an hour when the Arc opened the roof hatch and stuck her head out.

"You'll have to do something," she said.

"About what?" I asked.

"Op-whoever-he-is. He's been sniveling ever since he got into bed. Get him to shut the fuck up."

That's what I did. I leaned down from the roof and yelled in at him.

"Shut the fuck up! You hear me? You're a soldier now. Act like one."

I didn't hear anything from either of them for the rest of my watch. I even had to wake Op438 when it was time for him to take over.

✦

Before The Wipe Out, there used to be some sort of satellite navigation system. However, we no longer have the technology to access it, so

I have to rely on my eyes and my sense of direction. That's why I need someone sitting on the roof to help. Salt calls it riding shotgun. I hadn't heard that expression before, so when we stopped at our refueling node on the way to the Arc changeover, I asked him what it meant.

"It's what my mother used to say."

I'd heard cadets say that before. It meant nothing—just a stupid joke that regularly cropped up in group banter when one cadet wanted to take the piss out of another. OK. I'd slipped into calling him Salt, but that didn't give him the right to disrespect me.

"Cut the bullshit," I said. "I know you were made in a test tube. You didn't have a mother."

"Did you?"

"I'm a factory-born."

"You did then."

Although I was conceived in a womb and born naturally, like all factory-borns, I could've explained that I'd immediately been taken to a nursery and had had no further contact with the woman who gave birth to me. But that was none of his business. I ordered him to wipe the layer of dust and dirt off the ATU windows.

✦

We arrived at the changeover location on time and made the swap over. My new Arc turned out to be another female, younger than my last one, and a lot more talkative.

"Hey! Good to meet you. How long have you been out here? Found anything interesting?"

"Two years as an Operator Assistant and four as a Driver," I said. "And no. There's nothing out in this zone, only piles of rubble."

That shut her up.

But as Salt helped her pack her equipment into my ATU, I could see them chattering eagerly to each other. As soon as he'd finished, I called him over and warned him there was to be no familiarity with her.

It was dark by the time we got back to our sector. This time I took the second watch. Once again, Salt couldn't have been in bed for more than an hour when I heard him. I climbed down, reached into the cab, and dragged him out.

"What is wrong with you?"

How do you communicate with someone who won't stop crying? I slammed him against the side of the ATU.

"You'd better stop that right now. You hear me?"

Next thing, the Arc was out.

"Go easy on him."

What? No Arc tells me how to discipline an assistant. That's what I wanted to say to her. But maybe I had gone too far. That happens to me sometimes. I get this feeling of anger, frustration. I don't know what to call it. And I don't know why I get it. You're supposed to report things like that to your medical officer. I don't. No way. They'd call me back to Base—the Military Base, not the Earth History Base—and dump me in some boring backroom. That's the last thing I'd want. What I am now—a Driver in the middle of a shithole-nowhere—is the second last thing. I'm a trained soldier, but I'll never get to do anything important while I'm stuck out here. If I were in an urban zone, I could be working with Engineers and Scientists, helping to build our future. My life would have meaning.

"I'll deal with him," the Arc said.

Now I really wanted to hit him. Instead, I climbed back onto the roof.

I listened to them talking down below, but I couldn't make out what they were saying. A few minutes later, I heard the Arc return to her bunk. This couldn't go on. I'd never had an Op carry on like that. I would have to stop it.

✦

The next few days were like any first days with a new Arc. I showed her the extent of our sector on our maps. She already knew that all the former towns and cities had been burned to rubble by their own inhabitants during The Wipe Out. Now there was nothing but wilderness. But that didn't diminish her enthusiasm. She photographed every random pile of bricks we saw, no matter how small, and marked its location as best she could on the map. She even had us looking for roads long since buried under vegetation. I didn't bother telling her she was wasting her time. At night she wrote long reports into her notebook. She'd soon stop that when she realized that every day would be the same. Salt was already settling into a routine. He'd quit whining at night, and in the daytime, he only spoke to me when he had to in relation to work. I couldn't stop the Arc from talking to him, though. She spoke more to him than to me.

Then one night, shortly after we'd parked up, I realized I hadn't seen him since he'd come down from the roof. I checked with the Arc, but she hadn't seen him either.

"He's probably in the bushes somewhere."

I knew what she meant, but he'd been gone too long. I called his name a few times but got no response.

"Stupid kid," I said. "He knows he shouldn't wander off. I'd better go look for him."

The Arc knew how dangerous the bush is at night as well as I did. I advised her to stay in the ATU and keep the doors and hatches shut. Then I set out to look for him.

It's not easy following a trail through the bush with darkness falling. After nearly an hour of thrashing about, I had to decide whether to turn back and leave him to get eaten by whatever hungry, malformed monster might be out there or keep going and face a dereliction of duty charge if the Arc reported me AWOL. I decided to keep going.

That's when I heard the shot.

I instinctively crouched for cover, took out my gun, and listened for the slightest noise. Nothing. Not a rustle of leaves. Not a pounding of fleeing animals. No shout for help. It had to have been Salt. He must've gotten scared by something. At least I knew he was close by now. Should I call his name? No. He was already spooked enough. I cautiously moved forward, step by step, not making a sound. I'd wait until I had him in sight before calling to him.

But it wasn't Salt that came into sight. It was a big, grey hulk looming up in a clearing between the trees. Now I was the one spooked. It was some kind of building but not like any I'd ever seen before. All our new buildings are built underground with just the top layer of solar panels visible. But this was a square block stuck up above the ground, the height of four humans at least. I stopped and stared at it—my first fully intact pre-Wipe Out human dwelling. Salt had to be there. I called his name softly. No response. The silence was eerie now. I edged forward, my gun in my hand, and approached the house. I'd made it almost right up to the front door before I saw him. He was sitting on the top step and leaning back against the door. I called to him.

"Salt, are you all right?"

He didn't answer.

"What are you doing?" I asked as I got nearer.

He still didn't answer.

I tried again.

"Salt!"

He didn't move.

Oh, shit!

I ran to him and shone my torch on his face. He looked fine. Normal. And then I caught a glimpse of something glistening. I leaned over him for a better look and saw the bloody mess streaming down the side of his face.

I dropped to my knees in front of him. He looked straight at me. It was too late. Life had already faded from him.

"You stupid . . ."

There was nothing I could do. I backed off and looked up at the house. It was huge—two stories high and dark and imposing despite its dilapidated condition. The light from my torch reflected from a series of windows evenly spaced along its ground floor walls. Most were unbroken, though covered in moss and grime. I looked in one and recognized chairs, a table, some sort of ancient computer, shelving along a wall. It was precisely the sort of thing all the Arcs I'd had over the past six years had been looking for and had never found. I continued around the walls and looked in more windows at the rear of the house. But this wasn't the time for exploration.

I returned to the front and looked again at Salt's body. I would be in big trouble for having let this happen. His right arm lay across his lap, the hand still holding his gun. I removed his gun and tucked it into my belt. There was something in his other hand. A photograph of a woman and a boy. How or where did he get that? I put it in my pocket, then I left him and went back to the ATU.

✦

At least the Arc was still safe.

"It's not your fault," she said when I told her what had happened.

"That doesn't mean I won't be blamed."

"You won't. I know Salt was a very troubled kid. I'll tell them that. As soon as I can get a signal, I'll call it in."

I try to avoid driving in the bush at night, but not this night. I had to go back to the house. I drove us right up to the door. But there was no Salt. Now the Arc wanted to know if I was sure he'd been dead. Of course, I was sure. I showed her his blood on the doorstep and the door.

"Maybe he was only wounded. Maybe he's hiding somewhere."

Was she stupid? I pointed to a trail of blood along the ground leading away from the doorsteps.

"An animal has taken him," I said.

She shone her torch the length of the smear.

"Should we follow it?" she asked.

"We could, but I don't think there'd be much left to find."

She shuddered. Then she looked at the house.

"This is incredible."

I followed her as she walked around its perimeter, shining her torch on its walls and looking in the windows as I had done. When we arrived back at the front, she wanted to go inside. I stepped over the blood, turned the door handle, and pushed the door open. We entered a small hallway and opened another door into a long hall. Our torch beams bounced over a clutter of objects I didn't recognize. Something moved in front of us. The Arc gasped, and her beam swung wildly. I held mine steady and saw an eerie face looking back at me.

"Look. It's OK. It's us."

Her beam joined mine, and we both stared at our reflections.

"Maybe we should leave it until daylight," I suggested.

✦

We returned at dawn and stood once more in the long, narrow hall-way. There was a side table with a chair on either end along one wall, and on the other stood a grandfather clock. Something called a barometer hung near the door, and facing us at the far end was the huge mirror that had spooked us the night before. I'd never seen anything like it before, and, going by the expression on the Arc's face, neither had she, although she knew the names of everything the house contained.

In each room, the walls were covered in a soft, textured coating that had repeated floral patterns and, hanging on each, were images that the Arc called landscape paintings. The floor was made of wooden boards and partly obscured by a faded red and blue rug. The dust had piled up in thick layers and cobwebs hung in every corner. We saw armchairs, sofas, tables and chairs, cupboards stacked with plates and cups, pots and pans, bedrooms with huge beds, closets stuffed with clothes, bookcases full of books, devices for accessing music, televisions, old computers. There were mirrors everywhere, as if the people who lived here had always needed to see themselves.

Back outside, it took us a while to find a location where the Arc could get a good cell signal. I hung around to listen. I wanted to be sure she'd keep her word about Salt. First, she told them about finding the house and gave the coordinates for its location. Then she told them what had happened.

"Yes, definitely dead, but gone. Disappeared. An animal, we think. No, I mean, he shot himself. Then an animal took him. Suicide, yes. Definitely. He was very disturbed. . . ."

✦

We spent two days filming, photographing, sketching, and writing up everything we found inside the house. I couldn't help but catch her buzz. It was pretty amazing to see and handle all the stuff that had belonged to the people who had lived there so long ago. We even found photographs of them posing together—an older male and a female, two young females and a young male. The Arc was fascinated by the photos. She said they were proof that the people in them would all have lived here together as a family—something unknown in our modern world.

I don't know why I didn't tell her then about the photo I'd taken from Salt. I guess I wasn't ready to share it.

✦

A military convoy arrived at dawn on the third morning. We watched them from the door of the house as a Transporter and four ATUs parked up about a hundred meters away. A stream of heavily armed soldiers emerged from the Transporter and ran into the bush at the house's rear and sides. Even my Arc was surprised.

"What the fuck?"

That was my thought too. There could only be one explanation.

"They're going to arrest me," I said.

"But they weren't interested," the Arc said. "I told them it was suicide. They couldn't have cared less."

I wasn't so sure. I'd lost two Ops—one to a serious injury and one literally. There would be consequences.

CHAPTER

2

It was ages before the door of the Transporter opened. A hulking figure stiffly emerged encased entirely in some kind of hazard suit, making him, or her, into an 'it.' It lumbered towards us, lugging a heavy-looking metal box. When it arrived at the door, it gestured to us to get out of its way. I thought it was going to examine the now dried blood on the step and the door. Instead, the figure shuffled into the hallway, set its box on the hall table, unlocked the clasps, and opened up the lid. I just had time to catch a glimpse of an arrangement of vials before the figure turned and pushed the door shut, leaving us on the outside.

Two more hazard-suited figures emerged from the Transporter and came towards us. One took the Arc's arm, and the other took mine and gestured towards the transporter.

"Hold on. What's happening?" I asked.

"Contamination precaution," it muffled through its sealed helmet as it pushed me forward and almost ran me to the transporter.

Once inside, it shoved me into a plastic bubble kitted out as a medical examination room where another Haz-Suit was preparing a syringe.

"There's no need," I said. "I'm fully up to date. I'm completely immune."

I made out the word "precaution" again as he, or she, mumbled an instruction to sit on the examination table and roll up my sleeve.

"Where's my Arc?" I asked as the needle pierced my arm.

If there was an answer, I didn't hear it.

I regained consciousness, strapped naked to the table and with a line feeding blood from my arm into a tube. I watched a Haz-Suit take the filled tube and place it in a tray with several other blood samples—probably all mine. He, or she, removed the line, taped a wad of cotton to the puncture site, then picked up the tray, unzipped an opening in the bubble, waddled through, and zipped it back up again.

I lay still and tried to figure out what was going on. It must have to do with the house. But the place was so old. Nobody had lived there in such a long time. We'd seen the evidence—an ancient calendar hanging on the back of a door, the old-style clothing like the ones worn by the people in the photographs, the defunct communication systems. Could we have disturbed something? Could something have lain dormant, just waiting to attach itself to us? There was no way of getting off the table. There was no way of communicating with anyone. All I could do was wait. But for what was I waiting? I didn't know.

But some things I do know. I know I have an extra-strong immune system. I was bred from specially selected ultra-immune genes. When I was growing up, I was repeatedly tested until the Bio-Medics were sure of my strength. I regularly have my eggs harvested and frozen for use in the Ex-Vivo program. The Earth History Project accepted me based on my immune system. I get vaccines every six months to keep it strong. I can't be compromised. Any known germ can't touch me. They've invested too much in me to let some old house kill me, and I wasn't going to let them kill me. I had to get out of there. I had to get free of the straps. But the straps wouldn't budge. I could feel my panic levels soaring. My only chance was to stay calm—mind over matter. Be mindful. Be patient. Stay in the moment.

✦

The zip slides open. A woman comes in. She leaves the zipper open. She takes my wrist and feels my pulse. She smiles at me. She is not wearing a hazard suit. I know I am safe. I ask her anyway to make sure.

"Am I all right?"

"Yes."

She undoes the straps. I sit up. She reaches out beyond the zippered opening, produces a folded all-in-one suit and a pair of shoes, and gives them to me. They are not my clothes, but I put them on. When I'm ready, she stands back and allows me to go through the opening. I step out of the bubble into the back of the truck. There is a movement behind me. Before I can look, my arms are grabbed and pinned behind my back by two soldiers. They frogmarch me out of the Transporter.

We run across the tangle of grass and brambles towards one of the Armoured Cars. A soldier opens the rear door of the AC. My captors throw me in and jump in after. The door slams shut. I hear the driver's door and the passenger door shutting. The engine revs. We take-off. I jolt around on the floor. I roll up against one of my captor's boots. The other, a female, places her foot on top of me. I grab hold of her leg and pull myself into a sitting position. My head is clearer now.

"Where are you taking me?" I ask her.

A man's voice answers, "No questions."

I turn and see a Captain looking in at me from the front passenger seat. He turns away immediately. I look back at the female. She, too, turns away.

✦

We drove over rough terrain, smashing through bushes and saplings. I didn't ask any more questions. I even regretted asking the ones I did. It showed weakness on my part. I must remain detached at all times. Just like the two soldiers in here with me. But the female had helped me. She'd stopped me rolling around on the floor. She'd let me touch her to get my balance. Could I now risk sitting up on the bench beside her? Both she and her colleague stared straight ahead at the metal walls, she at the one behind him and he at the one behind her, their faces blank. It's what I would've done too. But I might've opened one of the viewing slits. I'd have wanted to look at something. I'd have wanted to let some light in unless I'd been ordered not to allow the prisoner to see out. I hauled myself up onto the bench. Neither soldier showed any reaction. I sat and stared at a bolt in the metal wall panel and made my mind a blank.

It was late by the time we arrived at our destination after a four-day journey in which, although my captors watched me night and day, no one spoke to me. I couldn't tell how far we'd come. I only knew that in about the last hour, the bumping and jolting had gradually reduced until we must've been driving on a smoother track leading into an urban center. When our engine noise turned into an echoey roar, I knew we'd entered a tunnel. I'd driven routes like this. We were heading down into a sub-base, probably military.

We stopped. I heard the front passenger door opening and closing as the Captain got out. Our door remained shut. I stayed calm. In control. A proper soldier. We sat like three androids, waiting. The Captain returned, and we took off again.

After only a few minutes, we swung to a halt. A new soldier opened the rear door. My two companions got out. I got out too. We were definitely in a military base but not one that I'd ever been in before. I allowed myself to fall into step with the new soldier while he led the way and my two companions followed. No need for aggression. Why would a prisoner even attempt to run down here? There was nowhere to go, nowhere to hide.

✦

We march along a corridor of closed doors and finally stop outside the last one. Our leader knocks on it and opens it. He does not enter but stands back to allow me to step inside. He closes the door behind me, and I find myself in a large office. A tall man with a Military Intelligence Commander's insignia on the shoulder straps of his crisp, white shirt sits behind a large, grey desk. He looks scrubbed-clean and radiantly healthy. He could be aged anywhere between thirty-five and forty-five. Even without seeing his badges, I would've known how high ranking he was by the pristine severity of his office.

"Sit down."

It's an order. Not an invitation. I sit. He picks something up from his desk and holds it up towards me.

"Who is this?"

I see that it's the photograph of the smiling woman and boy that I took from Salt. They must've found it in my pocket when they stripped me of my uniform.

"I don't know."

"Where did you get it?"

"I found it."

He narrows his eyes. Evasion is not the way to go. I decide to play safe and anticipate his next question.

"Op438 was holding it when I found him dead."

"Why didn't you report it?"

"I didn't have the chance."

"Why do you think Op438 had this in his possession?"

"I don't know."

"Didn't you think it was unusual?"

"Yes, sir. No one carries things like that around."

"But you did."

It wasn't a question, so I said nothing.

"Tell me what happened to Op438."

I told him everything, right up to Salt's body disappearing. He kept eye contact with me all the way through. I never wavered. Even when I'd finished, he kept staring at me. I knew he was testing me. I held his stare.

At last, he broke away. He turned to the computer on his desk. I watched his eyes flicker as he scanned the text on its screen. Then he looked at me again.

"You didn't tell your Arc about the photograph."

"No."

"Why not?"

"I felt it was a military matter."

That wasn't true. I'd watched the Arc get excited about the photos in the house. I'd listened as she put her interpretation on who the people were and how they would've lived their lives. I couldn't have articulated why but I didn't want her doing that with Salt's photo. It was my photo now. I couldn't tell that to an MI Commander. It's not in my remit to be sentimental. He could have me court-martialed.

The photo remained on the desk between us. He placed his middle fingertip on it and pushed it towards me.

"I want you to find out who these people are. You will be seconded to Military Intelligence for the duration of your search and subject to Military Intelligence secrecy and ethics. And you will report only to me. Do you understand?"

"Yes, sir."

✦

I understood only too well. To be assigned to Military Intel was beyond anything I would ever have thought possible. It was my big chance to be somebody. All I had to do was track down this woman. It wasn't my problem if she was guilty of having broken some rule and raised a son outside the official birth programs. She was my ticket to the future, a better future than I could ever have dreamt. She looked to be in her early twenties. It was more difficult to judge the age of the boy. He appeared to be sitting on the woman's lap with one side of his face turned towards her and the other partially obscured by her arm. He could have been anywhere between five and eight years old.

Was it possible that this was Salt and the woman was his mother despite the strict laws on procreation? Had he been telling the truth when he'd claimed to have had contact with his mother? It didn't make sense. Salt's generation was all Ex-Vivos. Even if he had been birthed naturally from this woman, he would have been immediately taken to a nursery facility, as I had been. Or had this woman broken all the rules and illegally raised a son outside the official birth programs? But that would've been impossible. We enforce our laws too well for that to happen.

"I'll need access to Op438's file."

"It's been arranged. Your biometrics have already been logged into the mainframe. All relevant information systems will recognize you from your fingerprints, iris, DNA, whatever."

Our meeting was at an end, but I had one more question.

"Do you know what's happened to my Arc?" I asked.

"No."

"Do you know if she's all right?"

"I have no information on her."

He dismissed me by turning back to his computer.

As a Military Intelligence Operative, I had my own private living quarters in the MI base and a computer to help me with my newly assigned task. I opened it up, logged in, and gazed at the screen, wondering where to begin. We're all given a seven-digit ID at birth, which we shorten to the last three digits. My designation is Military Operative 4279344, shortened to Op344. My Arc's designation was Arc3124371. I keyed her. She wasn't there. I tried again. There was nothing.

I keyed myself in. Yes. There I was: 'Seconded to HQ.' That made perfect sense. MI work would be highly classified. I rechecked Arc3124371. Definitely nothing—no file, no record. It was as if she'd never existed.

I tried Salt's designation, Op5351438, and got him immediately. "Missing. Presumed dead." Fair enough. Military-speak. What else could they say? His body is missing, and I know for a fact that he's dead. End of story. Goodbye Salt.

But what had happened to Arc371? Had something in the house contaminated her? Was that why they'd wiped her file? But how could she have been? She'd have had the same level of immunity as I had, the same vaccinations. Did something happen to her afterward? Or had she done something so traitorous that she was now a non-citizen? It was a mystery. But one that I couldn't afford the time to dwell on. So, goodbye Arc371 too.

I knew that Military Intelligence would already have checked the woman and boy through the face database, but I'd learned from my training to try the obvious first. The database didn't recognize them. I studied the photo again, especially the woman. Nobody makes an expression like that—all smiley. As if she knew me, her eyes all big and soft like she was trying to get inside my head. Weird.

I chucked the photo face-down into an empty drawer and looked around. I had a desk, a chair, a computer, a cell phone, and a proper bed. I had the use of any vehicle I wanted, and I could ask for an assistant any time I needed one.

✦

I didn't get much sleep that first night. The bed seemed strange after eighteen months sleeping in the hard bunk in the ATU vehicle, and I missed the shrieks of animal kills. All I could hear was the rumble of the machinery that supplies water, heating, and ventilation. I missed the darkness at night too. There's always a low-level artificial light in the private quarters in these underground military buildings in case of an emergency evacuation. Turning off the computer screens isn't possible, so they flicker every time a public information message comes in. I ignored the messages and lay on my back, going over everything that had happened in my head. Where did Salt get the photo? Why did he keep it? What did it mean to him?

I had no answers and no idea where to get them. But I had to start somewhere. I got up and set to work.

✦

First off, I got rid of the messages. All the usual exhortations from The Moral Code that I'd heard or seen all my life, urging us to be strong in mind and body. I'd have to participate in the daily physical exercise programs that would be beamed into my quarters now that I was no longer a field operative. But that could wait. I logged on to Military Personnel and keyed in Salt's ID number for a more in-depth search. His top page recorded his creation in Ex-Vivo Lab EV1 and the date of his death, but the identities of his semen and egg donors had been redacted. At two weeks old, he moved to Belfield Nursery, where he remained until three years of age. He attended Venter Junior School until he was fourteen and then Military Cadet School until he was eighteen. Nothing unusual there. His IQ was 134, and his particular aptitudes were Mathematics, Verbal Reasoning, Spatial Recognition, Strategic Analysis, and Problem Solving. His personality was introverted. His vitals suggested that he was of average height and weight for his age, and he was in good health. He had stated a preference for medicine as a future career and had spent a short time at the Medical Training Center in his last year at Cadet School. The Medical Training School had rejected him, so he was sent to the military. That, too, wasn't unusual—graduating cadets don't always get what they want.

I clicked on EV1 and brought up their records for the day of Salt's birth. Sixteen embryos had been created that day. Two died within the first hour, five were severely malformed and aborted, and four died within six days of birth. Of the remaining five, only three, including Salt, survived to full term. Not a very successful batch that day then.

The Belfield files merely recorded that he was there, along with 143 other successful Ex-Vivo products, and noted his vaccinations and regular medical check-ups—all satisfactory.

The Venter Junior School files extended to pages and pages of academic test results and, like the Belfield files, recorded the results of the almost continuous checks on his health. Far more tests and assessments than I had undergone at school. But then, I wasn't an Ex-Vivo. These were all also in order as far as I could see from scrolling through them.

The pattern was the same in Military Cadet School, only this time the pages included his various physical fitness tests. We'd all had to go through those in my time too. So, nothing unusual there either. I printed out a few essentials, then logged out of Salt's file and tapped in a vehicle request.

Ten minutes later, I was breathing the warm, sticky air of a late July morning as I drove a Lightweight towards Venter, seventy-eight kilometers away.

✦

Venter is situated within a heavily guarded, ring-fenced compound and has around a thousand pupils. Its large entrance area is glass-fronted and sits above ground while the rest of the building slopes back down underground, giving it a wedge shape. Each classroom has a hermetically sealed reinforced glass dome, which lets in natural light but keeps all germs out. The doors leading back from the entrance have similar seals, allowing the whole interior to be locked down in an emergency. The wedge point houses the bunker and has all the equipment necessary to withstand a sixty-day siege. This design is standard for all buildings, including residential complexes. The outdoor sports fields each have a tunnel that provides quick access directly into the bunker.

The Principal, a woman in her fifties and full of self-importance, made a big show of scrutinizing my MI credentials before settling back into her steel-framed armchair behind her steel desk. I could tell she'd no intention of being helpful. I began by showing her the Weird Smiley Woman and Boy photo and asking her if she knew them. She stared at it for several seconds, taking in all its detail as if she had to memorize it, then passed it back and asked me why I wanted to know.

I repeated my original question.

"Do you know them? Have you ever seen them before in any context?"

"No."

I showed her a photo of Salt that I'd downloaded from his file onto my cell phone.

"Do you remember him?"

She barely glanced at it.

"No."

"He was one of your students. He killed himself."

Now she was interested. She looked at the photo again.

"What was his designation?"

"You would've known him as 351438 from the EV1 program."

She called him up on her computer screen.

"Yes. A good but unremarkable pupil."

"Really? You didn't pick up on his mental issues?"

She frowned as she scrolled rapidly through the data on her screen. The school would be in trouble if it let a less than perfect pupil graduate without correction, especially one from an Ex-Vivo program.

"Were all his medical checks properly carried out?" I asked.

"Absolutely, they were."

"By properly qualified staff?"

"All my staff are fully qualified. If 438 had any defects, they would have been reported to me."

"And what would you have done?"

"He would have been sent for specialist assessment."

"Can you do that here?"

"No. We send defective cases to the Children's Specialist Services facility where they get all the support they need to become fully functioning Citizens."

"How long does that take?"

"Usually, a few months."

"Then what?"

"They return to complete their education."

"What if they don't?"

She stared at me. I repeated my question.

"What if they don't come back here?"

"Then, it's not my concern."

I asked her to summon the staff one by one. I wanted to show the photo of the woman and boy to each. She almost managed to conceal her irritation as she agreed to do so. I quizzed sixty-three, including teachers, medics, and ancillaries. None of them recognized the woman or the boy in the photo, and none had any thoughts on why Salt had their photo in his possession.

✦

I didn't think a visit to the Military Cadet School would be any more productive, so I returned to my quarters in the rabbit warren of Military HQ and emailed the photo to each of the one hundred forty-seven instructors. I didn't hold out much hope of any of them knowing anything.

Next, I downloaded a list of all the cadets in Salt's unit. I planned to track down each one and interview them on their impressions of him. Another waste of time probably, but I couldn't think of anything better.

Lastly, I emailed my pathetically dismal progress report to the MI Commander. I got a reply within minutes saying, 'Noted.'

Yeah. Thanks a lot.

CHAPTER

4

I didn't sleep much that second night either. I couldn't stop thinking about the circumstances of my birth. My progenitureship was as carefully manipulated as Salt's. My genes, my DNA, had been as predetermined as his. But I had an actual flesh and blood mother who grew me inside her. He didn't. At least that's what the evidence so far confirmed. None of this had ever mattered to me before. I couldn't allow it to matter now. Such thinking was subversive and disloyal to The Citizenship.

✦

I checked my emails, but none of the Military Cadet School instructors had responded to my previous evening's request. OK. It was still early. The instructors could not ignore any request from Military Intelligence. They'd get around to it as the day progressed.

Further research in the Military Personnel files revealed the identities and current locations of the thirteen other cadets' who had been in Salt's unit. I ordered up the Lightweight again and set off to find them.

✦

I started with Op298, who was on guard outside a meeting of The Grand Controllers in their Admin HQ in Urban Center One. I explained who I was to her boss, and he agreed to stand in for her while I asked my questions. Yes, she knew Salt. She didn't know that he was dead and said she had no reason to think that he was the type who might kill himself. I showed her the photo, but it meant nothing to her. I took a risk and asked her if Salt had ever talked about having or wanting to have a mother.

Her answer was swift. "Nobody has a mother. Mothers are obsolete."

"Did any of you ever talk about mothers?"

"Why would we?"

"Have you been harvested?"

"Yes."

"So, you could be a mother?"

She glared at me. "That's a very outdated concept."

I gave up on that line of questioning.

"Do you have a name?" I asked.

"April."

"Do you like your posting?"

"Of course."

"Salt wanted to be posted to Bio-Medics. Was he disappointed when he was rejected?"

"I have no idea."

I understood. Personal thoughts were to be kept private.

I found Ops 487, 189, and 891 on a multiple dome building project at a new urban center designated Urb Six. I'd already used my MI access privileges to look up the Engineering and Architecture files to find out more about it before I arrived. The new center was to be the most sophisticated yet. Its central dome would be the biggest hermetically sealed, reinforced glass dome ever built. I didn't doubt that as I drove around its perimeter in search of my three targets. I tracked down Op487, who gave his name as Axel, on the western face where he was helping to lay the foundations for the steel struts that would contain the shape of the dome. I went through my routine of showing the photo and asking how well he knew Salt. The photo meant nothing to him, and Salt had made no particular impression on him.

Ops189 and 891 were unloading struts from a truck and glad of a rest when I spoke to them. I got the names thing out of the way first. The male was called Tork and the female Faze. They were both tall and athletic-looking. It was easy to see why they were chosen for heavy building work. They looked at the photo together and agreed that the woman seemed strange. I pressed them on this. Faze said it was because of the way she was smiling. She tried to mimic the woman's smile, but it didn't turn out quite right. It's not normal behavior for us to smile, but I thought I caught a glimpse of a response smile from Tork. He said it was the woman's eyes that were strange, but he couldn't say why. I asked them if they'd ever witnessed Salt being upset about something. A glance passed between them before Faze answered.

"Not really."

"What does that mean?" I asked.

"He could be a bit. . . ."

She stopped. Tork took over.

"It was nothing."

"He's dead," I reminded them. "You can say what you like about him now. No one can touch him."

Tork continued. "He was OK until the last few weeks before we graduated. Then he turned a bit . . . I don't know. . . ."

"He backed off from everybody," said Faze.

"Why?" I asked. "Did something happen in those last few weeks? Did he become emotional? Or overly sensitive?"

Faze shook her head. "No. The opposite."

"Yeah," agreed Tork. "He just closed down. Made himself a blank."

I tried one more question.

"Was Salt close to anyone?"

Tork answered. "He was part of the team."

"But not friendly with anyone in particular?"

"We don't have one-on-one attachments," said Faze.

Right answer, but I could've challenged her on it for two reasons, one being that her answer came too quickly and the other being the bond she obviously had with Tork. I decided to say nothing. I could use this at a later stage if I needed to, but right now, I couldn't see any advantage in pushing them further. They had a story, and they were sticking to it. I had no reason yet to doubt them.

My next target, Op761, was on guard duty at a water treatment plant close to Urb One. Several soldiers, with guns at the ready, watched my approach. When I finally got their leader's permission to question her, Op761 offered nothing that I hadn't already heard. Salt didn't stand out from the crowd, he didn't appear to be in any kind of trouble, and if he'd gone a bit quiet towards the end of his final year, Op761 didn't notice. She had no idea who the woman and boy might be and looked like she couldn't have cared less.

The next day, I got the same level of indifference when I visited Ops 594 and 495 at the Computer Science lab located in Urb Five. They were both engaged in something mind-numbing, like checking how many times people like me completed their exercise programs or took their nutrients—indifference born out of boredom. As with Op761, names didn't arise during our brief and futile conversations.

I moved on to Urb Four and interviewed Op176 and Op184 in the Physics, Chemistry, and Math Labs. Neither had much to do apart from fetching, carrying, and cleaning for the scientists, so they were more than willing to break their routine and talk to me. I took a risk and began by admitting that I would hate their jobs. My apparent indiscretion worked in that it encouraged them to relax with me, but it didn't produce anything that I didn't already know.

My next interviewee, Op377, was on guard outside the Political Commissariat headquarters in Urb One. All the Nine Disciplines headquarters and their admin buildings are located in Urb One. By now, I expected nothing, and nothing was exactly what I got.

I returned to base to write up my report and plan my final interviews. I had three Ops to go—one in the Bio-Med Research Center, one in an Anthropology Lab, and the third on the same sort of Earth History recce that I used to do out in the wilderness zone. If none of these produced anything significant, I would have to admit defeat.

I decided to leave the wilds until last, mainly because of the difficulty of tracking the recce team's exact location and the several days' journey I would have to make to get to them. Also, I wanted to re-experience the freedom of driving through the bush again before my inevitable failure condemned me too to a lifetime of fetching and carrying or boring guard duty.

I opened up my emails to an avalanche of responses from the Cadet School instructors. No time for dwelling on failure now. I determined to get through all one-hundred forty-seven in one go on the off-chance that one of them might reveal something interesting and make my report a little less anemic.

It took a lot less time than I'd anticipated. Nobody knew anything and said so in the briefest possible terms. I completed my report and sent it off.

CHAPTER

5

The Bio-Med Research Center is a vast wire-fenced complex located about ten kilometers northwest of Urb One. Most of it is underground, but I could see the ceiling domes of several clusters of buildings, each isolated from the other by more of the same high-security fencing. I lost count of the number of security checks I had to go through before I finally got into the main building. By the time I was shown into an office and told to wait while someone went off to fetch Op267, I was completely spooked.

This place is germ city. No, more than that. It's the germ capital of the world as we know it. There were Biohazard warning signs everywhere—all along the outer fence, the main gate, and at every checkpoint on the way through. Direction signs pointed out the different level Biosafety zones and Biocontainment areas—the relatively safe to the lethal. Keep Out. No Unauthorised Entry. No Entry Without Full Bio-Protection. Even here in the Admin block, posters on every wall screaming at you to be vigilant. And soldiers on guard everywhere.

All the potential killers were in these labs—botulism, anthrax, yellow fever, chickenpox, measles, mumps, retroviruses, coronaviruses, rabies, and influenza. And all the actual killers like Marburg and Ebola. The ones that kill you from the inside out, that sear your head, your back, your whole body with pain and fever. The ones that clog up your liver, your kidneys, your lungs, your brain, and turn them to slime; that dissolve the tissues in your body; that peel the skin from your face, your hands, your legs. They burst your labia and rot testicles. And make you evacuate yourself in black vomit and shit as your intestines rip apart and your guts erupt. You bleed out from your ears, nose, ass, nipples, everything—every drop containing hundreds of millions of virus particles. As you die, you thrash in convulsions that explode what's left of you across the floor, releasing those hundreds of millions of particles into the air. The virus spreading and spreading. Unstoppable. Ten days from start to finish. No antidote.

And also, somewhere inside here, is the most prolific of all—the one that caused The Wipe-Out.

Op267 entered. She had to have been around Salt's age, but she looked much older. Her short, dark hair stuck lifelessly to her scalp, and her skin appeared grey against the stark white of her lab uniform. After an initial glance at me, she kept her head down.

"How do you work here?" I asked.

She shrugged.

I tried again. "What do you have to do?"

"I'm not allowed to say."

I showed her my Military Intel ID.

"You can say to me."

"I help look after the animals before they go into the After Labs."

"OK. What does that entail?"

"I feed them . . . clean out their cages . . ."

"Anything else?"

She shrugged again. It was evident that she didn't want to talk about it. That was fine with me. I didn't want to hear any more. I asked her name. It was Lake. She agreed that she'd known Salt, but she had no particular opinion on him. She said she was sorry he was dead but showed no surprise. Her answers were flat and brief. She was dull, too, as if drained of all her vitality. Nothing was going to surprise her anymore. I showed her the woman and boy photo. She looked long and hard at it. Why? What did she see in it? Was the woman's strange smile drawing her in too? She kept looking even as she shook her head to indicate she didn't know them. I'm not sure why, but I told her she could keep it if she wanted. I had plenty of copies. She quickly shoved it into her pocket as if she feared I might change my mind.

"Did you ask to be sent here?"

She shook her head.

"Why do you think you were?"

She shrugged.

OK. So, she hated her job, but this shrugging was starting to piss me off.

"Listen, soldier, when I ask you a question, you answer it. Why did they send you here?"

"I don't know."

I thought this was the most I was going to get out of her. But she continued.

"I didn't want to come here. Neither of us did."

"I don't understand?"

"This sort of work . . ."

"You said neither of us."

She looked at me blankly.

"Who else got sent here with you?"

"Clover. I mean Op285."

I scrolled down my list. There was no Op285 on it.

"Can you remember her full designation?"

"Military Cadet Op5929285."

I checked again. There were thirteen on the list I'd pulled from the Cadet School files. Salt would've made it fourteen in total. But no Op5929285.

"Where is she now?"

"I don't know. Working in the After Labs, I suppose."

She couldn't tell me anything more, but she insisted that Clover, aka Op285, had been in the unit through training. She couldn't think of any reason why she and Clover were posted together. Of course, they weren't really together since she hadn't set eyes on her after their first day in the Research Center. I let her go back to her duties and buzzed for a guard to let me out.

When the guard appeared a short time later, I asked him if I could interview Op5929285. He searched through the personnel list on his handheld and informed me there was no Op5929285 anywhere in the facility. I reminded him that I was Military Intelligence and asked him to check again. He rang someone somewhere, and we both waited while they checked. The answer came within minutes. There was definitely no one with that designation on record in this Center.

✦

I left the Bio-Med Research Center with a feeling I couldn't identify. Apart from my strange but infrequent sense of aloneness, I'm not prone to feelings of any kind, so I did my best to put my encounter with Lab Assistant Op267 out of my mind as I drove to the Anthropology Lab in Urb Three. By the time I got there, I had succeeded.

Op470 was very chatty and asked me to call him Ford straight off. I didn't. I made a point of using his numerical. He claimed he could give me a rundown on everyone in the unit. I told him I was only interested in Salt. No problem. Salt was a loner; he didn't even try to fit in. Hated sports, hated team activities, got into trouble all the time for not focusing. Nobody liked him much.

Op470's description of Salt confirmed what I'd already suspected. It also confirmed that Op470 had a high opinion of himself. I showed him the photo. Yeah, he'd seen loads like it. Of course, he had. There was nothing this guy didn't know.

"Where?" I asked.

"In this very building. I'll show you."

"Do you have authorization?"

I'd been hoping to put him in his place, but he turned it on me.

"You have."

I followed him into a room where two unknown Ops were retrieving various small objects from a large metal box and setting them out on a table where a third Op was photographing them and scanning them into a computer. There were a few more boxes stacked around the room.

Op470 introduced me as Military Intelligence and explained that the boxes contained material found at various archaeological sites by the Earth History teams. There wasn't that much. I already knew how little had survived, or had been allowed to survive, after the Wipe-Out.

But that wasn't what he wanted me to see. He grabbed a chair, pushed it up against another one already positioned in front of a spare computer, and asked me to wait while he fetched a Senior Anthropologist.

The Senior wasn't too pleased with being summoned by one of her most junior assistants, and I didn't blame her. But, as Op470 had predicted, my MI credentials did the trick, and she relented enough to key in a passcode to let us access the files we needed then left us to it.

Op470 took charge and typed in a "woman and child images" search. Within seconds he was scrolling through a seemingly unending whirl of images. I got him to specify mother and son images. They instantly flooded the screen—women with babies clinging to them, women holding boys in their arms, older women with tall young men at their sides. Some were photographic images of real people who had existed before our time, and some were hand-painted images made hundreds of years ago.

The photographic images depicted women just like Weird Smiley Woman—all staring out at us with big eyes, their mouths stretched in big, broad smiles. I found them overwhelming. Alien. Unsettling.

"There's not that many left now," Ford said. "Compared to how many there used to be."

"What do you mean?"

He explained that these were samples extracted from obsolete databases. The rest had been systematically destroyed. It didn't make sense to me, and it mustn't have made much to him either because he spared me his thoughts on the purpose of such sampling. We scrolled through several more photographic ones, but we didn't find a match for Weird Smiley Woman and Boy. I realized the Weird Smiley Woman and Boy photo could have been downloaded at any time from files like these by anyone with access to the passcode. I thanked Op470 for his help and allowed him to lead me back out to the reception area. I was about to dismiss him when it occurred to me to ask something that I hadn't asked any of the others that I'd interviewed.

"How many were in your unit at Cadet School?"

"Fifteen."

"You sure?"

"Yeah. Fifteen, counting Salt."

I asked him to list them all. He listed fifteen, including Op285, aka Clover.

I asked him, "What happened to Clover?"

He didn't know. There was no reason why he should. Unless cadets tell each other where they're going to be posted, there's no reason for other members of their unit to know. But if they are posted somewhere together, they would know about each other. Could Lake have been right? Had Clover been assigned to the Bio-Med Research Center, and if so, why was she not in their records?

I waited until after Ford returned to his duties, then I set off to search for the Senior's office. After apologizing to her for disturbing her again, I asked how many people had access to the images database's passcode. Only three was the answer—the Senior herself, her boss here in the Lab, and the Grand Controller for Archaeology and Anthropology. I showed her my photo again and asked if anyone was researching similar images. With exaggerated patience, she explained that while it was important to conserve evidence of historical beliefs and practices, there was no need to expend time and resources on studying concepts that were contrary to Moral Code principles.

✦

I drove away from Urb Three with my head spinning. Until then, I hadn't thought that the photograph that Salt had clutched in his hand as he died, and which I had since been distributing far and wide, could be a symbol of a subversive moral order and, therefore, extremely seditious. But where did Salt get the photo? Had he somehow gained access to the database of mother and child images and downloaded one at random? Hardly likely.

I became aware of being roughly jolted about in my seat as the Light-weight ran out of road. I'd been driving for I didn't know how long and with no sense of where I was going. I stopped and got out and discovered that I'd ended up on a track running around the lower side of a mountain. The land on the track's outer edge fell away in a long, gentle slope. The usual tangle of thorn bushes, grasses, and wind-bent trees clogged the valley below. A river flowed along the bottom of the valley. Across from the river, the land rose again in a thick forest of oaks, beech, chestnut, and birch, with clumps of pines and firs interspersed. Above the forest, a tall escarpment stood stark against an almost clear blue sky.

I sat down on the nearest boulder. I'd never before been out in the wilds on my own. And I'd never before really looked properly at my surroundings. I'd always been too busy speeding and bumping along, crashing through the undergrowth, and enjoying the adrenaline rush as the big ATU climbed halfway up a young tree before snapping it in two with its weight and power, my Arc strapped in beside me, and my Op clinging to the roof rails. I'd wanted to scare them. I'd wanted to scare myself. I'd wanted a reaction—any reaction. I wanted a reaction now. I wanted somebody to be here and to say, "I don't know what's going on either."

Was that what Salt had wanted? Was that why he'd cried at night? Because there was nobody? Only me. And the Arcs who didn't care. Well, maybe the last one—Arc3124371—did a bit. Now she was gone too, disappeared as if she'd never existed. Why? If she'd been contaminated at the house and died as a result, why isn't that recorded in her file? Instead, somebody pulled her file. Why?

There was something else bothering me. I'd been trying not to think about it, to dismiss it as nonsense. But wouldn't Military Intelligence know about the database of mother and child images? And if so, wouldn't it be the symbolism of the woman and boy image that was important, not their actual identities? What if Military Intelligence didn't really need me to find out who they are because it doesn't matter, but instead, they wanted me to find out who knew about them? But why didn't they say that? Was I being used in some way? Then something else occurred to me. Something I should've thought of when I was in the Anthropology Lab.

✦

I made it back just as the Senior was locking up. She wasn't exactly pleased to see me. Too bad. I asked her if cadets destined to become Archaeologists trained here along with the Anthropology trainees since both are classed as one Discipline. She confirmed that this was true. Prospective Archaeologists spent six months training in the Anthropology Lab before being allowed to continue their training as Archaeologists. She also confirmed that such trainees had access to all the archives held in the Anthropology Lab, including the files containing the mother and child images.

"Could a trainee print out one of those images?" I asked.

"Why would they?"

"Any number of reasons."

"No. There would be no possible reason to do so."

"But if they had a personal reason?"

"Such as?" she asked.

I hadn't a clue. Except that there was something about the woman in the photo, something that drew you to her. But I wasn't about to tell her that. Instead, I asked her if the Anthropology Lab kept records of all the archaeology trainees. She confirmed that it did.

"I'd like to see the files for the past twelve months."

"Why?"

"This is a Military Intelligence investigation. You are obliged by law to provide me with whatever information I require."

Thirty minutes later, I left the Anthropology Lab with a two-page report on Arc3124371's progress as a trainee and the same for four others who had trained alongside her.

✦

I returned to my room at MIHQ and ordered an ATU vehicle for the next day's expedition into the bush to find my final interviewee—Op675. I'd already calculated it would take me at least three to four days to drive out to his particular rural zone and then probably another day to track his exact location. I preferred investigating alone, but the bush could be dangerous, and I didn't want to have to fight off a pack of wild animals in the middle of the night without backup. I could pick any assistant I wanted from the General Operatives list, but it occurred to me that there might be an advantage in bringing along someone from Salt's unit, and there was one obvious choice—Op267, aka Lake. Of all the unit members I'd met, she was the weakest and, therefore, the most likely to reveal something she shouldn't. I put in my request to the Bio-Med Research Center.

It was some time before the reply came, not from the Research Center but in a phone call from my MI Commander asking why I wanted

Op267 when I could choose anyone from the pool that had been made available to me. I'd overstepped my authority, and the Research Center was not pleased. I almost panicked. Then it came to me.

"She has better immunity than any of the General Ops. I can't risk taking someone who might be vulnerable, but Op267's vaccinations are bang up to date."

Bloody genius! Her vaccinations were up to date because of where she worked. And it really would be foolhardy to expose a less than fully protected General Op to whatever germs might be lurking out in the rural zones. But would he buy it?

He obviously did because he issued the authorization there and then.

✦

With that sorted, I settled down to study the two-page reports on Arc371 and the other four anthropology trainees. Each recorded the date the trainee started, the results of their regular assessments, and the date they'd moved on to the Archaeology Lab to begin their training to become Arcs. Beyond that, there was nothing of any interest. What did I expect? If Arc371 had come across the Weird Smiley Woman and Boy photo in the Anthropology Lab files and made an illegal copy, there was no mention of it in her file. But who else could have given the image to Salt? Arc371 had had plenty of opportunities, and she had been sympathetic towards him. Did she give him the photo as some sort of comfort thing? And if she did, does it matter? No, because both Salt and Arc371 are dead.

CHAPTER

6

Lake was waiting just inside the Bio-Med Research Center's main gates when I arrived in the ATU. I'd instructed her to dress for bush conditions, and she had, meaning we were both armed and in military fatigues.

We were a couple of kilometers beyond the urban boundary and heading west before she spoke.

"Thank you."

"What for?"

"Getting me out of there."

"It's only for a few days."

"I know. But . . . thanks."

I let it go at that. If she thought I was doing her a favor, then all the better for me.

"How are your navigating skills?" I asked.

"Above average," she replied.

Really? I hadn't anticipated either gratitude or navigational skills. I handed her my map and told her the coordinates of our estimated area of destination. She pinpointed it immediately. I confirmed that she was correct. But first, I wanted to revisit the old house where Salt had met his end. I explained this slight diversion to her, and she eagerly searched out a route for us. She was on an adventure, and she intended to enjoy it.

✦

We hit the edge of the bush by mid-afternoon. I swung the ATU off the road and plunged into the undergrowth, racking through the gears to fit the terrain and maintain maximum speed. Out of the corner of my eye, I saw Lake clinging to the handrail above her door. I intended to enjoy myself too.

A conversation was impossible as we bounced along, smashing through all before us. Occasionally I heard Lake gasp as the nose of ATU rose into the air over a bank before slamming back down again with a bone-shaking thud. I kept the pace up until almost dark, then pulled up in a clearing somewhere deep among a tangled forest of trees and underbrush. I was about to hop out when Lake finally spoke.

"Did I pass?"

"Pass what?"

She shrugged.

Yeah, she'd passed better than I had expected, but I wasn't about to tell her that. I explained the look-out system as we set up camp and instructed her to get some sleep while I took the first watch.

✦

A few clouds were scuttling about and only a crescent moon for light. I knew I'd have to rely on my hearing more than my sight if I was to keep us safe. But a sudden metal clunk right beside me made me almost jump out of my skin as the roof hatch opened and Lake's head appeared.

"Can I join you?"

"It's not your turn yet."

"I know. I can't sleep."

She was already out on the roof before I could stop her.

"There's no need for two of us on watch."

"But if there's something out there . . ."

"There is."

"Aren't you scared?"

"I know what I'm doing. I've spent a long time out here at night. I know what to look for and how to deal with it. You work in much more dangerous conditions every day."

"Not without protection."

She had a point. The most obvious danger out here hadn't bothered me before my experience with the Bio-Haz team in the Transporter, but there could be grossly infected creatures sniffing us out, stalking us, and just waiting to sneak up on us if we let our guard down. We were fully prepared for an attack by a hunting animal, even a hunting pack, but would our vaccinations be strong enough to protect us against a virus-riddled one?

"OK. Stay up if you want. But when it comes to my turn to sleep, you're on your own."

A couple of weeks in an urban center, and I'm turning soft already.

✦

At first, Lake was jumpy. She held her gun constantly at the ready and continually twisted this way and that at the slightest noise. I let her. She'd soon learn to relax. I was trying to figure out a way to get her to open up about her cadet unit when she got in before me.

"Do you know why Salt killed himself?" she asked.

I'd been avoiding thinking about Salt since my moment of weakness on the side of the mountain. OK, he'd been miserable in his posting with me, but how had it escalated to the point where he'd felt there was no way out? Why had Military Cadet School let someone like him graduate? I had tried to show him that he needed to toughen up. Was that why? Had it backfired? Was it my fault?

I sidestepped her question with, "You didn't seem very surprised when I told you."

She shrugged. Then she fumbled in her pocket and brought out the woman and boy photo and peered at it.

"You shouldn't carry that around with you."

"Why not? You gave it to me."

"It may not be as innocent as it seems."

"She reminds me of somebody."

"Who?"

"I'm not sure."

"You didn't say that when I first showed it to you."

She held the photo up to catch what little light there was.

"It's the eyes."

"What about them?"

"I don't know. Nothing, I suppose."

I knew what she meant. I avoided looking at the photo as much as possible because the eyes made me, too, think that I knew the woman. I didn't. But if it were a way to get Lake talking, then I'd go with it.

"It's the way she looks straight at you," I suggested.

"Yeah, that's it," she agreed. "I don't know her, but she makes me feel like I want to know her. Is that crazy?"

"Maybe that's what Salt felt," I said.

The look she gave me reminded me that I hadn't told her how I'd found the photo. When I did, she looked at her copy again.

"Poor Salt."

She had no thoughts on how Salt might have gotten hold of the photo.

I asked her about the other members of the unit. Her answers were brief and non-committal. The sort of bland answers any cadet unit member would give to an outsider. I revealed that I'd tried to talk to Clover at the Bio-Med Research Lab.

"Did they let you?" she asked.

Why would she suspect that they wouldn't? I couldn't see her face well enough to read her expression, but she seemed genuinely interested.

"They said there was no one there with her designation."

"She'll have been re-designated."

"What?"

"They change your designation when you go into the After Labs."

"Why?"

"Because you don't get out again."

"What do you mean?"

"You disappear."

"How do you know that?"

She shrugged.

"OK. Supposing that's true, why would they do that?"

"I'll tell you everything I know if you promise to get me out of ever having to go back there."

"I don't have the power to do that."

"You got me out for this. They didn't like it. They were really pissed. You pulled strings."

"I've told you it's only for a few days. A week and a bit at the most."

"Do you think they're going to let me just settle back in as if nothing had happened?"

"Why wouldn't they?"

"One of us will have to pay for it, and it won't be you."

She was trying to manipulate me. I could stop it right now, or I could play along.

"How would I know if what you tell me is true?" I asked.

"How do I know I can trust you?" she countered.

I decided to stop it.

"Since you're so wide awake, you can stay on this watch. I'm not going to lose out on my sleep."

I dropped down through the hatch and hoped our conversation wouldn't distract her from being vigilant. I mightn't have found out much about Salt from her, but I'd discovered she was more intelligent than our first meeting had suggested.

✦

We didn't talk much the next day. Our progress was slower as we drove deeper into the bush, but I had a reasonable idea of where I was heading, backed up by Lake's map skills. We use accurate topographical maps showing all landscape features and contours and geological maps showing soil and rock types. The only thing they didn't show was the territories known as The Sick Lands, where The Wipe Out viruses were thought to be still present. There was no need. No one would ever want to go there, so they had been blanked off.

Lake could read the maps as well as I could. Probably better, if I'm honest. But this terseness wasn't what I'd planned. I needed to get her to relax if I was ever going to find out more from her.

"What type of animals do you look after?"

"Rats."

"Just rats?"

"I'm the lowest of the low. I get the rats."

"Don't you need something bigger? More humanoid?"

"Primates."

She didn't offer anymore, but this was the only angle I had. I tried a different approach.

"I think Tork and Faze have the best jobs."

"And you."

OK. She was still sulking.

We stopped a few times to check our bearings and stretch our legs, and by nightfall, I was confident that we were in the area where the old house was located. Lake took the first watch without complaint, and I snuggled into my bunk and fell asleep instantly.

✦

We found the house relatively easily the next day. Or rather, we didn't. All that remained was a mound of scorched rubble. They'd blown it up after we'd left, in the same way that all houses had been destroyed back in the time of The Wipe-Out.

We viewed the rubble, and I showed Lake approximately where the front door had been where I'd found Salt. She wandered around a bit in the surrounding undergrowth, probably trying to get a sense of what might have happened to him. I didn't pay her much attention. I was preoccupied thinking about what could have happened to Arc371. She'd been so excited by the house and especially by all its contents. It should have been the highlight of her career. Instead, it looked like it had killed her. Was it possible that she hadn't been fully vaccinated? Did she not consider the risks? But then I hadn't either. It was just a house, empty for many generations. Could a virus have survived inside it that length of time? Not without a living host, but we hadn't found any evidence of animals or birds living inside. Could it have survived in insects? Probably.

A shot startled me. Lake! She must've fired. Where was she? I couldn't see her anywhere. I called her name. No reply. Which direction? There. I was certain. I wasn't stupid enough to run into the bush, but I had to do something. I fired into the air and called her name again. She appeared out of an area of shrubs to my right, still holding her gun.

"Did you see it?" she asked.

"What?"

"You fired . . ."

"I fired so you could orientate."

I replaced my gun in its holster, but she still held hers at the ready. She couldn't tell me at what she'd fired. I asked her to describe it.

"It was big."

"How big?"

"Tall."

"Like a human?"

"No. Yes. I don't know. Maybe."

"Or an animal?"

"It was coming right at me through the bushes."

"Probably an animal. It's gone now, whatever it was. I warned you to be careful out here. You have to stay alert."

"I'd been thinking about Salt," she admitted. "About what had happened to him—his body. Then this thing . . ."

I hadn't previously given much thought to what type of animal might have dragged Salt's body away, but it would have to have been one that was big enough, so whatever it was Lake had seen could have been the same type. Maybe even the exact same animal. In the bush, there's always some hungry creature watching, waiting for an opportunity to pounce. But only a desperate one would face a human in daylight. A mother with cubs hidden somewhere might take the risk. Lake was right to be scared. I should've stopped her from wandering about on her own. I wouldn't have let an Arc do it or any of my previous Op assistants. I'd allowed myself to become distracted by my thoughts about Arc371. I needed to focus. I could see Lake was shaking. I couldn't let anything happen to her. She was my responsibility. I had to protect her. I needed her for information, for her navigation skills, for her help on night watch.

"You did right to fire. We can't take any chances out here," I assured her.

But there was something else on her mind.

"We're not supposed to care. They keep us together in the same unit for two years, and we're supposed to be able to leave it and forget each other."

"It gets easier."

"It didn't for Salt."

"We have to be able to control our feelings."

"Anger's a feeling. Don't you get angry?"

"Not without reason. Anger's rational."

"Is it?" she asked. "What about love?"

"Completely irrational. That's why it has been eradicated."

"But, it hasn't."

"Look. You're still very young . . ."

"I'm nineteen."

"OK. But . . ."

"You can't help your feelings."

"Then you shouldn't be allowed out into the real world until you can. That's why Salt's dead. He couldn't control his feelings."

"So, you know?" she asked.

"I know he was crazy," I said.

"He couldn't help it," she said. "They loved each other."

What did she mean? I couldn't ask her outright, or she'd realize we were on different wavelengths.

"Did he say that?"

"No. She did."

Who was she talking about? Another unit member, obviously, and she thought I already knew.

"Why didn't the instructors put a stop to it?" I asked.

"They did. That's why she's been disappeared."

"You mean Clover?"

"I told you. People who are sent to the After Labs are never seen again."

Could she be right? If the Cadet School had indeed found out about any kind of bond between two of its cadets, they would have acted swiftly and very decisively.

"Did any of the other cadets know about this?"

She shrugged.

"Salt used to cry at night," I said.

"He wasn't the only one," she said.

I didn't ask any more questions. I needed time to get my head around what she'd already revealed.

CHAPTER
7

Although I had contacted the Earth History Project Base to get the coordinates for Op675's team, I'd had no way of contacting the team itself to advise them of my visit. Even now, if I managed to get them on my cell, it would be challenging for them to direct me to their location because of the thickness of the bush. I would have to rely on my tracking skills and Lake's observations from her look-out position on top of our vehicle.

After several hours of driving, Lake spotted something. I stopped, and she swung down to inform me that she could see a line of broken branches cutting through the undergrowth off to our left. We checked the map to confirm that it was within the correct coordinates and headed towards the break.

It was tough going. Sometimes gaps in the undergrowth caused us to lose the trail and waste time heading off in the wrong direction, thinking we'd pick it up again. This happened several times, but with Lake on the roof and our determination to keep going, we made it through the worst of it and arrived out on a more open plain where the tracks were easier to follow.

Driving was easy now. Automatic even. Too much time for thinking. And too much to think about. Why would Salt and Clover risk everything for . . . well, for what? What about Tork and Faze? Were they doing the same? I'd turned a blind eye to the possibility because I'd wanted information from them. But there was something about them. They'd somehow drawn me in. I liked them. Like. Love. It's all wrong. It's too dangerous. It's anti-citizenship. But I didn't like Salt. Did I? No. I was indifferent to him. Liking, not liking? Loving, not loving? It's ridiculous. It has no meaning. I'm indifferent to Lake. She's useful, for now. She's an Operative. That's all she is—a cog in a wheel. That's all I am too. I don't need to care about any of this. It's not my fault that Arc371 has died or that Clover has disappeared. It's not my fault that Salt killed himself. He was weak and stupid. It's not my concern. I need to get my priorities in order. I've allowed a simple mission to identify a woman and a boy in a photo to fool me into imagining mysteries and conspiracies everywhere. Nobody knows who they are. They've never seen them before. Why would they? They're a relic of a time lost and utterly meaningless to our world. I'll find Op675, show him the photo. Complete my task. Return to HQ. Make my final report. Job done. Move on to the next job.

A thump on the roof jolted me out of my thoughts. I braked, and Lake's face appeared upside down in my side window.

"When are you going to stop?"

"What?"

"It's getting dark. I can't see anything anymore."

I'd been so deep in thought that I'd been driving with full headlights, but I couldn't remember having switched them on. I stopped, and we prepared to rest up for the night.

✦

I took my turn on the first watch and planned what I would say in my final report. But no matter how I shaped the words in my head, there was no way I could make my investigation look like anything other than the abject failure it was. I couldn't go back to Military Intelligence and say I'd found nothing. It would be the end of my MI career. That's when it struck me. I'd been so full of my own importance and flashing my MI ID at everybody that I'd unwittingly ensured that the people I'd questioned told me as little as they could get away with, especially the cadets who'd known Salt. They'd all only graduated a short time ago. Their loyalties were still to each other. The world outside was an alien place that they were still trying to figure out. Was Lake right? Did they cry themselves to sleep at night after they left the security of their unit? I had only one more chance to get the answers I needed, and I had to make it count. I waited until Lake appeared to take over the watch, then I put my plan to her.

"If I promise to help save you from having to go back to the Research Lab, will you do something to help me?"

"What?"

"I don't want Op675 and his team to know that I'm from Military Intelligence."

"Why not?"

"I can't promise to get you reassigned, but if I can solve the mystery of who the woman and boy are, then I'll have more influence with my superiors. I can say in my report that you were of significant help and that you deserve to be rewarded with a new posting more suited to your skills."

She stared at me, weighing up the likelihood of my proposal's success.

"Who are you supposed to be then? And what are we doing out here?"

I hadn't figured that out. I'd wanted to be sure of her cooperation first. I told her I'd think of something.

I'd just settled into my bunk when she appeared at my window again.

"Cale knows I was assigned to the Bio-Med Research Center. Right?"

"Cale?"

"Op675. That's his name."

"OK."

"Right. So, this is what we say. We're on a scouting mission to find new lab subjects for the Bio-Med Research Center. We're plotting their hunting grounds on the map so the trappers will know the best places to come to catch them. I'm the scout, and you're my driver."

It wasn't a bad idea. It just needed one adjustment.

"OK. You can be the scout. But I'm the Recce Coordinator, and I'm in charge."

I detected an alarming change in Lake's attitude towards me as we prepared to set off the next morning. She had adopted a casual swagger as if she was now my equal. I had to explain that everything, including my proposal to help her, depended on both of us taking our pretend roles seriously. She agreed. But she alarmed me even further by making a point of assuring me that I could rely on her to keep my secret. I warned her that she'd better for both our sakes. But I noted the undertone. I would have to keep a close eye on her.

✦

We eventually found Op675's team near a small waterfall. As soon as Lake spotted them, I ensured they knew of our approach by pumping the ATU's horn. Lake helped by standing on the roof, waving her arms, and shouting towards them. They merely stared back at us in irritated bemusement, but I wanted them to see us as a couple of simple adventurers and a complete non-threat.

After introductions, when Lake greeted Cale with an embarrassing enthusiasm that he didn't reciprocate, I revealed my previous experience on an Earth History Project like theirs. I told them everything about finding the old house and about Salt going crazy and shooting himself. I even told them about the Bio-Haz team holding my Arc and me for virus testing. I claimed I'd asked for reassignment after that and that I'd ended up working for Bio-Med Research. This lie allowed me to explain our bogus mission. I made a big deal about asking the Senior Op, who, as a Driver, was in an equivalent post to the one I had held, about how much territory they'd covered and what type of animals they'd encountered. He revealed that he'd come across bears, deer, wolves, squirrels, and foxes but not at close quarters. He'd also heard rumors of primates living in the thick forest that spread up beyond the bush and into the mountains, but he hadn't seen any down here, and he didn't want to. He went off to get his map, and his Arc, who was female and probably around thirty, returned her attention to a pile of old bricks and rusted iron railings that, as she'd already explained, had once been connected to the flow of water emanating from the waterfall. I took the opportunity to stroll over to where Lake and Op675, or Cale, as Lake called him, were deep in conversation. As I got closer, I heard Salt's name mentioned. Lake called out to me.

"Hey, Hazel, I've been telling Cale we were at the house where Salt shot himself."

I cringed at her familiarity, but this was the game I'd agreed to play, and I had to accept it.

"Yeah. Nothing left of it now."

"I never would've thought he'd do that," Cale said.

"I did," said Lake.

I kept quiet to see where she was leading.

"He wasn't like the rest of us," she continued. "He had no self-control."

"Yeah," agreed Cale warily.

My presence was making him unsure of himself.

"What did you think of him, Hazel?" Lake asked, with a contrived innocence apparent only to me.

"I barely knew him," I said.

I became aware that the Senior Op and the Arc were hovering close by and listening. Lake was on a roll. She looked directly at Cale as she continued.

"Hazel doesn't know about what went on between him and Clover, but we all knew, didn't we?"

"Who's Clover?" asked the Arc.

Lake repeated what she'd already told me about Salt and Clover. She had everybody's attention now—even the Senior Op's—and she was milking it.

"Clover was sent to the Bio-Med Research Lab and hasn't been seen since," Lake said. "And Salt killed himself because he knew he'd never see her again."

✦

"But what about the photograph?" I blurted out without thinking.

"What photograph?" asked the Senior Op.

Lake produced her copy with a flourish and passed it around.

The Arc asked the obvious question, "Who are they?"

I did a Lake-type shrug as if I couldn't have cared less and said, "I don't know. Salt had it."

"Maybe that's him and his mother," said Lake. "Isn't that what you think, Hazel?"

I expected a snort of derision from the others.

Instead, Cale said, "Couldn't be. We don't have mothers."

"I did," said the Senior Op as he stared at the photo.

He was much older than the rest of us. Probably early to mid-forties.

"I was part of a Natural Births Experiment."

"You mean a factory-born? Like me?" I asked.

But that wasn't what he meant. He explained that there had been an experiment to see if a return to natural conception and birth and natural childrearing would be feasible, and he had been born in that experiment. Too many children birthed through the factory system had proven to be vulnerable to developing various mental and physical incapacities. Several females were selected to give birth naturally and raise their children until they reached ten years of age. Then the children were removed from their mothers. They spent many months in intensive re-education to help them adjust to their new 'orphan' status. After successful completion, they entered Military Cadet School, just like children from the general population. Zac and five other boys from the experiment were retained as soldiers after they graduated Cadet School.

"It's been thirty-three years since I saw my mother," he said as he handed the photo back to Lake. "But I'll never forget her. I still dream about her."

None of us spoke. What could we say?

"I felt like killing myself, too," he confessed. "But I couldn't. I was a coward."

This was too much. He needed to pull himself together.

"You've got the map?" I asked.

I followed him to his ATU. He spread his map out on the bonnet and showed me all the marked-up areas where they'd been. I had to struggle to hide my inability to concentrate. I couldn't allow myself to dwell on what he'd just told us. At least not yet. I was in turmoil, and I'd no idea why. But I had to ask the obvious question.

"Did anyone ever take photos of you with your mother?"

"All the time. They monitored everything."

"What did they do with the photos?"

"I don't know. I suppose they must be on the system somewhere."

I knew they weren't. If they were, I'd have found them by now. Unless they were so top secret that only a very select few knew about them. Or they'd been deliberately destroyed and all evidence of the experiment deleted from the records. Had this one escaped destruction? Had someone seen it in a recovered file and made a copy for themselves? We only know what the Grand Controllers allow us to know, and they only know what relates to their own Disciplines. We know there is a twelve-member body called The Implementers above The Grand Controllers, and, at the very top, there is the six-member, self-appointed Supreme Council, which rarely appears in public.

"We were only allowed one copy each."

What? Did I hear him right?

"You have a copy? A photo of you and your mother?"

"No," he said. "My mother had."

"Where's your mother now?"

"She's dead."

He hadn't even looked up from his map.

"How do you know?" I asked.

Now he looked at me.

"I don't," he said. "Not for certain. But she might as well be."

Like mine. Like my mother. She was dead too. Except she wasn't. She was only dead to me. Somewhere she was probably still alive. I'd realized a very long time ago that there was no point in wondering who she was, or what she was like, or even if she ever wondered about me. I'd learned that I'm not part of a lineage, and that's a good thing. I may not possess the Ex-Vivos' scientific purity, but I'm free of kinship traits or characteristics and misplaced loyalties. I'd learned that I don't need a mother. I am an individual. I am complete. I don't need anybody. I'm strong. I am The Future.

I became aware that he was speaking again.

"I'm not supposed to remember."

"What do you mean?"

"When they took us from our mothers, we were put through a massive brainwashing program to make us deny that our mothers ever existed."

"Why?"

"Because it was a failed experiment. A hundred women took part in the experiment, but only thirty babies were successfully born from it. The state doesn't accept failure. We either had to accept the new story they were telling us or face the consequences."

"What were the consequences?"

"Do you have to ask?"

I didn't. I knew the state allows only the physically and morally fit to survive. I understood that. If we are to rebuild our population, we have to eliminate the weak. That includes the morally weak—those who can't or won't follow the rules.

"I shouldn't have said anything," he said.

No, he shouldn't. He'd been left out here on his own too long. He'd become de-programmed. I wanted to reprimand him. Tell him who I really was. But I also wanted to know more. Here was that turmoil again. And an increasing and disturbing suspicion that things had been kept from me all my life. Important things that I had a right to know. Was I being manipulated by a system that I only thought I understood? Before my posting to Military Intelligence, I had been content. I still would be if I could have faith that the system is right. The system has to be right. If it's not, what else is there?

"Do you know what became of the others?" I asked.

"No. Look, forget it. It's all in the past."

Why was he clamming up now? Had I been too direct? Was I giving myself away? I hadn't Lake's knack of appearing utterly naïve while being utterly devious. But I could try.

"What you said earlier . . . about being a coward because you wanted to kill yourself? That's not true. Salt was the coward because he did it. You didn't. You're a survivor."

He didn't answer. He didn't need to. I knew I had him. And he had me. I had to stay now and keep him talking. But I also had to keep up the scouting charade. I knew from watching other Arcs work that he wouldn't be leaving this location for at least another day, so I made up a story about wanting to trek into the bush on foot for a better look at a nearby area he had marked on his map. It meant that Lake and I would have to leave our vehicle and take our chances unprotected, except for our personal firearms, but it also gave us a valid reason to return and spend the night in the company of the Senior Op and his team.

8

Lake wasn't happy with my plan. She'd already had a scare and, not unreasonably, feared another. Tough. She'd have to do as she was told, or our deal was off. Anyway, I only intended going far enough into the bush to be out of sight and earshot of the others.

We soon came to a suitable clearing and sat down to assess all the information we had so far gleaned. Lake had continued her chat with Cale and managed to ingratiate herself with the Arc while I'd been quizzing the Senior Op. Cale hadn't provided anything more than we already knew, and the Arc, of course, knew nothing about Salt or even about my team having discovered the old house. She'd probably been somewhere out in the field when my Arc sent her information through to Base. But we both agreed that the Senior Op's revelation was explosive.

"Don't say anything to alert him when we get back," I advised.

"Alert him to what?" Lake asked.

"That we have to report him. I want to get as much out of him as I can first."

"You're going to report him?"

"I have to."

"Why?"

"I have a duty."

"Seriously? You're going to drop him right in it?"

"He's a security threat."

Anyone who reveals something they know they shouldn't is a threat. But I was also thinking that by reporting his revelations to Military Intelligence, I could show that I had achieved some success towards discovering Weird Smiley Woman and Boy's identity. They had to have been part of the Natural Births Experiment. The Senior Op would be unlikely to be able to tell me much more than he already had. Still, I intended to get as much as possible from him and persuade Military Intelligence to order the release of all information on the Experiment to me. Then I could simply go through all the successful births until I found them. I still had no idea how they were connected with Salt, but I was confident I could work it out. Progress at last.

Lake didn't see it that way. I tried to explain it to her.

"He's breached the rules. He's talked about something that he shouldn't."

"Yeah. People do. Welcome to the real world, Hazel."

How dare she speak to me like that? But she wasn't finished.

"We all talk about stuff we shouldn't. Maybe you don't. You're like a zombie. But normal people talk about things all the time. And normal people have feelings. OK, we have to learn to pretend we don't, but we do. And we have to learn who we can trust and who we can't. And sometimes it gets so hard that you just have to take a chance and let it all out."

I had nothing to say to that. I had nothing to say to her ever again. I would not be confiding my plans to her, and I would not be sharing my thoughts. This was my mission. Not hers. She had no right to challenge my decisions. I had a good plan for justifying my continued presence in the Senior Op's zone and for spending another night in his company, and I intended to carry it through.

I got out my map, on which I had marked up the areas that the Senior Op had shown me on his map, and set off to see if I could find any animal tracks or sightings. I didn't have to, but it's what I'd said I was going to do, and I would do it. I might have to prove to him that I'd done it, so it made sense. I'm not a zombie. There's always a sound, logical reason for everything I do. I'm a good citizen. I follow orders. I do my duty. I said I was going to look for animals; therefore, I will look for animals.

I heard Lake following behind me. She was scared of being left alone, probably. Too bad. I ignored her. She caught up with me.

"Can you not see that that guy could help you track down the woman in the photo? If you report him, he'll never tell you anything. You've got his trust. Use it."

She was right, but I wasn't ready to admit it. We plowed on in silence on our pretend venture.

✦

We didn't see any animals. We had nothing at all to report when we got back. Lake took herself off to sit with Cale. The Arc sat a short distance away, writing up her notes, and the Senior Op busied himself twiddling with frequencies on ATU's radio. I had no idea what he was trying to do, but this was my chance to talk to him in private. I asked if he needed any help. He declined and stopped twiddling. We talked a bit more about our respective vehicles and their quirks. Mine was fresh out of maintenance, so I made up a story that it tended to pull to the left. He offered to look at it for me, but I assured him that I'd gotten used to it. He said his was a nightmare with a mind of its own, but he'd learned to fix every damn thing in it. We soon exhausted our vehicle stories. There was nothing else for it but to plunge right in.

"What was your mother like?"

He stayed silent so long that I thought he wasn't going to answer. Then he did.

"Ordinary. Average."

He picked up a cloth and began cleaning the inside of the ATU's windscreen. OK. He was still wary. I'd have to try harder.

"I often wonder what my mother was like," I said.

He said nothing. Did he know I was bluffing? Probably not. But was I bluffing? No. I really did want to know. I kept talking.

"I mean, do I look like her? I suppose I must. Even if only a little bit."

He still didn't answer.

"At least you knew yours," I said. "You got to be with her. Ten years. That's a lot. You have your memories."

At last, he spoke.

"Do I?"

"That's more than I have."

"What good are memories?" he asked.

"I have nothing," I said. "I look at my hands, and I wonder, are they like her hands. And then I wonder how her touch must've felt. I don't know."

"Touch. That's what I missed most at the start," he said. "Her touch."

"What was it like?"

He stopped cleaning the windscreen and looked at me. Had I gone too far? Was it too soon? I held his gaze. He looked away before he answered.

"Warm. Soft. She could make everything all right with her touch. Not just her hands. Her whole body. She could pull you in, gather you up, wrap you in softness. Make you feel safe. Like nobody could ever harm you. Like she'd be there. You know?"

I didn't.

He stepped out of his vehicle and stood in front of me.

"Hold out your hand."

I had no idea what was in his mind, but I played along and held my hand out.

"The other way," he said.

I turned my hand so that my palm faced up.

He reached out and slowly placed his hand, palm down, on top of mine. He didn't press or grasp. He let his sit lightly on mine. I looked at him and saw that his eyes were closed. OK. I could go along with this. See where it led. I closed mine too. I felt his skin, surface soft, warm, melting into mine. I had a sensation that our hands were lifting, floating. I wanted to look. But I liked it. I didn't want to spoil it. I let it happen. Whatever it was. He took his hand away. I stood with mine still held out, and my eyes closed and felt the coolness of his absence.

"Nobody touches like that anymore," he said.

I opened my eyes and looked at my outstretched hand. My mother's hand?

He retrieved the cloth from his ATU and rubbed the outside of the windscreen. I watched him for a little while. I felt the familiar turmoil again. So much more I needed to know. Words jumbled up in my brain. I couldn't line them out into the questions I needed to ask.

"You heading on tomorrow?"

"What?"

He was talking to me, making normal conversation. I couldn't get my head around his words. He tried again.

"To a new zone?"

"Yes. I mean . . . I don't know. Probably."

"Not much to be found in this one, then?"

"No."

I wasn't thinking straight. I couldn't move on tomorrow. I didn't know how to handle this anymore. Not without the authority of my Military Intelligence status. I'd have to reveal myself. Interview him formally. Make him tell me everything.

"What was her name?"

Was that me? Did I just ask that?

"Tora. She was an engineering technician. She had to give it up for the Experiment."

"Do you know who your father was?"

"No."

"How long did the Experiment last?"

He indicated to me to follow him. When we were far enough away from the others, we sat down on a fallen tree trunk.

"The thirty of us were born within a few days of each other. We were all raised together in the same compound, somewhere in the middle of nowhere. We knew we would be separated. We'd been told all our lives—prepared for it. We thought it was something exciting. I mean us children. We thought we were special. We didn't know what it really meant."

I didn't have to ask him anything. He told me he had known all the other children and met the other mothers growing up in the compound. Unlike children on the outside, they had all been educated together and returned to their mothers every afternoon. Their mothers played games with them, talked to them, read from books, and fussed over them when they were sick or injured. Closed-circuit television cameras watched them at all times. Most mothers were like his and were kind and affectionate towards their children, but one or two were often bad-tempered. The mothers helped prepare the children for the separation. But the children never really believed that they'd never see their mothers again. That all changed after they were taken away. They were put in a re-education program designed to convince them that their mothers were aberrations from the past and were of no further use to them. But Zac knew that his mother was not a useless aberration. She loved him, and he loved her. The thought that he would never see her again had almost driven him crazy with grief and had even led him to thinking about taking his own life. The only way he could survive was by finally giving in and accepting that his mother was just someone who took part in an experiment. He would never see her again, and she would not be seeking to see him ever again. But last night, the woman and boy photo brought it all rushing back to him. Everything that he had buried deep inside was now out on the surface like a raw wound. He had to talk about it. He knew it would do no good. But there it was. As painful as ever.

He was right. It would do no good. I'd listened to him without interrupting, but it was time for both of us to leave sentimentality behind. I was clear in my thoughts now and clear about what I needed to do. I thanked him for sharing his story. I wanted to tell him to do as he had been taught and put it out of his mind again, but he didn't need advice from me.

It was almost dark when we re-joined the others. As usual, I ordered Lake to take the first watch on our ATU as the Senior Op took up lookout on his, then I climbed into my bunk and wrote up everything he'd told me.

✦

I awoke to a loud banging on the roof above me and the sound of Lake yelling my name.

"Hazel! Hazel! Get up quick."

I shot out of the bunk, grabbed my gun, dived into the rear of the ATU, and hauled myself up through the already open hatch.

"Look!" Lake was shouting hysterically and pointing.

She didn't need to. I'd already spotted them. They were up on two legs, long arms waving, balancing their top-heavy bodies, darting through the bush. Five, maybe six. Coming closer and closer. Searching. They'd be on top of us any minute. I fired. Shots rang out from the other ATU. No time to turn and look. The things kept on coming. I'd have to kill one. I steadied myself and aimed. I heard a scream and saw Lake's body disappear over the edge of the roof. Then a crescendo of screaming. From them. They'd got her. No, they hadn't. Not all of them. Just one. The others hung back, afraid of the shots still blasting from the other vehicle. I could see this one dragging Lake away, towards them. I could hear Lake still screaming, still fighting. I leapt from the roof. Bullets whizzed over my head. I flung myself at the thing, battering at it with the butt of the firearm I now held in both fists. It screamed even louder than Lake. Not in pain. In excitement. In rage. Another scream. Loud! Loud! Louder! Me. Screaming in a fury. Fear! Survival.

Just me and the thing now. I batter and batter it. I'm roaring. I don't recognize my voice, shouting, screaming. I've no control over it. I jam my gun into the thing's belly. I pull the trigger and fire. Suddenly I'm free. The thing has dropped. It's writhing on the ground. I'm still roaring. I fire again. I hit it smack in its forehead. My eyes are streaming. My throat is raw. Something grabs my arm. I turn—no time to aim—I swing with my gun. The blur of a man's face as he dodges the blow. I hear him shouting.

"Hazel! Hazel! It's all right. They've gone. Can you hear me? They've gone."

It's the Senior Op. I've almost cleaved in his head. He dodged in time. Blood pours down the side of his face. He knows I'm staring at it. He wipes it away. It smears his cheek, but only a trickle comes from the wound. It's nothing—a graze. I'm shaking. My whole body. Faster and faster. I look at my arms. They're vibrating almost. I can barely keep hold of my gun. A hand reaches out. It's the Arc. I let her take it. She touches my elbow to lead me away. I can't let her. I hear my voice, hoarse.

"Lake? Where's Lake?"

I turn and see Lake lying on the ground with Cale bending over her.

"She's dead." I'm not asking. I can see she's dead.

The Arc answers me. "No. She passed out. She's unconscious."

I don't believe her.

"She's dead," I repeat.

I watch the Senior Op shove Cale aside. He lifts Lake. She hangs limp in his arms. He carries her towards his ATU. Cale runs ahead and opens the rear doors, the Senior slides Lake inside. I hear him speak gruffly to Cale.

"Stay on watch."

Cale climbs onto the roof, gun at the ready.

The Senior calls to the Arc, who now has her arm around my waist, holding me steady, holding me up.

"Get her over here."

I let her bring me to the open doors. She helps me inside.

"Stay with them," the Senior orders the Arc.

I come to my senses.

"No," I say. "I'm all right."

I try to get out. I need to be on watch too.

The Senior shoves me back in.

"You do as I say. I'm in charge here."

He can't talk to me like that. I'm Military Intelligence.

"No. You don't know . . ."

"Hazel."

It's Lake. She's alive. She struggles to speak.

"Hazel, shut up."

I shut up. The Senior closes the door. There's just me, Lake, and the Arc inside. The hatch above us is open. I hear the Senior take up position beside Cale on the roof. I watch the Arc remove Lake's blood-soaked shirt. Deep gashes run across her face, arms, and upper body. I know where to find the Emergency Medical Kit. I pull it out. The Arc prepares an antibiotic, tears open a syringe pack, loads it into the syringe, and injects it into Lake's arm. We clean Lake's wounds. We work quickly, desperately, applying pressure to stem the bleeding.

CHAPTER

9

Daylight. We're exhausted. Lake's bleeding has finally stopped, but she is in hemorrhagic shock. We must keep her still and safe to give her body the chance to replace the blood loss. I ache all over. I'm covered in welts and bruises. My face has deep scratches. I have a vague memory of the Senior Op talking to me in the night. He told me his name is Zac. The Arc's name is Tern. She took over the watch from Zac to let him rest. He couldn't. He'd only stayed with me an hour or so before he went back up to the roof again. Apes. That's what they were. None of us had seen the one that sneaked right up to my ATU and pulled Lake from the roof. They'd have eaten her. Torn her apart and gorged on her. I put that thought out of my mind and eased myself out of my bunk.

Outside, Zac is examining the dead ape. I go to him.

"They must've followed you back," he says.

Yes. That's what I'd thought too. That's why we never go into the bush on our own. I'd been careless.

"Sorry I couldn't get in a good shot," he continues.

"I know," I say. "But you scared off the rest of them."

"You'd better send for the Bio-Med people. Your scout needs proper medical attention."

He is right. But if I request assistance from Bio-Med, Lake will end up back in the Research Lab. How can I explain my increasing unease about that place to him? He is being perfectly reasonable, concerned even.

"She could be infected. So could you. You'll need to be checked out."

"We're fully up-to-date," I assure him.

"Even so. You don't know what those things may have picked up."

"They looked OK," I say. "Strong and healthy."

"You've achieved your mission. You've found primates. The real thing. Not just spoors. Chances are there's a lot more out there. We'll stay with you until the Bio-Meds arrive."

"I can't send for them."

"Why not?"

It makes no sense to him. Lake needs more than just what's available in the ATU's Emergency Medical Kit. I should give in. Make the call. They'll send a field ambulance and a team of medics. Or will they? They didn't want to let her go in the first place. Maybe I should contact Military Intelligence. Get them to organize medical assistance. The outcome would be the same, though. Lake would have to go back to the Research Lab.

"You have a responsibility to her," he says.

"Yes," I agree. "That's why I can't make the call."

"Is she in trouble?"

"She could be if she goes back in that state."

I expect him to ask why. He doesn't. He stares at me a moment. Then he makes a decision.

"Right. She can stay where she is in my ATU so Tern can look after her. Do you think you'll be able to drive?"

I assure him I can, even though my whole body aches.

"OK. Cale can ride with you."

"Where are we going?"

"Just follow me."

He strides off to explain his plan to the others. I watch him talk to Cale and Tern. I see Tern questioning him. She'll want to know what's going on. She's his Arc. This is her assignment. Not his. He is responsible for her safety. That's all. It's not his job to tell her what to do. I need to help him. I hurry towards them. I arrive in time to hear Lake struggling to speak from her bed inside Zac's ATU. Her voice is barely audible.

"I can't go back there. They'll disappear me. Like Clover. That's what they do."

Tern looks at me.

"Do you think that could be true?" she asks.

"After the Bio-Med field team held my Arc and me captive, I never saw her again. Her records have been completely disappeared from the system."

Tern turns to Zac.

"How long will it take to get there?"

"We can be there before nightfall," he says.

I don't know what they've discussed, but I'm prepared to go along with it.

Tern signals her assent by climbing into the back of Zac's ATU to be with Lake. Zac nods to Cale to go with me. We hurry to my ATU. I fire the engine and wait for Zac to pull his vehicle out in front. I swing in behind him and follow.

✦

There wasn't much conversation between Cale and me as we drove. That suited me. I didn't want to offer any more explanations, and I didn't think there'd be much more he could tell me about Salt and the unit. I did ask if he had any idea where Zac might be heading, but of course, he hadn't. He hadn't had any real experience of the bush until now, and he hadn't been with Zac long enough to know Zac's routes. I only knew the routes within the zones where I'd worked, and, as far as I could tell, we were heading away from those areas.

We stopped a couple of times to stretch our legs and to check on Lake. Tern kept her well topped up with tranquilizers and painkillers, so she remained mostly out of it. I saw Zac check his map and compass each time we stopped, but I resisted asking him anything about our destination. He had trusted me, and now it was my turn to trust him. At least for the time being.

By evening I was completely disorientated. I suspected that Zac might have backtracked or side-tracked several times to confuse me deliberately. We were maneuvering through brambles and weeds between a long line of ancient trees when I realized we were now on an overgrown track. I couldn't see much beyond Zac's vehicle, but I got the impression that although the weeds and bramble grew thick, they were not as impenetrable as they would have been if they had been a long time undisturbed.

I was right. The trees cleared, and we drove into an area strewn with long strands of bramble snaking through tall weeds and bushes. Zac stopped. I stopped behind him and got out. We had arrived at our destination—a house similar to the one where Salt had died. Tern and Cale had also got out by now and joined me as I stared at it.

"What is it?" asked Cale.

"Don't go near it," I urged. "It's too dangerous."

But Zac was already striding towards the front door. I ran in front of him to stop him.

"There are diseases in these old houses. Don't go in."

"I've been in before," he said. "There's nothing."

"But the Bio-Meds . . . they came in hazard suits to the last house . . . they took us away to decontaminate us."

"They're not going to take us away because they're not going to know, are they?"

He was right. I'd already admitted I couldn't send for the Bio-Meds. I watched him shove the door open and go inside. Tern approached. I tried to stop her, too. But she was too overawed by discovering such an important artifact to listen to me. OK. Maybe Zac was right. Perhaps this house was safe. I asked Cale to stay with Lake and followed Zac and Tern inside.

We shone our torch beams around in the fading light. It all looked so familiar to me now—the same sort of furniture, the framed photos, the pictures on the walls, everything that I'd already seen in the other house. I stood, letting it all come back to me as Tern flashed her torch beam over everything, wanting to see it all, to understand it all. Zac carefully checked the house—every room, every corner—making sure we were safe, alone. We were. He was in charge now. He organized Tern and me to fetch blankets from the ATUs and make up a bed for Lake. Then he and Cale carried Lake into the house and placed her in the bed. She was so doped up that she barely registered where she was.

"We'll be safe here," said Zac.

Right now, Tern was more interested in the house than in Lake.

"Why didn't you tell me about this place?" she asked Zac.

"I've never told anybody," he replied.

"It should be preserved."

"They don't want to preserve places like this," said Zac. "I've seen it happen before. They photograph everything, and then they destroy it. They hide the photos in a computer file that nobody ever gets to access."

"That's still preservation," said Tern.

But Zac didn't see it that way.

"No," he said, "You think you're working on a history conservation project. You're not. You're working on a history destruction project. That's why we're sent out here. To find things like this so they can destroy them. And if we find something that they don't like, they can destroy us too. She knows that."

He meant me. But they hadn't destroyed me. I told him that. He countered with the inevitable.

"What happened to your Arc?"

I had no answer. It was one thing for me to suspect that Arc371 had been deliberately disappeared and for me to use that to get Tern to co-operate with helping Lake, but it was another to accept that someone had killed her. Why would they do that? She'd only been doing her job. Zac must've seen my confusion.

"Look, the house is safe. I've been here a few times now. Nobody knows about it."

He looked pointedly at Tern as he continued, "If I had my way, they never would. But that's not my decision."

✦

We settled in for the night. Zac and I volunteered to take the first watch, although there was no need as we were perfectly safe all in the same room inside the house. I asked him if he knew of any other houses. He didn't. Or at least he said he didn't. He'd come across this one entirely by accident after one of his previous Arcs had taken ill, and he'd had to return him to Base. There were no other Arcs available for a short-term secondment, so Zac and his Op assistant were offered a vacation. His Op assistant chose to stay at the Base while Zac preferred to return to the bush. Zac was allowed to retain his ATU on the understanding that he would do some reconnaissance on his own. He'd found the house and kept quiet about it because, as he said, he'd been fascinated by it and its contents. It still held the evidence of the people who had lived in it. They had sent their breath into its atmosphere; they had spoken their words to each other in here; their skin had touched the surfaces and flaked off to make the dust. Strands of their hair, lashes from their eyes, all were still in here. It was a living history. Not like his own, which had been buried. That had been almost eight years ago. He'd been back twice since during periods when, as a trusted senior, he'd been tasked with scouting out possible new zones for inclusion in the Earth History Project.

As I'd been listening to him, I had become increasingly aware that once again, he was unsettling me by introducing me to thoughts and ideas that I'd never before considered. OK. I got it that an old house full of stuff was interesting—my Arc371 had shown me that—but I'd never have been prepared to risk my career to try to save it. Now I found myself in sympathy with his notion of the house as a living thing. It was nonsense, of course, but that wasn't the point. It meant something to him because he felt he had a personal connection with it and its one-time occupants—its family. I suppose you could say he felt its sense of loss. But that was ridiculous. I rarely felt a personal connection with anything. I'd never wanted to. But was I the one missing out?

"I'm sorry," I said.

"What for?"

"Causing you all this trouble."

"You needed help," he said.

It was that simple to him. And it was true. Even if Lake could have endured the long drive back to an urban center, where could I have taken her? Military Intelligence was never going to stop her from being sent back to the Lab. I'd known that all along. I had no way of saving Lake from whatever fate might await her when I took her back. My only plan had been to find the information I needed to fulfill my mission. And I had. Zac's big revelation was the key. All I had to do was use that as the basis for persuading Military Intelligence to let me into the secret files on the Natural Births Experiment, and I would find Weird Smiley Woman and Boy. I was convinced of that. But to do that, I would have to report Zac's indiscretion, and I would have to take Lake back with me. Even if I didn't reveal what I now knew about the very likely source of the photo to save Zac, I still couldn't save Lake.

How has this become my problem? Lake has nothing to do with me. And neither has Zac. I'm letting things get out of perspective. I need to get back in control of myself. I need to stop listening to Zac. Lake will soon be well enough for the journey back. In the meantime, all I need to do is wait. Zac and Tern can decide between them whether or not they report the house. I can't tell them I will have to reveal it when I make my report because I can't blow my cover with them. They'll have to take the consequences of whatever they decide. I've made my decision, and I'm sticking with it.

Zac's voice broke through my thoughts.

"They must have seen something in the photos she sent back."

"What do you mean?"

"You said your Arc photographed everything she saw and sent the photos back to Base. Somebody there must've spotted something that neither you nor she knew about. It set off alarms. They had to do something quick, so they sent a Bio-Hazard team to make you think the house was contaminated. But maybe it wasn't. Maybe they were really trying to find out what you knew, what your Arc knew. What questions did they ask you?"

I told him I couldn't remember them asking me questions about the house or what my Arc might have found.

"No. But you would've been. You gave the answers they wanted to hear. You proved that you hadn't been aware of anything significant in the house. They let you go."

"But you think my Arc may have seen something?"

"Maybe. Or at least they thought there was a risk that she had."

"So, they disappeared her?"

"It's just a theory," he said.

"What do you think we might have found?" I asked.

He had no idea. Not much of a theory if he couldn't provide a basis for it. But interesting. Someone else found it interesting.

"So, when we find something and call it in, we risk being disappeared too?"

It was Tern. She'd been listening. And so had Cale.

"Why would they do that to us?" he asked.

"We're expendable," said Zac. "They want to build the future by eliminating all traces of the past and all the weaknesses of the past."

I didn't know if he was right, but I had nothing else to offer. One thing was sure, though. That old house had set off a chain of things I couldn't explain. The discussion went around in ever-decreasing circles after that. I dropped out and left them to check on Lake. She had remained asleep, her breathing stable, her pulse still weak. I sat down beside her rather than go back to the others and fell asleep almost instantly.

✦

When I awoke the following day, I knew I had to come clean with everyone. I had put them at risk, and they had willingly gone out of their way to help me. They had taken my word when I'd said I couldn't let Lake go back to the Bio-Meds. They could've sent for them themselves, but they didn't. I didn't understand why. I realized that I couldn't go on with my deceit. I told them everything. Zac disclosed that my revelation explained some things that he'd found puzzling, like why we'd suddenly appeared out of the blue so ill-equipped to carry out our scouting mission. Tern was still too perturbed by the events and theorizing of the past couple of days to pay much attention to what I was saying. I could tell that she was becoming as confused and disillusioned as I was.

Zac was the first to recognize the potential in what I'd revealed. He knew that if I were to report what he had told me about the Natural Births Experiment, I would be able to persuade Military Intelligence to allow me access to the Natural Births Experiment files. He even suggested that I could claim my interrogation skills had gotten him to open up. That was precisely what I'd planned to do before I'd decided to let them in on my secret. But Tern was having none of it.

"Are you insane?" she asked him.

"The files will show what happened to our mothers after we were separated from them," he replied.

"They'll arrest you for treason."

"Only if they can find me."

A look passed between them. They knew something I didn't. But I could guess what it was because I'd seen that look before when I'd talked to Tork and Faze.

"Won't they expect you to have already arrested him and brought him back with you?" Cale asked me.

"She can say I escaped," said Zac.

I couldn't go along with Zac's suggestion. I'd be doing myself no favors if I had to say that I had arrested a traitor and then lost him. I kept that thought to myself, but I did voice my concerns about Lake. I admitted that I hadn't been totally sure that I believed her story about Clover being deliberately disappeared until last night. Zac had put thoughts in my head that, although I found them hard to believe, they did cause me to wonder if there might be something in them. I couldn't risk letting Lake return to the Research Lab until I knew she would be safe. Right now, I couldn't be sure. Then there was the question of what had happened to Arc371.

Like Zac, Tern now also suspected that Arc371 and I may have stumbled across something so threatening to the status quo that our debriefing resulted in Arc371's death. OK, maybe Tern was becoming paranoid, but she was the one most likely to one day find herself in a similar situation, so she had good reason to be concerned and to want answers. But how could we find out? I could visit the Archaeology Base and use my MI creds to access the photos that Arc371 had sent in. Maybe I would see something I hadn't spotted before. But if there were something, they would want to know why I was interested. I, too, could be disappeared. We were indulging in wild, crazy speculation, and it was scary.

It was also stimulating. Challenging. Despite everything, I was enjoying pitting my brains against the insurmountable. There had to be answers.

"How far are you prepared to go to find them?" Zac asked.

It was a fair question.

"I don't want to die," I answered.

"Neither do I."

But I couldn't let it go at that.

"What have you in mind?" I asked.

CHAPTER

10

We'd been walking underground for almost an hour through a maze of passageways and caves with no discernible plan. I suspected we might have doubled back on ourselves a few times, but I couldn't be sure. The only light came from the torch held by the man I was following. I didn't know who he was.

Earlier, Zac had driven me to a spot in the forest where we waited until the man appeared. I don't know how he knew we were coming. Zac introduced me and my concerns regarding the now-demolished house and my Arc's disappearance, but he didn't introduce the stranger to me.

We entered yet another cave. There was some sort of structure in the corner. An iron framework. A cage. We entered it, and the man set it in motion by hauling on a system of chains and pulleys, and slowly we moved upwards towards natural light; welcome after so long in darkness. The light came from a grime-covered glass dome high above us. Beyond the glass, I could see a lattice of tree branches. The cage stopped at a small landing. Two doors led off the landing, and a narrow staircase continued up towards the glass dome. We went through one of the doors and arrived in a room furnished with armchairs, a sofa, table, straight chairs, cupboards, and, to my surprise, a computer. All the furniture was old and shabby, like the furniture I'd seen in Zac's house and in the previous old house that had been destroyed. There were window panels high up in the walls, and I could see that the trees outside surrounded this room, and probably the whole building, protecting it from detection. I felt myself warming up after the cold and dampness of the underground passages. I could see the man properly now. He was bearded, his hair longer than would be allowed, and his clothes were old and scruffy. I guessed he was around the same age as Zac. He opened a cupboard and lifted out two large glasses, which he took to a small barrel with a tap. He filled each glass with a cloudy, purple liquid from the barrel and held one out towards me.

"Drink?"

I didn't know what it was, and I'd no intention of drinking it, but I took it from him. He held his glass up to the light and examined it.

"It'll be better in another few days. Ten at the most."

I had no idea what he meant. He flopped down on an armchair.

"Sit," he commanded.

I sat in another armchair across from him.

"So," he said. "You're a spy."

I didn't know what to say.

He laughed, the sound loud and grating. Confusing. I understand a smile, even a slight giggle. But this was beyond me.

"I'm an intelligence operative," I said, repeating what Zac had already told him.

He laughed again.

"You're a flunky."

I'd never heard the expression before, but I got the meaning.

He raised his glass of cloudy stuff and drank.

"What do you want?" he asked.

I was no longer sure what I wanted. I only knew that I did not like this man. Zac had told me nothing about him. I answered him with a question of my own.

"How do you know Zac?"

"Zac and I go back a long way."

"To childhood?"

"Is this how you do it?"

I hesitated.

"Don't play games with me," he continued. "If you want to know something, ask me directly. Now, try again."

"Who are you?"

"Call me Ethan."

"Why do you live here?"

"None of your business."

"Were you born in the Natural Births Experiment?"

"No."

"But you know about it?"

"I've heard about it."

"Why are you in hiding?"

"To get away from people like you."

"Then why did you agree to meet me?"

"For the diversion."

I liked him even less then, but I was determined to make the best of my visit to him.

"I want to find out what happened to my Arc."

"What's her name?"

"Arc371."

"Her name," he repeated.

"I knew her as Arc371," I said.

"You don't know her name, yet you expect me to believe that you care what happened to her? Well, I'll tell you. She's dead. Or as good as."

If he'd been expecting to disconcert me by saying she was dead, he'd failed. It was his second thought—that she was as good as dead—that did that. I put my dislike aside and told him everything—about Salt killing himself, how excited my Arc had been about the old house, about the Bio-Haz team's arrival, about my reassignment, and about my mission to find the woman and boy in the photo I'd taken from Salt. I even showed him the picture. He glanced at it but did not comment. I also laid out Zac's theory about us having come across something, the significance of which we'd failed to recognize but which had caused my Arc's disappearance. He waited until I'd finished before he spoke.

"Yep," he said. "That's a worthy diversion. First, we have to make a list of everything you saw."

He scrabbled around until he found pen and paper.

"Take it from when you heard the shot."

I told him how I'd immediately taken cover and how careful I'd been moving forward. He listened but didn't write anything down. He wanted to hear about the house. I told him about seeing a big square block among the trees, but that wasn't good enough for him.

"Be more precise."

I closed my eyes and tried to bring myself right back. I waited for the pictures to come to me. That's how I think. In visuals. Like a film playing in my head. He paused, letting me take my time. I began speaking.

"Nettles. Thistles. Tall grass. Hacked. A pathway through. Made by Salt. Easy to follow. Trees to the side. Bushes. Brambles. I go through a gap, and I see it. Big, square, dark. Dark windows."

Now he was writing.

"How many stories?"

"Two. Slate roof. Some missing. Chimneys at either end."

"The boy?"

"Sitting on the doorstep."

"Dead?"

"Yes."

I recounted everything I'd done, including walking around the house. He wanted to know why I'd done that. What else could I have done? I needed to calm myself. I told him about looking in the windows. He wanted to know everything I'd seen through them. I listed as much as I could remember, but he kept pushing me to keep going, keep remembering until I had nothing left.

"OK. You came back to the house the next day with your Arc. Take me into every room and tell me what you see."

"No, I came back with my Arc that night but Salt's body had gone."

"Yeah, but leave that for now. How did you get into the house when you returned the next day?"

"We shoved the porch door and the front door open."

"They weren't locked?"

"No. But they were stiff."

I take him through every room and describe everything I saw. I know how to name the things because my Arc told me. I describe everything as if I'm looking at them right now—the furniture, the photographs, the pictures on the walls. He keeps prompting me, urging me on. What else? What else? The useless ornamental things, the old computers, the televisual receivers, the radio receivers. Suddenly a strange feeling comes over me. I have a sensation of being unable to move, of being on my back, strapped down. I leap up.

"What is it?" he asks.

"I've done this before. I remember someone asking me questions. Over and over. 'What did you see? What do you remember?'"

"Who?"

"I don't know. A Bio-Med in the Transporter where they were holding me."

"What made you think of that now?"

"You. Your questions."

"Yes, but something else. Something you saw when you were describing the inside. Something you told them. What was it? Where are you? What have you just seen?

"I'm in a kitchen."

"OK. Take your time. What do you see?"

"Cupboards, a table, chairs, some sort of storage thing. My Arc called it a dresser."

"Describe it."

Tall. Wooden. Shelves on top, cupboards below."

"Did you open the cupboards?"

"No."

"What's on the shelves?"

"I can't remember."

"Yes, you can. Close your eyes."

I close my eyes.

"You're looking at the shelves. They're right in front of you. What's on the shelves?"

"Old pots, jugs, plates, dirt, and dust on everything."

And then I remembered. There was something that shouldn't have been there. I'd reached out to pick it up. But my Arc had come up behind me, and I'd moved out of her way.

"What is it?" Ethan asked.

I couldn't answer because something weird was happening inside my brain. All the pictures in my head—my visual memories—were slipping and sliding over each other, merging and separating. I remembered the kitchen as a dark, dirty place thick with dust and great whorls of cobwebs. But now I had an equally strong memory of it as cobweb free, except for the webs high up and out of reach in corners. I remembered fingerprints on the shelves and footprints on the floor. I kept my eyes closed.

I heard myself say, "It's all wrong—all mixed up."

And I heard Ethan saying, "Stay with it, Hazel. Concentrate."

There was something important I had to remember. Something on the shelf. Something that shouldn't have been there. That was why I'd wanted to pick it up before I'd had to step to the side to let my Arc photograph it. I tried to imagine the photograph. What would it show? And then I remembered. It was a small package, already opened. Like you'd have in an Emergency Medical Kit. But not pills. Not bandages. The sort of thing you'd need to administer an antibiotic intravenously. The kind of thing Tern used on Lake.

"I saw a syringe pack. Modern. The type we have today."

"Did your Arc see it?"

"Yes."

"Did you talk about how it could've gotten there?"

"Yes. We couldn't figure it out."

Now all the images in my brain flashed into place. I had two different sets of visual memories for each first floor room in the house. Each set showed the same old furnishings in the same places, but one set showed them covered in dirt, dust, and cobwebs. In contrast, the other showed them relatively dirt, dust, and cobweb free as if someone, no more than one, several people, still lived in the house—the sort of people who weren't bothered about keeping it clean and who had left their fingerprints and footprints all over the first floor. But not the upper floor. I had only one set of memory images for up there, and they were all of rooms where the dirt and dust and cobwebs were undisturbed. I didn't know how I could explain this to Ethan when I couldn't begin to explain it to myself.

"FMI," he said. "False Memory Implantation. They'd have done that to your Arc too."

"So, she's alive?"

"Maybe. Somewhere. Her old memories wiped out, and new ones implanted. Or maybe she wasn't a good FMI subject, so they disposed of her. They don't like losing trained personnel in any Discipline—it's a waste of resources—but sometimes it's necessary when secrets have to be kept."

"But it worked on me? I replaced my real memories of the house with false ones that they implanted into my mind?"

"It works better on some people than on others. If it hadn't worked on you, you'd have been disappeared too. Instead, you were given a ridiculous pseudo promotion and sent on an inconsequential mission to keep you out of the way."

"But they gave me resources, Military Intelligence status, and ID, anything I wanted to help me with my investigation."

"All that supposedly because of an image that the kid could've made on any computer during his cadet training?"

"The mothers and children from the Natural Births Experiment were photographed just like that."

"That photo is a distraction tactic. Can't you see that? They're reinforcing the FMI by making you concentrate on something completely different and irrelevant. And it's working. You've been successfully brainwashed. You're not even curious about why they want to keep what you saw in the house a secret. Supposing you do succeed in tracking down the mothers from the Natural Births Experiment? What do you think will be gained? Will they be rewarded for their sacrifices, held up as heroes of the Citizenship? Will they be reunited with their long-lost offspring? No. They won't. Go back to your spy bosses and tell them the photo is a hoax. Tell them you don't know where Salt got it, and you've been unable to find anything more about it. They won't care because they never cared. They expect a negative result. You'll be thanked for your efforts and given a nice posting somewhere and you'll fade into the background and live happily discontented ever after, like everyone else."

"Go fuck yourself."

"Yeah, you too."

"Take me back to Zac."

"I can't."

"I'm not staying here."

"You have to stay tonight. Zac will come for you tomorrow. That's the arrangement. In the meantime, you can help me prepare some food. You do eat, don't you?"

✦

During my training, before I took up my assignment with the Earth History Project, I'd been taught which of the plants in the bush were safe to eat in case we ever got so badly lost that we ran out of our pre-prepared rations. It had never happened, so I'd forgotten most of it. However, as I discovered when he insisted that I went out with him to pick some for the rabbit stew he intended cooking, Ethan knew them all. He'd caught the rabbit in a trap sometime previously and said it was 'ready for the pot.' The idea of eating unprocessed plants and animals was obscene to me.

We took the plants back to his hideout, where he chopped them up and put them and the skinned rabbit and some water into a heavily smoke-blackened pot. The whole procedure seemed to give him inordinate pleasure.

Next, we returned to one of his caves, where he lit a fire from a pile of twigs that he had stacked up inside to keep dry. He said he couldn't light a fire inside the building because there was no chimney to let the smoke out, but the smoke would dissipate more slowly and be less likely to be noticed in here. He set the pot on a metal, open-lattice stand he'd made for placing over the flames, and together we watched the water come to the boil. As the water bubbled, the foul smell of boiling flesh filled the cave. Ethan merely laughed and promised me that I would find the stew to be the best thing I'd ever eaten.

It was not. Back inside the building, I tried a mouthful and instantly retched. Ethan's disappointment was unfathomable. I didn't care. Nothing would induce me to try it again. I couldn't even bear to watch as he scooped huge spoonfuls of the mess into his mouth. I gratefully reverted to my ration pack and watched as he finished off with another large glass of the cloudy liquid that I'd ignored earlier.

A silence descended after we'd eaten. On the one hand, I didn't care. I had no wish to bear the brunt of any more of Ethan's resentments that had nothing to do with me and everything to do with his inability to cope in the real world. On the other hand, there was so much I wanted to ask him about his friendship with Zac. They obviously knew each other well and trusted each other, or at least Zac trusted Ethan enough to send me to him to seek answers. But I hadn't found any answers, only more questions. These techniques that Ethan used—he must have been trained in them. Why? How did he know about False Memory Implantation? What was his role before he deserted? Why did he desert? I accepted that he'd probably been right when he'd said I'd been subject to FMI, but I didn't want to think about it. I had one job to do, and I would do my best to complete it. Everything else could wait.

I could see that he found it increasingly difficult to keep his head up and his eyes open. Finally, his chin dropped onto his chest as he fell asleep where he sat on the floor across the room from me. I had no idea where he usually slept, and I had no intention of waking him.

I made myself comfortable on the sofa and went over everything I could remember about finding Salt at the old house. Could someone else really have been there? Did that someone kill Salt? And what did any of it have to do with Arc371's death?

✦

I wake with a start. Something's wrong. It's dark. Where am I? I remember. I'm in a room. Warm. Claustrophobic. I find my beam and switch it on. Something in the room. Ethan. Just sitting there, staring. At me? Yes. Wide awake and staring at me.

"What's wrong?" I ask.

"You don't know, do you?" he asks.

"What?"

"I eat natural now."

I have no idea what he's talking about. I barely recognize his voice. Thick. Slurred.

"I'm a full man again. I have desires. You don't, do you? You have no idea. You're too chemmed up."

Now I get it. I know about desires. Some people experience them to a greater degree than others. However, we all have a duty to suppress them and never speak about them to anybody except our designated Medical Officers.

"What do they give you now?

"What do you mean?" I ask.

"It's in your ration pack. That rubbish you consume. It's full of it. Chemicals to keep your mood up and your cock down. Or, in your case, your legs closed."

I don't know what to say.

He hauls himself up off the floor.

"Don't worry. You're safe. Go back to sleep."

He staggers out of the room.

There's no way I can go back to sleep.

✦

It was daylight when he returned. I watched him take a jar of water and drink from it until he had almost emptied it. He turned and looked at me.

"You all right?" he asked.

"Yes."

"Good girl. Forget last night—too much jungle juice. I've been thinking about your Arc. She's the reason you came here, isn't she? If we're to try and figure out what happened to her, you'll need to tell me everything you know about her."

I could tell he was trying to make everything normal again.

"Where was she trained?"

That's what I wanted too, so I went along with it. His analytic questioning did work so far as it forced me to remember and rethink things that I'd failed to notice previously. Besides, he seemed calmer now, more rational and focused. But what did I really know about Arc371?

"Six months in an anthropology lab and a year in an archaeology lab. She's been removed from the Archaeology personnel files as if she'd never existed."

"You know she did. Other people will know too."

"I'm aware of that."

"Right. Let's concentrate on what you don't know you know about her."

I told him what I could. She was full of enthusiasm and seemed to know a lot about old houses because she could name everything she saw. He asked if there was anything she couldn't name. Yes, sometimes she made guesses, and sometimes she just took photographs and said nothing. Anyway, I wasn't by her side all the time we were in the house. I was just repeating what I'd already revealed about the place from my point of view. I hadn't gotten to know Arc371 well enough even to attempt to guess at her perception of what she saw.

"OK. Forget about her. Tell me more about the boy."

I told him everything I could about Salt's delusion of having had a mother and how that had been the starting point for all the bad stuff that had since happened. Ethan asked why Salt thought he'd had a mother. I explained Lake's theory that Salt had been crying over the loss of Clover and that he'd invented a mother as a cover. Ethan immediately asked me if Salt had ever claimed that he'd been crying for his mother. He hadn't.

"But that's what you thought?"

"I don't know. Maybe. I mean before Lake told me about Clover it seemed to fit."

"Why?"

"He said he had a mother. He told me."

"Did he tell you that he was missing her? That he missed her so much that he couldn't control himself?"

"No. Not exactly."

"But, you made that assumption."

He was right. Salt's only reference to having a mother was his claim about hearing her use an outdated expression. I'd known at the time that couldn't be right, that he couldn't have had a mother. But I'd been too proud to challenge him. I'd been determined not to appear to give his stupidity any credence. But then the photo had changed that. The photo was the credence.

"What do you think that says about you?" asked Ethan.

I knew what he was getting at, but I wasn't going to give him the satisfaction of hearing me admit it. But, of course, he knew that.

"Ok. Let's try and glean something from the actual facts."

I knew Zac wasn't due to return for several hours yet, so once again, I allowed Ethan to subject me to his intense form of questioning. He was primarily interested in Salt's school days and his subsequent time at Military Training School. He thought it odd that Salt had been rejected for medical training, given his relatively high IQ, and assigned to the military instead.

"I have a high IQ," I pointed out.

"But you asked for the military. You're classic military material. Salt wasn't."

I had to agree. So, was it significant that the Medical Training School had rejected Salt? Ethan thought it was.

"The main purpose of medical training is to teach future practitioners how to identify the weak, or potentially weak, and eradicate them at the earliest opportunity. That means all medical students must be able to satisfactorily demonstrate their own mental and physical capabilities before they are allowed into the Medical Training School."

Ethan had wanted to practice physical medicine, but in his first year at Medical Training School, he scored so highly in all the mental manipulation assessments he had been assigned to the mental medicine field. One of those assessments had been on the topic of false memories. Students were required to distinguish between actual past events in their lives and fake events planted by the instructors. If they couldn't and held on to the fake memories, they were considered too intellectually and emotionally weak to continue with any type of Medical Training. Ethan's theory was that Salt may have been exposed to a false memory of having had a mother and that it had become deeply embedded despite the evidence to the contrary. That was why he had been rejected for medicine and sent instead to the military.

"Do they use props when they're planting false memories?" I asked.

"Of course."

"A photograph?"

"Ideal."

"So, the photograph that Salt had could have been given to him by whoever planted the false memory?"

"Or he could just have been playing you."

"What do you mean?"

"Having a bit of fun. Spinning you a story to see how you'd react."

"So, where did he get the photo?"

"Had you seen him with it before the shooting?"

"No. Are you saying someone put it into his hand?"

"What if someone had?"

"Why would someone do that?

He didn't answer. "You mean his killer put it in his hand?" I asked.

"You don't know there was a killer."

"But you think there was."

"I've never said that."

"Who else could have given it to him?"

"Anyone at any time. Just because you didn't see it doesn't mean he didn't have it."

"That doesn't help."

"Concentrate on what might. If you didn't give it to him . . ."

"Arc371?"

"She seems most likely. What else do you know about her?"

"I've told you everything."

"OK. Time to stop talking and start thinking. Have you been taught how to meditate? How to access your deep unconscious? I can show you."

But there was something else on my mind.

"What about Zac? How many of his memories are real?"

"All of them. He lived for ten years with his mother. That's ten years of genuine memories. The purpose of his re-education was not to erase them completely but to reduce their importance to him. To eliminate the emotionality his mother brought into his life. To make him like everybody else."

That had the ring of truth. But his being right still didn't make him any more likable.

"How long before Zac returns?"

"What's your hurry?"

"We're done here."

"And I had such plans for us."

"What plans?" I asked.

He burst out laughing. I guessed he must've made some kind of joke.

"Zac will be here when he's here," he said.

"I need fresh air."

"Can't bear to be in the same space as a traitor like me? Can't wait to get back to civilization so you can report me? Tell them where I am? Lead them to me?"

The thought had occurred to me. But if Zac trusted him, there had to be a good reason for his trust. He saw that I wasn't going to rise to his goading, so he changed tactics.

"I'd advise you not to go out on your own. It's too dangerous."

"Why do you live like this?" I asked.

He laughed.

"What's wrong with the way I live?"

"You've made yourself an outcast, a fugitive. You live in fear. Why?"

"Because I know what there is to fear."

"There's nothing. Not if you live by the rules."

"And you believe in the rules? You think everything out there is good? All you have to do is obey the masters, and life will be perfect?"

"Not perfect. We haven't achieved perfection yet."

He shook his head. I thought he was about to laugh again, but it wasn't scorn I saw when he caught my eye. It was despair.

"We have to work towards it," I argued. "We have to be disciplined. We have to suffer some hardships—"

"You haven't a clue. People like you are so stupid. You destroy all hope of decency, of common humanity. It would've been better if we'd all been wiped out. Then you and the likes of you wouldn't exist."

"Neither would you."

He stared at me a moment before answering.

"Yes. It would've been better if I had never existed either."

"Why? What have you done? Why are you in hiding?"

I didn't expect him to tell me. Why would he? But then again, why wouldn't he? He had nothing to lose. He'd already lost it all. His life here in this self-imposed prison was pathetic. No structure. No purpose. No value to anybody. No normal person would want to live outside the Citizenship. The Citizenship provides everything we need and keeps us safe. That's what I'd always believed. It had never occurred to me that people deliberately broke the rules. I mean ordinary healthy people like Zac. Fetuses were always scanned for indicators of delinquent genes, and those displaying them were aborted. Anomalies should not arise. At least that's what we were told. Everything should be perfect. We should be a healthy,

highly intelligent population working in unison for The Future. Now I
was beginning to discover that wasn't always true. There were flaws in
the system. Not many, surely? But definitely a few. Zac was flawed. But
Ethan? What he told me revealed he was way beyond flawed.

✦

After proving himself so effective in the brainwashing programs,
Ethan, or Op2433543 as he was then known, was sent to Bio-Med
Research Center headquarters. There, he trained the medical team
researching the effects of various bacteria and virus strains. The senior
researchers had been frustrated in their efforts to source sufficient suitable
subjects for study. Animals such as rats, rabbits, foxes, pigs, or dogs could
be obtained relatively easily through in-house breeding, but their useful-
ness was limited. Larger primates, which more closely replicated human
physiology and biology, were more useful but were difficult to breed and
control. There had been numerous breakouts from the cages, and many
lab assistants had suffered vicious attacks. So, although animal subjects
were useful for training lab personnel and in the initial development and
testing of antibiotics and anti-viral inoculations, human subjects would
be much more manageable. A new Directive was issued ordering the
collection of non-viable humans for participation in the experiments'
final stages.

I assumed he meant humans who were already infected and who
were willing to try out whatever new drugs the labs were developing
in the desperate hope of being cured. But that wasn't it. According to
the Directive, any human whose profile was considered below standard
could be regarded as a suitable subject. That meant anyone who suffered an injury that they could not recover from within a reasonable time
and within affordable resource expenditure, whether mental or physical,
could be rounded up and taken to the lab.

I immediately thought of Op931, who had fallen off the roof of my
ATU and broken her pelvis. But Ethan assured me that she would not
have been considered a candidate providing she'd made a full recovery
and was not compromised in any other way.

"So, the terminally ill and the insane?" I asked.

He answered me with a question.

"How many times were you put through physical and psychometric tests when you were in school?"

"Once a year, every year."

"How many failed?"

"Only two that I know of."

"What happened to them?"

"They were sent to specialist units for extra training."

"Did they come back?"

"Yes."

"They were lucky."

"You mean they take children?"

"If they're below a certain IQ. They take babies, too, if they seem in any way substandard. But you already know this."

"I know they euthanize the non-viable at birth."

"And some they keep for experiments."

"Who authorized this?"

I knew I'd asked a stupid question. What did it matter who authorized it? We have no say in how things are done. When a Directive is issued, we all fall in line because we have no other choice. Not if we want to remain Citizens. And we do because that's all there is. The Citizenship protects us. Ethan didn't even bother answering me. The authorization came from somewhere higher up the chain, and that's all he, or anyone else at his level, would have known.

"Why did they need you?" I asked.

"To convince the medical researchers that it was the right thing to do."

"How did they convince you?"

"The same way you've been convinced to do what you're doing. They gave me power and status."

"What went wrong?"

"Nothing. It's still going. Fully operational. Their greatest success."

"I mean, why aren't you still working there?"

"Do you really have to ask that?"

I did. I needed to understand how I felt about what he was telling me. I needed to hear his view because I was totally confused about my own view.

He told me that he had designed the series of tests that the medical researchers had to complete to determine which ones would most likely accept human subjects. Those chosen then had to undergo another set of tests, also designed by Ethan, to discover which of them would be prepared to experiment on babies and children. Then the subjects were chosen. The babies came as rejects from the Ex-Vivo program. Older children came from the schools. A few adults arrived. The experiments began. The medical researchers played their parts without any misgivings. If the Ops who looked after the subjects in the Before and After Labs had any qualms, they knew better than anybody what could happen to them if they revealed them. The program was a success. Not because subjects were recovering from whatever diseases they were being infected with, but because they were the ideal breeding ground for the infections. Each baby, child, and adult became an incubator for every naturally occurring known disease and every artificially concocted disease that the researchers could imagine. Subjects died at a ferocious rate. I knew what that meant. Inevitably, the demand for human subjects rose at an equally ferocious rate.

Although Ethan had no active part in the actual experiments, he'd witnessed some of them on visits to the labs and had become increasingly disturbed by what he saw. Humans from a few weeks old to those in old age dying in agony. More and more humans were brought in and subjected to more and more extreme trials. And more germs and viruses were created and stockpiled. Some of the subjects were older people who had refused to give themselves over to the Euthanasia Program that everyone beyond a certain level of capability must accept. Many were adults who had been found guilty of criminal activities and had been perfectly healthy before entering the lab. Healthy humans made better subjects than those already compromised.

"Like my Arc?"

"Possibly," he agreed.

"But not me. Why not me?"

"Because she was smarter than you? She realized the significance of what you both saw. You didn't, so you were no threat. Or she really could have been contaminated by something in the house, but you weren't."

"And now they have her in one of their death labs?"

"It's what they do."

"This is why Zac sent me to you."

"I'm the horse's mouth."

"What?"

"You needed to hear it from me to believe it."

I asked him if he thought Lake knew about the human experiments and if that was why she was so afraid of going back to her lab. He didn't. He thought she'd probably be aware of the terrible atmosphere of the place, but as a new entrant, she wouldn't know what was really going on. That would come later as she was drawn in further by having to carry out increasingly unpleasant duties. That's when someone like him would complete the brainwashing process by persuading her that there was nothing wrong with experimenting on her fellow human beings. I told him what Lake had told me about Clover. He agreed that if the military authorities had found out about Salt and Clover's relationship, Clover could also be an experiment in a human research lab.

So, I'd been one of the lucky ones. Not just when the Bio-Hazard team let me go, but throughout my life, right from the moment I'd been created. A dropped IQ score, an unexplained illness, a mental lapse, or just somebody's whim could have sent me to the lab too. If I wasn't careful, it still could.

"How do you know Zac?" I asked.

"He was one of my guinea pigs."

"In the lab?"

"No. I came across the audio-visual files of the re-education of the Natural Births children during my training. He stood out from the others."

I asked why, and Ethan explained that Zac had initially been the most distressed of all the children going through the brainwashing process. Ethan had felt sympathy for him then. But when Zac finally succumbed and accepted everything his brainwasher told him, Ethan suspected he'd been bluffing to make the brainwashing stop. Ethan had then secretly admired the little boy who couldn't be broken.

"But he is broken," I suggested.

"No. He's damaged. We're all damaged. Most of us know that. It's those who don't know that are broken."

Did he mean me? I dismissed the thought and asked him how he then got to know Zac as an adult. He revealed that he remembered Zac many years later when he was a trained psychoanalyst carrying out his research into why some subjects are easier to manipulate than others. He used his authority to have him tracked down and sent to him. By this time, Ethan had discarded all notions of sympathy for his subjects and was prepared to exploit Zac to suit his own ends.

"What ends?" I asked.

"The same as the ones you still believe in."

"I just do my job."

"That's what I mean. You think you're helping build 'The Future'—a Citizenship free of illness and disease. A super race that can't be contaminated by germs, viruses, emotions, or feelings. I've listened to the broadcasts too. I know the stuff they feed you. I've even designed some of it. But that's what it's for—to create a race of super-idiots that will do exactly what their masters tell them."

I didn't argue with him. You can't win with people like that. Instead, I asked him to continue with what he was telling me about Zac. He told me Zac had cooperated fully with his experiments. Or rather, he played along, as Ethan soon began to realize. When Ethan showed specially constructed film clips to Zac and then quizzed him about what he could remember, Zac's recall proved almost faultless. When Ethan began implanting false variations into Zac's remembered accounts, Zac resisted long enough to be convincing but mostly gave in and accepted the altered version.

"False Memory Implants?" I asked.

"That's what I was trying to do. But, as I said, it doesn't work with some people."

Ethan began to recognize a pattern in Zac's apparent acceptances. Zac was playing a game with him. Zac still couldn't be broken. Now Ethan had even more respect for the adult Zac. He kept Zac with him in the lab for several weeks until Zac's military superiors demanded to either have their Operative returned to normal duty or to be provided with evidence of the continuing need to keep him in the lab. Ethan knew that keeping Zac any longer would put them both at risk of unwelcome scrutiny, so he signed off on the experiment, and Zac returned to the rural zones. But not before they'd set up a system of coded radio communications.

I'd seen Zac fiddling with the radio in his ATU. I'd heard the beeps and squawks that came from it and thought them just static. My own ATU radio rarely worked, so, like all the other Driver Ops that I knew, I didn't bother much with it and left my Arc to take care of communications with Base via their cells. So, somewhere in this building, Ethan had a system for sending and receiving radio messages and, probably, a generator supplied with fuel by Zac.

"Zac didn't just send me here so you could help me find out what happened to my Arc, did he?"

Zac arrived at Ethan's hideout mid-afternoon, taking me by surprise as he entered unannounced. Ethan had known precisely when he was coming and greeted him nonchalantly. I was ready to leave, get away from Ethan and not have to be in his company ever again. But by now, I'd realized that the two of them were up to something. Zac settled into an armchair and spoke directly to me.

"Did you remember anything?"

Ethan laughed from the background.

"She remembers everything."

"Just like you do," I said to Zac. "You sent me here so he could see the photo, didn't you?"

Zac switched his gaze to Ethan then back to me again. I knew I was on to something.

"Why didn't you tell me you knew who they are?"

"We have to be careful," Zac said, looking towards Ethan.

"He's pretending he doesn't know," I said.

Ethan moved into my line of sight.

"I don't. They were faces in a file. I saw dozens. I don't remember who they are now."

OK. This was possibly true. It was a long time since Ethan had worked with the audio-visual files from the Natural Births Experiment. He'd only selected one—Zac—to investigate further. There was no reason for him to remember the names of the other twenty-nine children and their mothers. But I also knew Zac would've told him whom the photo depicted when he arranged for me to visit him. Why was he so reluctant to name them?

Zac provided the answer.

"Their names mean nothing. We need their numerical designations."

He was right. If I could access the files, I could track their whole lives since their births via their numerical IDs.

"Where are their files stored?" I asked Ethan.

"I haven't seen them in almost twenty years," he replied.

"But they're somewhere in the system."

He laughed. "Good luck with that. They'll be highly classified. Not for your eyes."

Zac spoke, "The boy's name is Ferris."

"What?"

I couldn't believe he'd said it.

"At least that's what we called him. I never knew his mother's name."

"You knew him?"

"In junior school. Yes."

"Why didn't you tell me before?"

He didn't answer.

"We don't know why they're looking for them," said Ethan. "And neither do you."

This was also true. I'd been so wrapped up in fulfilling my mission and making a good impression on my MI Commander that I hadn't given much thought to why he was seeking the woman and boy. Then something else struck me. When I started my search, I hadn't known about the Natural Births Experiment, and my MI Commander hadn't mentioned it. But Military Intelligence would have access to all the biometric info on the Natural Births participants. If they wanted to find the woman and boy, they only needed to get permission from the appropriate government level and go through the bio-records. That would tell them where the woman and boy are now and what they're doing.

"Exactly," said Ethan when I voiced my thoughts aloud. "So, what's going on?

Zac supplied the answer.

"It's not an official search," he said.

"Which is why they've brought someone like you—an unknown outsider—in to do it," said Ethan.

The thought that the Commander had picked me for my naivete had been niggling in the back of my mind ever since he had assigned me to the search. Why me? Why not an experienced MI operative?

"If the top levels aren't the ones looking for them, then they aren't in danger," Zac said.

But Ethan didn't see it that way. He'd witnessed, on videotape, the efforts that had been put into brainwashing the Natural Births children so they would accept the huge emotional change in their lives. He'd been trained in using brainwashing and manipulation techniques himself. He knew not to believe anything nor to assume anything. To him, everything and everyone was suspect.

"Nobody ever knows what's really going on. Motives and counter motives. Reasons and unreasons. Truths hiding untruths. That's what this society depends on—nobody ever thinking beyond their own small remit. Nobody knowing who's really in charge."

"Maybe if you told us everything you can remember about this boy, Ferris, we could figure out what's going on," I suggested to Zac.

"Doubtful," said Ethan.

"It's worth trying," I persisted. "It's what you made me do."

"It's pointless," said Ethan.

"I've been thinking about him a lot since you showed me the photo," said Zac. "But it was a long time ago. I don't remember many details."

"That's OK. Just tell us what you do remember. Anything at all. Did you play sports together? Did you talk much to him? What sort of things was he good at?"

Ethan intervened. His professional pride won out over his contempt for my quest. He advised me to slow down and take one thing at a time. Between the two of us, we got Zac to recall everything he could about the boy. Yes, Ferris was sporty and athletic. He was a good team player who never got into fights with his teammates or the other side. He was also clever and never got into trouble with his instructors. But that was all Zac could recall. No intimate details, no quirks of character, nothing that would identify him as an adult.

I asked Zac if he could remember the names of any of the other children. He remembered some of them, but he couldn't remember the mothers' names, so he couldn't match mothers to children.

But I potentially could. I explained that by using Zac's numerical ID—Op 2411215—as a starting point, I could work out the other twenty-nine Natural Births children's numerical IDs by counting twenty-nine forward from Zac's and thirty back. That would give fifty-nine possibilities ranging from 2411186 to 2411245, and the target group would be within that.

"What if you find that more than sixty were born within that range?" asked Zac.

"She won't," said Ethan. "Even factory birth rates were so low back then that a week with sixty would've been an exceptional week."

"OK," I said. "All I have to do is go through the same personnel files where I found Salt's and my records, and we'll find them."

"And then what?" asked Ethan.

"We find the man who was the boy in the photo."

"And you report him to Military Intelligence without even knowing who exactly wants to find him or why?"

"It's my job. I have to."

"How can you be sure that your memory of Salt having the photo is real?" Ethan asked.

I wasn't prepared to consider any other scenario. I had only one in my head regarding finding Salt dead on the doorstep of the old house and taking the photo from him, so I knew it was real.

Zac had concerns of his own.

"What about the boy's mother? What if it's her they're after?" he asked.

"What do you think I should do?" I asked them.

Ethan replied immediately. "Do nothing."

Zac agreed. "Hold off until we try and figure it out."

But I couldn't hold off. I'd gone too far. I had to complete my mission. My future career depended on it. I couldn't say that to them, but I had to find a way to get more information from them.

"What if I do the search but don't report it?"

"Why would you?" asked Ethan.

I directed my answer to Zac.

"I might find a link to the mothers. To your mother."

"Their identities will be redacted," said Ethan.

"On the military files, yes. But not in the files you saw when you were in training."

"I didn't have access to all the files. I was only interested in the videos of the children. I saw nothing relating to mothers."

"But those files must exist."

"Yes," agreed Ethan. "In the Psychoscience Training Unit. But each Discipline guards its own information from all the others. They don't share—they obstruct. Only very senior Psychoscience staff would get anywhere near their records, so you can forget about that. Anyway, there are more important things we should be talking about."

"Like what?" I asked.

"I have a theory about how your assistant died. I don't think it was suicide."

I shut up and listened as Ethan revealed he wasn't the only one to have escaped the Bio-Med Labs. He explained that first, it was apes when apes were the only primates in the Research Labs. Then it was the humans who had been sent to the After Labs—the Labs Lake feared so much. Like the apes, the humans who'd escaped the After Labs were already contaminated and quickly died. They were found easily, and their remains cremated. But others survived. Ethan explained that these were people who had been deliberately infected and then treated with various experimental cures. They were in the in-between stage of being allowed to recover from the original infection before being reinfected with different viruses. Ethan referred to these people as Re-Cos because they were, at least temporarily, in the process of recovery. Some lab workers had stolen medication and guns and joined with a group of Re-Cos and escaped. These Re-Cos survived and made it to the forests along with the lab workers. No one outside the senior lab officials and the military's Specialist Search Units sent to track them knew this.

"How do you know they've survived?" I asked.

He pointed to his computer.

"I can spy too."

"You've hacked into the lab computers?"

"No. The Search Units' computers."

"The SSUs take no prisoners. And they take no chances," said Zac. "They don their Bio-Haz gear, move in, and kill.

"Tell me again about hearing the shot," instructed Ethan.

"I can't tell you anything more than I already have," I said.

"Tell me why you thought he'd killed himself."

"He was still holding his gun."

"Show me."

I shaped my hand as if I were holding a handgun and laid my arm across my lap.

They both stared at me.

"Are you sure that's exactly how you found him?" asked Zac. "His arm definitely in that position?"

"Yes."

"Unlikely," said Ethan.

"I'm telling you it was," I insisted.

"He means it's unlikely that his gun arm would've fallen across his knees like that," said Zac.

"It's more likely it would've fallen on the same side as his head wound," agreed Ethan.

"Did you check if his gun had been fired?" asked Zac.

Did I? I'd assumed it had been. But I hadn't checked. Had it been warm? I couldn't remember. I hadn't touched it until well after I'd heard the shot. I'd spent at least ten, maybe twenty minutes going around the house looking in windows. The gun could've had time to cool before I came back to the body. Had I smelt gunpowder? Maybe a whiff? Not much from a single shot. I wouldn't have noticed. Or would I if it had been Salt who'd fired? But I was too aware of the wound, the blood, the iron smell of the blood. But did I also smell gunpowder? I couldn't be sure.

"So you do think someone shot him?" I asked.

"Could have been a Re-Co," said Ethan.

"Why didn't they shoot me?"

Ethan explained his theory. The existence of the syringe strongly suggested that Re-Cos had been in the old house very recently. What if a group of them had been using it as their hideout? Maybe they had been out hunting or foraging when Salt had appeared? One Re-Co may have been left on guard or even been too unwell to go with the others. Maybe he or she saw Salt and thought he was an SSU soldier. Salt may have heard something or been aware of something after he'd sat down, and that was why he'd taken out his gun. The Re-Co couldn't risk discovery, so he, or she, shot him, and that's what I'd heard. I'd taken my time creeping up to the house. That would have given the Re-Co time to flee and warn the others. Maybe, after I'd gone, the Re-Cos returned and realized Salt wasn't from the Special Search Unit, but they couldn't risk staying at the house any longer, so they left sometime in the night. Either they took Salt's body away to hide it, or an ape took it for food.

"Are you saying that the Re-Cos planted the photo on Salt?" I asked.

"Forget about the photo," said Ethan. "Don't you see there's a much bigger issue here?"

"The escapes?"

"The labs," said Ethan. "They have to be shut down. You can help."

"How?"

"If people really knew what went on in them . . ."

"I came here looking for information on a woman and boy, that's all."

"And a missing Arc whose name you didn't even bother finding out," said Ethan.

I ignored him and continued speaking to Zac.

"I'm sorry about your mother and what happened to you. If I can help you find her, I will. Maybe when I find Ferris, I'll get a lead on all the mothers. But that's it."

"You don't care what suffering people are deliberately being put through?" asked Ethan.

"Did you care? You helped set it up. You're responsible. Not me. You do something about it."

"We intend to," said Zac. "Even before you were able to tell us what you saw in the house, we were making plans."

"I don't want to know," I said.

But I so did.

"Anyway, what can two people do against the whole system?" I asked.

Zac looked at Ethan, checking how far he should go. Ethan answered.

"We're going to take over the public broadcasting system. You know all that guff that's fed to you every day through your computer? We're going to replace it with the truth."

I did an Ethan-style laugh of scorn.

"You think you can walk into the Office of Information and Communication, grab a microphone and start talking?"

"We don't have to do that. We can pre-record."

"Nobody listens to those things anyway," I said.

"Oh, but they do," said Ethan. "They think they're not listening, but they are. They can't help it. It's unconscious. Subliminal even. It's the ultimate form of control of the masses, and it's supremely effective."

"Which is why we need you," said Zac.

How did I get into this situation? If I say I'll help, I'll get caught up in something way beyond my control. But if I say I won't, will they let me simply walk away and risk me reporting everything to my superiors? I didn't think so.

"I don't know anything about broadcasting. I've never been to the Info and Comms office. I wouldn't have any authority there."

"You have MI clearance," said Ethan. "You can go wherever you like."

I'd given away too much about myself. Now I kept quiet and waited to see where this was leading.

"We don't need you to go anywhere near the Info and Comms office," said Zac.

"What do you need?" I asked.

"Now that we know, from what you've been able to remember, that there are still Re-Cos alive somewhere in this zone, we need to contact them and get them to help too," said Ethan.

"This zone is huge. They could be anywhere," I said.

"You have tracking skills," said Zac. "So have I. They're on foot. We have vehicles."

"No. No way. I can't do that. It's way beyond my remit."

"The escaped Re-Cos are the proof of what's going on in the labs," Zac continued. "We need them to tell their stories. When we find them, we will film them. We'll get them to reveal everything they've been through. We have all the equipment we need."

I saw a glance go from Ethan to Zac. One that signaled 'Say no more.' That was fine with me. I didn't need to hear anymore. I'd heard enough to figure that they'd been preparing this for some time. Zac had probably been able to get hold of what they needed by stealing it from stores somewhere, and Ethan had the technical knowledge to utilize it. How dare they involve me? What made them think I would go along with this? I could understand why Ethan wanted to do something. He needed to assuage his guilt. And Zac bears a grudge. He'd do anything to hit back at the system. But the system works for me.

"You don't have to decide right now," said Zac.

"She's already decided," said Ethan.

"I'm sorry," I said.

"If you understood . . ." Zac began.

I cut him off.

"No. I have a job to do, and I intend to get on with it."

"In that case, I'll take you back to the others," said Zac.

✦

And that was it. There was nothing more to be said. Zac led me back through the cave system to where he'd hidden his ATU.

My head was reeling as we climbed on board and set off on our way back to join Lake, Tern, and Cale. After an uncomfortable silence, Zac began talking as if nothing of any significance had just taken place. I had to make an effort to pull myself together and listen. He told me that Lake was recovering well and could travel as soon as I was ready to leave. This, at least, was good news. In my head, I'd already planned to leave at the first opportunity and report back to my MI Commander. I still had to work out what exactly I would say. Would I tell him about the lab escapees? That maybe one of them shot Salt? Probably not. He'd want to know how I knew about them. Did he know about them? Did he know what went on in the labs? I became aware of Zac speaking.

"I know that was a lot to take in, and I understand your fears. You don't have to get involved. But will you just think about it? About what's happening in those labs every day. Until people see it for themselves, they won't believe it."

"Then you should be filming in the labs and showing that. Not just broadcasting hearsay from a few alleged escapees."

"Yes! So, you agree we must do something?"

Of course, I did. Just don't drag me into it. That's what I wanted to say. But I didn't. Every way I looked at myself, I realized more and more how weak I was. If I joined with Zac and Ethan, I would be risking everything. I would become an enemy of The Citizenship, a traitor. I, too, could be sentenced to become an experiment in an After Lab. I couldn't do it.

"Where were you? You left me alone with these weirdos. I thought you weren't coming back."

"They're not weirdos."

"You're all weirdos. That guy Zac told me you were out scouting for monkeys on your own. I knew that couldn't be true."

"You're feeling better then?"

"They've been trying to keep me doped up."

"They've been trying to help you."

"How long have you been away?"

"Only two days."

"Is that all? I thought you'd been gone a week at least. Where were you?"

I'd been wondering how much I should tell her. Given her present state, I still wasn't sure, so I opted to say as little as possible about where I'd been.

"Never mind that now. Do you think you're well enough to travel?"

"Yes! Get me out of here. But not back to the lab. Right? You promised."

That wasn't exactly what I'd promised. I'd only said I would recommend to my MI Commander that she be offered a new post as a reward for her help. There was no guarantee. I'd known that when I'd said it. She knew it too. But she'd been desperate. She'd wanted to believe I could do it. I'd used that to get her to go along with what I'd wanted. Now that I'd decided not to tell my Commander anything that Zac had told me, it would be even less likely that he would grant me any favors.

"Look, Lake . . ."

"Don't do this to me, Hazel."

Of course, I didn't want to send her back to the lab. Not now. Not after what I'd just found out. I mightn't be able to help Zac and Ethan with whatever mad plan they were hoping to concoct, but I wanted to do something to save Lake. But what? I couldn't say she'd died in the ape attack because I couldn't hide her forever, and I couldn't leave her with Zac and put him and his team at risk if the Earth History bosses were to check on them. I had to take her with me.

I watched her say goodbye to Zac and Cale. Her fondest goodbye was for Tern. No surprise there. Tern had nursed her back to health.

✦

On the way back to MIHQ, I decided to come clean. I told Lake what I'd found out about Ferris from Zac, and I admitted I had no intention of revealing any of it to my MI Commander. Instead, I would explain to him that I had done everything possible to identify the woman and boy, as my regular reports would have already confirmed. I could only conclude that there was no information on them anywhere in existence. I would tell him that the woman and boy photo was a relic from a lost past and its subjects were no longer extant. I assured Lake that I would make a strong case that she should be reassigned to a post more suited to her abilities, as I had said I would, but she would have to take her chances on that. I also had to admit that I didn't know what I could do if he refused. That's when I truly realized how useless and ineffectual I was. I could talk and plot and plan in my head, but it all meant nothing. I wasn't even a cog. The machine could function perfectly well without me. But could I, or Lake, or any of us, function without the machine?

"Tell him you want me to stay working with you."

"Doing what?"

"Anything. Whatever you're doing."

"You're not getting it. I'm going to him to admit failure."

"But you haven't failed. You found out about the Natural Births Experiment. You even found somebody who was born in it and remembered the boy. Don't dump yourself right in it. You've got a lead, Hazel. Use it."

She was right. I didn't have to admit defeat just yet.

✦

It took us four days to get back to MIHQ. We arrived in the middle of the night. I'd planned it that way because I wanted to have a plausible reason for taking Lake to my accommodation quarters rather than returning her immediately to her post at the Bio-Med Research Center. I also wanted to get on my computer and search the personnel files before losing my MI status.

Zac's records were easy to find, and I had no difficulty searching through the twenty-nine numerical IDs before his and the thirty after. I immediately eliminated the thirty-three females in the batch, leaving twenty-six males, excluding Zac. Ferris had to be one of them. It was that simple. Why wouldn't it be? Who, beyond a very few in the know, would ever seek such information? I isolated the male ID numbers and printed them out. But should I go any further? Were Zac and Ethan right to be worried about why security services were searching for the boy and his mother? Zac had initially wanted me to reveal what he'd told me about his own circumstances, but even he had changed his mind when he thought of the possible consequences for the other natural borns and their mothers. What should I do? Report everything and keep my status? Or claim that I'd been unable to find anything and risk my career. After much agonizing, I hid the printout in the back of my drawer.

The following day, I instructed Lake to stay in my quarters while I went to MIHQ. I had a long wait as my visit had not been prearranged. Even then, I was still unsure if I was doing the right thing by not revealing that I'd found the Natural Births children's identities.

I was shaking when a soldier eventually ushered me into the Commander's office. I never shake. The Commander stared at me, waiting for me to begin. I couldn't.

"What do you want?" he asked.

"I want to make my final report."

I began to explain all the lengths I had gone to in my search, but he interrupted me almost immediately.

"I know all this. What have you actually found?"

"Nothing. The woman and boy are not known—"

He rose from his seat before I could finish.

"Destroy all evidence of your research."

"I can't. I mean, I sent so many emails."

"Indeed. Destroy everything you can, including any copies of your reports."

"Sir."

It was obvious he wanted me to leave. But I had to ask him.

"My assistant . . ."

"Who?"

He glared at me.

"Op267. You approved her secondment from the Bio-Med Research Center. Could she be reassigned to a different posting? She was very helpful to me. Very capable. More capable than her present job demands."

I was babbling, but I had to go on.

"Do you think she could be posted to something more suited to her skills?"

"What skills?" he asked.

Fair question. I wanted to say being a nuisance, being stubborn, cunning, manipulative, a complete pain in the ass. Instead, I listed map reading, navigation, problem-solving, courage, determination. I told him that I could see that the lab work—working with rats and such—wasn't bringing out her full potential.

"She doesn't see a future. I mean, she's worth more. Could do more useful work."

"Tell her to make a formal request."

"And you'll approve it?"

"It's not up to me."

"But, you got her seconded to me."

"As a temporary aide only. I have no further use for her."

"She can't go back there."

I'd blurted it out without meaning to.

He glared at me a moment then sat down again.

"Why not?" he asked.

Oh shit! I was making this worse. What should I say? He was waiting for an answer. But at least he'd stopped glaring.

"Why can't she go back?" he asked again.

How much did he know about what went on in the labs? If I told him what I now knew, he would want to know how I knew. I couldn't betray Zac and Ethan. I couldn't tell him anything.

"She has asked me to get her a posting to the Medical Training Center."

"Any particular reason?"

"It was what she had requested before graduating from Cadet School. She was disappointed to be sent to the Research Lab instead. I would like to reward her for all the work she did for me in my search."

I was still ad-libbing. He didn't look in the least interested. Then it occurred to me that there was another angle I could try.

"During my search for the woman and boy, I discovered that Op438—the boy that had the photo—spent some time at the Medical Training Center going through a pre-med assessment before being assigned to the military. There's a chance that Lake, I mean Op267, might find out something useful if she were posted there. It could work to our advantage."

He stared at me as if I were crazy. I didn't blame him. But I had to try anything to get him to agree. I knew from Ethan that the Psychoscience Training Unit was housed within the Medical Training Center.

"Maybe that's where he got the photo. They use things like that to test people's credibility, their vulnerabilities."

The Commander sighed.

"Can't you just ask them?"

"Yes, sir. I could. But . . ."

But what? I was talking nonsense, but I couldn't stop now. I had to use whatever I had, whether I believed it or not.

"Something caused some sort of mental breakdown in Op438 that led to him killing himself. There's no record of him having any problems at junior school or in cadet training. I checked. But maybe something happened in the Medical Training Center during his assessment. If it did, they'd be unlikely to tell me anything. Somebody innocently working on the ground and perceptive enough to pick up on the sort of things that might be significant could find out a lot more than an MI operative coming in asking questions."

"You really think that's where he got the photo?"

"I haven't been able to find any other source. So, yes. I think that may be where he got it. He may have stolen it, or it may have been part of an exercise."

"So, sending Op267 to the Medical Training Center is your idea?"

It so wasn't. And, after listening to Ethan, I no longer believed that Salt had killed himself. I was making this up as I went along. But he was buying it.

"It suits us to take advantage of Op267's aspirations."

"And you're sure she'll comply?"

"I'm certain of it."

"And what about you?"

I stared at him. What did he mean?

"What are your aspirations?" he asked.

"To do my job to the best of my ability for the good of the Citizenship," I managed to reply.

"Very good, soldier."

Our meeting was definitely at an end this time. I left the Commander's office furious with myself for not having been prepared for the obvious question of what I wanted to do next now that I'd had to admit my failure to find Weird Smiley Woman and Boy. It rankled all the more because I had found out so much that I couldn't reveal.

✦

I returned to my quarters and told Lake what had happened.

"What? You mean you actually did it?"

"I promised, didn't I?"

"Yeah, but . . . the Medical Training Center!"

"Don't get too excited. It's only as an admin assistant, not a medical trainee. You're still a Military Op. You'll be doing data processing and coding. Do you think you can do that?"

"No problem. Listen, thanks. I mean that, Hazel."

There was something about the way she was looking at me. Like her eyes were holding me. I couldn't look away. I didn't want to look away. I was . . . what? Flustered? Embarrassed? Scared? Why?

She broke contact and turned away. I felt I'd missed an opportunity. I'd wanted to reach my hand out to her the way Zac had shown me. I'd wanted her to reach hers out to me. And she would have. I knew that. I could sense it. If I'd taken the initiative, she would have responded. That was what had scared me. I had to pull myself together and get back in control. Or maybe I'd completely misread her. Perhaps I'd imagined it. Or maybe I hadn't. It was too late now. The moment had gone. There was nothing I could do about it now.

"There's something else. I had to tell my Commander that you would keep an eye out for any reference in the archives to Salt or anything that would indicate that the woman and boy photo originated in the Medical Training Center. It was the only way I could swing it for you."

"Sure."

She didn't care. She would go along with whatever I said. She was just happy to have escaped the labs. I decided not to tell her I had other plans for her, which I hadn't revealed to my Commander. They'd been developing in the back of my mind all the time I'd been talking him into assigning her to the Med Training Center. But they could wait until she was properly established in her new role. I gave her one of the encrypted cell phones that my Commander had procured for both of us to communicate findings and instructions and advised her to keep it hidden and charged.

✦

The next morning, I dropped Lake off at her new posting. I didn't know when I would see her again, if ever. I couldn't let her walk off without acknowledging that.

"Lake, be careful. You know you don't have to do anything. I only made that up about sending you in to look for information. You don't have to."

Already I was backtracking, getting softer and softer.

"But if I do happen to find any, you want to know about it."

I'd promised myself I wouldn't reveal I had a plan. But I couldn't help myself.

"If you ever get access to the Psychoscience Training Unit archives, let me know."

"Why?"

"I'll tell you if you do."

"Is it likely?"

"Very unlikely."

"But you want me to try?"

This was madness. I couldn't ask her to put herself in that kind of jeopardy.

"No. Forget I said that. Don't do anything. I want you to stay safe."

"I'll be safe away from you."

And with that, she strode off to report for her new duties. I knew she'd been joking. I hoped she was right. But if she could get access to those archives? No. It was too dangerous. And Zac had agreed with Ethan that I shouldn't. But I hate leaving a job unfinished.

✦

I returned to my quarters. I'd never thought about it before, but I'd spent all my life in the company of other people. First, the staff and the other infants in the nursery, then the staff and children in junior school, and then the staff and cadets during my military training. Even when I took up my Earth History post in the bush, I always had an Arc and an Op assistant. So why did that feeling of loneliness haunt me? Could I now cope alone in my quarters with no role, no status, and no idea of what was coming next? I'd been so concentrated on setting Lake up with the Medical Training Center that I'd talked myself out of my job. I thought again about how I should have answered my Commander's question. What were my aspirations? Did I still have any? Everything that I'd discovered in the past couple of weeks had turned what I'd always believed upside down. People didn't always behave in the way they'd been taught. Some only pretended to follow the rules. They didn't seem to care about The Citizenship or The Future. They cared only about themselves. The Moral Code meant nothing to them. Worst of all, it wasn't just the lower tiers of the Citizenry that behaved like that. Our leaders at the very top didn't seem to care either. I could have asked to return to my former duties with the Earth History Project. So what if that would be a step backward in my career?

I'd enjoyed driving through the bush, exploring new places, free to have my own thoughts. But my contact with Zac and Ethan had soured that. They'd shown me a world out there that I could never have dreamt existed. Frightened, disease-riddled escapees desperately fleeing for their miserable lives from ruthless Specialist Search Units. And what had happened to Arc371? Was she really dead? Or alive and in pain? Suffering some terrible disease inflicted on her by another Citizen? And who were these Citizens who could do such things? People whom the likes of Ethan had brainwashed? People too weak to say no? No. Not weak. Too afraid. Or people like me. People who wanted to succeed. To be the best. People who will do whatever it takes. Who will do whatever they're told. Who will believe whatever they're told. We must secure The Future. We must eradicate all diseases, all viruses, all vulnerabilities. There will inevitably be mistakes. We must inevitably make sacrifices. If I want to progress—to be a good soldier and a good Citizen—I must accept this. If I don't, I won't survive. I have to make myself immune to other people's suffering. I have to concentrate only on The Future. Mine as well as The Citizenship's.

I opened up my computer and began deleting all my reports as my Commander had instructed.

✦

The call came that evening. I was to pack up my belongings and report for a secondment at the Political Commissariat.

CHAPTER

13

I had not been expecting the Political Commissariat. Or the promotion to Senior Op. I still held my Military Intelligence ID, so I supposed my MI Commander wanted to keep me available to him if Lake and I did manage to find any further information on the photo. That would be unlikely as I had no intention of disclosing what I already knew, at least not to him, and, at this moment, not to anyone else.

My Pol Com Commander was female, thirties, and suitably stern. She did not seek to meet with me as my MI Commander had done. I viewed that as a good thing. I was determined to keep a low profile and stay out of trouble. It would be easy. I was now part of a team. I did not have separate instructions. Like everyone else of my status, my job would be to investigate low-level Ops in any Discipline suspected of Anti-Citizenship behavior or Moral Code breaches. I was not unaware of the irony of my appointment.

Six of us were appointed simultaneously, including one of Salt's class-mates from Military Cadet School. She'd been on guard duty outside Pol Com HQ when I'd interviewed her about Salt and had revealed abso-lutely nothing about him. I'd known then that she was an ideal Pol Com operative. Now she'd been allowed in from the cold and was training to become an investigator. I nodded at her. She ignored me.

The remaining four trainees were just as cold. At one time, I wouldn't have noticed. I'd have been the same. Not now. Now I hoped for conversa-tions, revelations even. They wouldn't be forthcoming. Nobody cared who I was. Or who I'd been. My fellow trainees didn't know I was on second-ment. My MI status meant nothing. I was a rookie now. Even I was aware of that. I'd been shoved in here because I'd failed to complete the only thing my MI Commander had asked me to do. But I hadn't. I'd come so close, and giving up was the most difficult thing I'd ever had to do.

✦

As Pol Com trainees, we had to show that we completely understood what was expected of a Citizen, and we had to show that we could recite The Moral Code from memory. Reciting The Moral Code was no problem as we'd all been taught it at school. Every morning began with us standing and reciting it in unison—six trainees and at least one instructor declaring "The Future is Survival. We are The Future" and then listing The Moral Code's twelve tenets:

The Future can only be assured by The Citizenship acting as one for the good of all.

All Citizens must obey the directives of The Nine Disciplines.

The only authorized alliance is The Citizenship, guided and directed by The Nine Disciplines. There must be no other alliances of any kind without the written approval of The Grand Controllers or above.

No Citizen is permitted to engage in personally motivated pair or group bonding activities.

All procreation is for the sole purpose of ensuring The Future and must be designed and controlled only by The Supreme Council. No Citizen is permitted to engage in any sexual or reproductive activity without the Supreme Council's written approval; otherwise, they will be deemed to have committed treason against The Citizenship.

All manufactured and intellectual property, whether historical or contemporary, belongs to The Citizenship. No Citizen may take, or use, any item or idea whatsoever for any unauthorized use.

No Citizen may slander The Nine Disciplines on penalty of death.

No Citizen may slander another Citizen on penalty of death.

No Citizen may physically or mentally harm another Citizen on penalty of death.

A Citizen who becomes unwell must report to the nearest medical unit immediately.

Any Citizen who becomes aware of another Citizen's failure to report an illness must immediately inform his/her superior.

It is the duty of all Citizens, at whatever level, to report any and all breaches of The Moral Code to their superiors.

✦

After our initial training, we were each assigned to an experienced investigator and sent out into the field. I got Sig—a twenty-eight-year-old male. One of our regular jobs was to provide escorts for Citizens sent to Re-education Centers for mind adjustments. We also escorted criminals bound for the high-security Pol Com Holding Center.

The Holding Center sat on its own campus beyond the perimeter of Urb One. We worked in teams of six when escorting someone there. We wore our full military uniforms with Pol Com insignia and regulation balaclavas, presumably to make ourselves look as intimidating as possible, and we carried semi-automatic submachine guns. I had assumed all this was because people being taken to the Holding Center were liable to be violent, but the few I helped escort were more frightened than aggressive. Neither Sig nor I had ever heard of anyone attacking an escort or any group of soldiers. But then we wouldn't. If such a thing ever happened, The Moral Code ensured nobody would dare talk about it.

When we weren't on escort duties, my job was confined to driving and making notes while Sig conducted interviews. Sometimes all we were required to do was show up at a facility and walk around so that everyone would see our Pol Com insignia and be aware that they were under inspection. I could sense the tension in the air when we did that. Had I not had the experiences I had in my previous MI post, I would've enjoyed the feeling of power. Now I felt as queasy as the workers in the facilities must have felt when they saw us watching them. As an operative out in the bush, I'd been spared this scrutiny. I'd had nothing to hide and nothing to fear. Now I had so much to hide, and fear controlled my every thought. Was this to be my life now? Yes. Because this is what everyone's life becomes sooner or later. Fear, I was beginning to realize, is what holds The Citizenship together.

As Pol Com Ops, Sig and I couldn't allow any familiarity to creep into our association. Still, I couldn't help myself revealing to him that I was on what I termed temporary secondment from Military Intelligence. I didn't intend to allow him to get too superior with me. Like a good Citizen and Pol Com Op, he expressed no surprise and asked no questions.

✦

I didn't attempt to make any contact with Lake during this time. As an unexpected insert into the Medical Training Center, someone like me would be watching her for any potentially unconventional behavior. I accepted that I had been effectively silenced. Now I was silencing her to keep her safe.

Part of my job required me to transfer our reports into the Pol Com database, so I regularly took the opportunity to read some of the reports filed by other field investigators. The reports were listed under their locations with a brief description of the crimes being investigated. They weren't very interesting—just more of the same sort of stuff we were investigating. There were no names in the reports—only numerals—so I couldn't identify anyone. One location caught my eye, Urb Six—the new urban center under construction. I'd been there as part of my Weird Smiley Woman and Boy search. The crime was suspected treason, as defined by The Moral Code tenet on unauthorized sexual activity. I already had a feeling that I knew who they meant even before I opened up the full report. I was right. Ops5932189 and 5877891. Tork and Faze. Why didn't I warn them at the time? If it were obvious to me, it would've been obvious to others. All I cared about back then was getting what I could from them. Now they'd been listed for further investigation. That was all the information available to me through my Pol Com access code. I needed to find out more. Since I still belonged to Military Intelligence, there was a good chance my biometrics might still be logged in to the mainframe. But if I did get in, would someone in Pol Com want to know why I was snooping beyond my remit? Maybe. Could I come up with a plausible reason? Probably. Did I need to know what was happening to Tork and Faze? No. It was none of my business. They knew the rules. They broke them. Now they're paying the price.

But I had to know. That evening I used my Military Intelligence ID to log into the computer provided with my new Pol Com living quarters. I brought up the Tork and Faze report I'd read earlier and clicked on the

permission to deep access button. My face appeared on the screen. I held
my breath. Would it still work? I watched the sensor move down my face
and saw my eyes seem to light up as both the facial and iris recognition
systems performed their tasks. My face disappeared and was immediately
replaced with the opening page of Case No PC9671187—Tork and
Faze's case. I hesitated before entering further. I was about to snoop into
the private lives of two Ops. But we're not supposed to have personal
lives. Feelings must be suppressed; emotions must be controlled; otherwise, you're in big trouble. Why am I doing this? OK, I'd liked Tork and
Faze when I'd met them, but they are nothing to me. What good will it
do me to know the details of their indiscretions? No one tasked me to do
this. I was tasking myself. I wanted to know why two bright young Ops
would risk everything for a friendship bond. If that's what it was. Or was
it more than that?

I was no clearer on the why by the time I'd finished reading. But I
now had a lot of information on the how. Someone at their workstation
had reported them, and despite warnings, they had continued their anti-
Moral Code behavior. The Pol Com investigators were not identified, but
their conclusions were clear. Tork had been relocated to another building
project, but he had gone AWOL within a week and been recaptured on
his way back to see Faze, who was still located at Urb Six. Now Faze was
under strict supervision while Tork was held at the Pol Com Holding
Center pending redesignation. Redesignation? I knew about relocation
and reassignment, but what exactly did redesignation mean?

I asked Sig the next day. After a brief look of uncertainty crossed his
face, he told me not to worry about it and that it would be covered in a
further training course if I ever made it to the senior investigator level. I
got the feeling he didn't want to admit that he didn't know.

I couldn't stop thinking about Tork and Faze. It was ridiculous. I'd
only met them for a short time, but I couldn't help feeling connected to
all the young Ops I'd talked to about Salt. OK, some had been reluctant
to engage, but I understood why. If only I'd known then what I know
now, I would've used a different approach, been more patient with them,
less aggressive in my attitude.

I went about my work in the usual way but that word "redesignated" kept niggling in the back of my mind. That night, after I'd gone to bed and couldn't sleep, it came to me. I had heard it used before. I knew exactly what it meant. It was the word Lake had used when she and I had been talking about Clover. I'd told her about being unable to find any record of Clover in the Bio-Med Research Lab, that there was no one there with Clover's designation, and Lake had said, "They change your designation when you go into the After Labs." A change of designation! A redesignation? This was what I'd feared. Now there could be no doubt. Tork was about to be disappeared into a germ experimentation Program in a Bio-Med Research Lab. Botulism, anthrax, yellow fever, chickenpox, measles, mumps, coronaviruses, rabies, Marburg, Ebola, and all the other deadliest diseases awaited him. His body wracked with pain and fever; his liver, kidneys, lungs, brain, every organ destroyed in continuous experiments; endlessly cured, then re-infected in a cycle of torture.

Was this what had happened to Salt and Clover? One taken away for the severest form of punishment, and the other left to continue alone. No need for The Citizenship to lose two Operatives. Punishing one by disappearing him or her was also punishment for the other. If I were right, Salt and Clover's investigation would be in the Pol Com records. I had the necessary access to find it.

14

I used Salt's ID number as a starting point and soon had his and Clover's case on my screen.

*   *   *   *   *   *   *   *   *   *   *   *   *   *   *   *   *   *   *

Political Commissariat
Investigations Branch
Case No. 8423945

Accused: Military Cadet 5351438 Male Age 18
Military Cadet 59294123 Female Age 18

Charge: Immoral behavior contrary to the Moral Code

Specifications:
1. Cadets 5351438 and 59294123 mutually formed an exclusive bond to the detriment of their fellow cadets.
2. Cadets 5351438 and 59294123 did absent themselves from their unit without authorization on three known occasions.
3. Cadets 5351438 and 59294123 did engage in mutual sexual activity on the occasions of their unauthorized absence from their unit.
4. Cadets 5351438 and 59294123 did conceive a child without authorization and in contravention of The Laws of Citizenship.

Accuser: REDACTED

Investigators: REDACTED

Recommendations:
1. Cadet 5351438 to be held at Military Cadet School for re-education.
2. Cadet 59294123 to be re-designated and assigned to the Bio-Medical Education Department.

*   *   *   *   *   *   *   *   *   *   *   *   *   *   *   *   *   *   *

The recommendations seemed so benign, lenient even. I knew better. There is no Bio-Medical Educational Department. There is only the Research Center and the labs. If Clover, or Cadet 59294123 as the report refers to her, was sent there, it means Lake was right. Clover was sent to an After Lab.

The rest of the four-page report set out the specified charges in more detail. The biggest puzzle was the child. They had conceived a child? How? What had become of it? Was it allowed to be born? Had it been born in the Bio-Med lab? Was it there now undergoing some awful experiment? Would Salt have known that? Probably not. But he'd had every reason to be in the state he was when he'd arrived with me. None of his classmates had mentioned that he'd been held back for re-education, but they may not have known. I needed to recheck his education records.

Sure enough, Salt's Military Personnel file revealed that he had hadn't graduated until three months after everyone else in his unit had gone off to their postings. The date hadn't registered with me when I'd first looked at his file. But, when my previous Op Assistant broke her leg, it provided the perfect opportunity to send him as far away as possible from the urban Centers. It all made sense now—the crying in the night, the running away. Lake was right. Salt had known that he'd never see Clover again. But it didn't explain the photo. Where did he get it, and why did he keep it? And did it matter? No. Not right now. What mattered now was stopping Tork from being sent to an After Lab. But how? I needed to talk to Lake.

✦

I used our secret MI phones and arranged a meeting with Lake after she'd finished work. I began by asking her why she hadn't told me everything she knew about Salt and Clover.

"You weren't interested."

"Of course I was. How can you say that?"

"As soon as Zac told you he'd had a mother, that was all you cared about. You never gave me a chance to tell you about Clover."

Was she right? Yes, she was.

"OK. Tell me now."

We were sitting in my Lightweight a couple of kilometers away from the Medical Training Center.

"What do we say if someone sees us?" Lake asked.

She was deflecting, but it was a good question. We had no authorized reason to meet.

"I still have my Military Intelligence ID. I'll show it and say we're on MI business. My MI Commander will back me up if necessary."

"You sure?" she asked.

I wasn't.

"Yes," I replied.

"OK. I knew something was going on between Clover and Salt."

"How?"

"Everybody knew. You could just tell. You know?"

I wasn't sure that I did. Could other people know what's going on in someone's head? Could she know all that was in my head right now, like how pleased I was to see her? She looked good. Better than when I'd first met her. She still had a few scars on her neck and face from the ape attack, but they would eventually fade. I had to stop looking at her and focus on what she was telling me.

"Including the instructors?" I asked.

"I don't mean them. They didn't know. Not at first."

"But somebody reported it."

"Yeah. Some crawler."

"You don't know who?

She shook her head.

"Why are you interested now?" she asked.

I told her what I'd found out about Tork and Faze, though not what I knew was about to happen to Tork, and how that had led me to look up Salt and Clover's case.

"I hope I never have to wait on you to cop on to something."

OK. Maybe I should've taken her Clover story more seriously.

"So, you knew she was pregnant?" I asked.

"No. At least not before we graduated."

"You found out after? How?"

"I liked Clover," she said. "She didn't care about anything. She played the game when she had to. But she did her own thing too. She didn't let them get to her. Salt took everything so seriously. It was him that gave them away—always looking at her, following her around. I mean, she felt the same, but he couldn't keep it hidden. No self-control. She used to get so pissed with him. Then they both disappeared."

"What do you mean?" I asked.

"In the middle of the night."

"They were arrested?"

"Yeah. I guessed it was something like that. Only Salt came back. They kept Clover. I didn't see her again until I was assigned to the Bio-Medical Research Center."

"None of this went on in my Military Cadet unit."

"Would you have noticed?"

I was thinking about that as she continued.

"Probably just as well you wouldn't, or you'd have reported it."

Would I? I wouldn't knowingly have sent someone to an After Lab. But I didn't know about such places and what went on in them back then.

"I thought you said you and Clover were sent to the Bio-Med Research Center together?"

"Not literally on the same day. She was already there when I arrived."

"When did you find out she was pregnant?" I asked.

"I met her coming out of some sort of office. She was scared. She told me then that she was pregnant. She thought they were going to abort it. She knew she was going to be sent to a lab."

"So, she knew where she was going?"

"We just thought it was an ordinary lab like the one I'd been assigned to. But they'd already changed her numerical. We both thought that was odd. I didn't have mine changed."

"Redesignation."

"Yeah. I suppose. Then a woman came out of the office and took her away. I never saw her again. That's why I think she was sent straight to one of the After Labs."

"Can you remember her new designation?"

"I'm good. But I'm not that good."

"Lake, do you know what goes on in the After Labs?"

"It's where the rats and monkeys that I used to look after go to have horrible things done to them."

"Not just rats and monkeys."

I told her everything Ethan had told me, including how some people had managed to escape and were hiding out in the bush. I kept Ethan's name out of it and hoped she wouldn't ask me how I knew all this. She didn't. Instead, when I'd finished, she kept on staring out the Lightweight's windscreen. I knew she wasn't seeing anything but the terrible images I'd put in her head. We sat like that for a long time. She didn't even turn to me when she finally spoke.

"Do you think Clover's dead?"

"She may be."

"And the baby?"

"I don't know."

"And now they're sending Tork there."

"Yes."

She turned to me.

"Why have you told me all this? Why did you think I needed to know this? What do you want from me? What do you think I can do about it? I'm not going back there. Is that what you want? You want me to go back. I'm not. Not ever."

"I don't know what to do about it."

"Take me back to the Medical Training Unit."

✦

We drove back in silence. I understood Lake's anger. I wanted to give her some sort of reassurance. I thought of saying that there was a chance that Clover had been one of the ones who had escaped. But I couldn't. She wouldn't fall for that sort of false hope.

"I don't suppose you've come across the Psychoscience Training Unit archives yet?" I asked.

"Seriously? Are you for real?"

OK. Wrong time. But I did have a good reason for asking. I tried to explain it to her.

"It's just that if I can impress my MI Commander, I might have a better chance of getting him to ask for leniency for Tork."

"Yeah. Like he'd care. He's one of them. It's people like him who send people to the After Labs. And people like you."

"I'm not like that."

"Really?"

We'd reached the Medical Training Center. She got out before I could reply and strode off. I watched her disappear into her accommodation block then I drove off. That was that then.

✦

What could I have said? She wouldn't have listened to me. But I'm not like that. OK, I believe in discipline. Correction. Re-education. But not that. Not torture. Not cruelty. But I didn't know. I could've been the person she'd accused me of being. I still could be. I'm only a junior Pol Com Investigator. I'm only on secondment. But if I progress, I could be just a few steps away from being the one who carries out the in-depth interrogations. I could become the person she's accused me of being. I would have to, to survive. But would I want to stay at that price? This is too much. I wish I'd never encountered that idiot Salt. Why did they have to send him to me? I always had good Op Assistants, good Arcs. We didn't mess up each other's lives. We did our jobs. No fuss. No problems. Then he came along. Whingeing and crying. They should've sent him to the After Lab too. In fact, why didn't they?

What am I saying? I'm not that person. I'm not. Everything was simple in the bush. All I had to do was drive. Why couldn't I have been content with that? Why was I always looking for more? Why did I think something was missing? Nothing was missing. Nothing is missing. This is it. This is life. We're all alone. That's how it is. There's nothing I can do for Tork. Or Clover. I don't even know Clover. I'd already put Arc371 out of my mind because what was the point of thinking about what happened to her? Thinking about it was unbearable. Images I didn't want. I wanted instead to remember her in the old house. Her excitement. How she pounced on things in each room we entered. She couldn't hold back. Telling me to look at this, look at that. Things I'd never seen before. Things I didn't know. She knew. She explained them to me. The photographs with mother, father, children—a family. All were living there together, all smiling. Happy. All beyond me. Unimaginable.

I had to stop. I couldn't see to drive anymore. Tears filled my eyes. I couldn't breathe. I felt like I was choking. This was not me. I'd lost complete control. I was breaking into pieces. What was wrong with me? Why was this happening? Ethan would laugh if he could see me. But Zac wouldn't; Zac would know. I wished I could go to Zac. I wanted to reach out and feel the warmth of his hand. I wanted to feel the warmth of Lake's hand. I'm not one of those people, Lake. Don't think that of me. I had to tell you. I wanted to tell you. I needed you to show me that it's all right to feel angry, sad, and helpless. I needed you to understand that's how I felt. I couldn't say it. I don't know how to say what I feel. I don't know how to show it. Why am I so messed up?

I'd never cried before. At least not since I was an infant in the nursery. I'd soon learned it got me nowhere. Now I was ashamed, exhausted. I drove back to my quarters, very glad not to meet anyone on my way.

I was too agitated to go to bed. I needed to get back in control of myself. I needed to decide on a course of action and stick to it. I had effectively, though unintentionally, shut myself off from Lake. I had already told Zac and Ethan that I wanted nothing to do with their plans, so I was shut off from them too. I owed them nothing, and they knew to expect nothing. Even my MI Commander wasn't hoping for much more from me. I was free of them all. I had an opportunity now to make a promising career in the Commissariat if I kept my head down and got on with it. I didn't need to waste time worrying about things over which I had no influence. We all knew the rules. We knew if we broke them, there would be consequences. I needed to put what I learned out of my mind and get on with the job.

✦

I reported for duty, as usual, the following morning. The days that followed involved more visits to various facilities, more strutting about, more interviewing Operatives who weren't sure why they had been singled out or by whom, and more stupid, inconsequential nonsense. I knew I couldn't do this for the rest of my life. I couldn't keep on pretending that I didn't know the possible results of what I did. Or that I didn't know the things I now knew. Or that I hadn't had feelings stirred up inside me that both frightened and thrilled me. I no longer wanted to be the perfect soldier if being perfect meant being so alone and so isolated from everyone with whom I came in contact. I was so isolated from myself. So unable to respond when someone touched me, reached out to me, needed me. So ignorant of how to react. So unaware of how to care about anyone or anything but my self-interest. I'd given up on what I could do. I'd walked away from the chance of finding answers. Answers to my questions. The ones I dared not ask. Who am I? Who gave birth to me? Is my mother still alive? Who is she? Where is she? Does she know about me? I'm a factory born, so she knows I exist. Does she care? Do I have a child, children, from the eggs they harvested from me? Probably. Somewhere. Where are they? Did they survive? Did they keep one, or two, or even all of them for experiments? In the Ex-Vivo files that I'd consulted for information on Salt, I'd seen that of the sixteen embryos in Salt's batch, two died almost immediately, five were severely malformed and aborted, four died within the following six days. Only three, including Salt, survived. That left two others unaccounted. What happened to them? Were they healthy? Were they kept back because they were healthy? Fit and available for experimentation because nobody cared enough to say no? Or nobody dared? But what can I do? Nothing. I have no power. I only have myself. There is nothing I can do. But that must be how everybody thinks. People who let these things happen tell themselves there is nothing they can do. They make themselves helpless. I'm not helpless. I have strengths. I have resources I can use. But have I the courage? I didn't know. But there was nothing to stop me from thinking that if I had, what would I do?

By the end of the day, I had a list in my head. Zac and Ethan were resources. They were way ahead of me in wanting to put a stop to the labs and the experiments. They were already making plans. I could help. Lake was a resource. She knew at least something about the labs' layout and workings, and she was familiar with the relatively safe part of the Bio-Med Research Center. That could help us gain information, maybe even entry to the rest of the Center. But my most significant resource, or asset, was my MI status. I had to regain full MI status, which meant I had to get out of my Pol Com secondment. Only my MI Commander could help me with that. I had to regain his confidence. That meant that I had to go back and use the information I already had and find Ferris.

And through him, find Weird Smiley Woman. OK, I didn't know what the consequences would be for them. I could be putting them at risk, as Ethan thought. But I didn't know how else to do it. I had to show I could potentially fulfill my mission before expecting my Commander to reinstate me fully. It wasn't my risk, but it was still one I had to take because I knew I couldn't continue not doing something.

I retrieved my list of ID numerical designations for the twenty-six males from the Natural Births Experiment that I'd copied from my previous research. Then I opened up my computer and began the slow process of entering each ID into each of the Nine Disciplines' personnel files. When I'd finished, I found that eight had been assigned to Computer Science and Technology, seven to Engineering and Architecture, one to Biology and Medicine, three to Math and Physics, two to Agricultural Sciences, and five to Security. Now I would have to visit each one at their respective locations. The problem would be how to find the time given that I still had to fulfill my regular duties with Pol Com. But I couldn't let that put me off. I started with those located closest to my present location and arranged my list accordingly. I'd been through the list so many times now that I almost knew each of the twenty-six ID numbers as well as I knew my own. One, in particular, held my attention: 2411228. Why? What was so familiar about it? It wasn't Zac's number because I'd had no need to include Zac in my search. Maybe it was similar to a number I'd come across when I'd been checking the list of cadets from Salt's unit. But their seven-digit numbers began with 5, not 2. Could it be someone I'd emailed about the woman and boy photo? Could Ferris be a Military Cadet School instructor? I'd deleted my emails to and from them on the MI Commander's instructions but not their email contact addresses. I opened up my contacts list. And that was as far as I needed to go. There he was: Military Op2411228. He wasn't some anonymous instructor. I knew who he was. I should've recognized the number when I first saw it. I'd sent so many emails to this address. But after the first time, I'd only had to key in the first three digits, and the rest entered automatically, which meant the whole number didn't embed in my head. Ferris—Military Op2411228—was my MI Commander.

15

It was late, but this couldn't wait. I immediately went to MI HQ. He wasn't there, and he wasn't going to be there for the foreseeable. That was all the woman who was deputizing for him would say. She had no idea who I was. Nor did she care. I apologized for disturbing her and asked her to let my former Commander know I had reported for duty and awaited his instructions. Now she looked at me with a spark of interest.

"What duty?" she asked.

"I'm sorry," I said. "I'm not at liberty to say. It's highly secret."

"Get out," she growled.

I didn't care if she believed me, she probably didn't, but I'd enjoyed my brief moment of defiance. I also didn't think she would bother getting in touch with my former Commander, but if she did, it would alert him to the fact that I wanted to speak with him. Hopefully, he would realize I had something worth saying.

At least I now knew why he'd tasked me with finding the woman and boy. It was the woman—his own mother—he wanted to find. But why hadn't he been able to track her down himself? Surely, he would've tried? Then it struck me. He couldn't because if he had, he'd have risked being found out. Then he discovered that I, an unknown Op from the bush, had her photo. That must've shocked him. And where did I get it? From some crazy, unhinged kid. Bloody Salt!

My mind was racing as I drove away from MI HQ. Now that I knew the MI Commander was Ferris, it changed everything. What I'd thought was an assignment from Military Intelligence to hunt down a subversive was an assignment from a man seeking to find the woman who gave birth to him. If I could find him, I could persuade him to help Tork. He would do it for me because I'd done so much for him. He didn't even know how much I'd done for him. I'd have to tell him everything. But hang on. What have I done for him? I'd found out that he was the boy in the photo. Big deal. He knew that. That wasn't what he'd wanted.

But what if there was a state organization involved? What if, somehow, Pol Com had found out what the Commander had been doing? Could that be why he'd ordered me to delete my reports? He'd let me send emails to the nursery, the junior schools, and the Military Cadet School. Was he so desperate to find her that he'd been prepared to risk everything? Had he, too, been disappeared? Had his mother? Had all the mothers? Or could Salt have somehow been in contact with Ferris' mother? Could she have given him the photo? How? What possible contact could Salt have had with Ferris' mother? So many questions and no answers. Just speculation. Maybe I had it all wrong. But I had nothing else to go on besides my imagination. And it was going crazy. I needed someone to bounce against—someone more in tune with the world than I was.

✦

I waited until Lake finished her duties at the Medical Training Center before I contacted her. I told her I had a plan to help Tork. It was the only way I could get her to agree to meet me again.

I drove us safely out of the urban area and stopped. She turned on me with predictable anger.

"I told you. There's no way I'm going back into the lab."

"Wait. Listen to me. I'm not asking you to go back. That's not where he is. At least not yet."

"What are you asking then?"

"He's in the Pol Com Holding Center. It's where the Commissariat sends people who are under investigation. They'll keep him there until the Bio-Med Research Center have a use for him."

"You mean the torture labs."

"If I can persuade the guards to let me in, I could maybe find a way to get him out."

"How?"

I explained my plan. I would use my MI ID to get into the Holding Center. I would say that Military Intelligence had ordered me to bring Tork to MI HQ for interrogation on a separate matter, unrelated to his current charge. That this matter was top secret and that Tork could only be interrogated under strict MI conditions.

Lake stared at me.

"You're mad. You're going to go in there, on your own, and just walk out with him?"

"Do you have a better idea?" I asked her.

I hoped she did. I was counting on it. I could see her thinking, working it out in her head. At last, she spoke.

"Everybody in our unit liked Tork. Or at least nobody actively disliked him."

"Somebody did."

She shrugged. OK. I got it. We couldn't let that stop us.

"We'd need at least five to make a convincing-looking arrest party," I explained. "Me as the Officer-in-Charge and you and three others as security. And we need two more for backup afterward. Who can we trust?"

She made a list of all the members of the unit and immediately crossed out Clover and Tork. I crossed out my new Pol Com colleague Op377 and number one suspect for reporting Salt and Clover. Also, Ops761, 487, and 298 because I had found them uncooperative when I'd interviewed them about Salt. And Op470, aka Ford, who'd been a complete know-it-all and most unlikely to risk his future as an even greater know-it-all. Also, Cale, Op675, since he was too far away in the bush for us to be able to track down in time, and Faze because she would be under severe scrutiny now. We agreed on Ops 176, 184, 594, and 495 as solid possibilities. Although I'd dismissed Op298, aka April, Lake was determined to include her.

"You've got her wrong. April's OK. She minds her own business, and she knows when to keep her mouth shut. And she's loyal to her comrades."

That narrowed our list down to five Ops. I thought it significant that the only one whose name I knew was April. Had the other four been cleverer than I'd realized and deliberately played dumb? I could check their personnel files and get their IQs and aptitudes, but I didn't need to. I had Lake provide the rundown on each of them.

Op176, known to her friends as Nea, had come top of the unit in every mental and physical task they'd been set, yet she had been assigned to fetching and cleaning duties in the Physics, Chemistry, and Math labs. Same with Op184, known as Adar. He, too, had been a very bright member of the unit, but he worked alongside Nea, carrying out only menial duties. The pattern was the same with Ops 594 and 495, known as Reyn and Peak. I'd met them in a Computer Lab where their job was to input the most boring statistical data imaginable even though they too had performed very highly in all their Military Cadet School tests. Even April, with the highest IQ of the lot, was assigned a relatively low position as a guard outside civic buildings. Why?

Lake explained that each of them had fallen foul of their instructors in some way. In Anthropology lectures, Nea had queried the instructor's interpretation of human development too many times. Adar was regularly accused of not paying attention when he was simply bored by a lesson that he'd already mastered. Reyn had been discovered using cadet training school equipment to conduct unauthorized chemical experiments, and Peak, as Lake expressed it, had an allergy to being told what to do. She wasn't sure what exactly April had done to offend. However, she suspected it might have been her unwillingness to join in the weekly self-humiliation of confessing your previous week's indiscretions to the whole unit. None of them had committed any serious offenses. They hadn't breached The Moral Code. But any type of defiance during military cadet training is always punishable.

We had to act fast. We went to my quarters to access my computer to track our chosen Ops in their accommodation blocks. The distance wasn't a problem, but persuasion might be.

At Lake's suggestion, we approached April first. It was relatively easy to dodge the security cameras at her accommodation block. Their purpose was to deter rather than to detect. I let Lake do the talking while I stood back looking, I hoped, rational and sensible. That didn't stop April eyeing me suspiciously. Even when I joined in and told her everything I dared about the After Labs, she looked like she didn't believe me. Lake took her cue and revealed what we were both convinced had become of Clover. I watched as April swung from disbelief to horror, to outrage. When Lake had finished explaining that Tork's punishment would be the same and how we planned to free him from the Holding Center, she asked the inevitable.

"What happens then?"

I did have a plan in the back of my mind that I hadn't even fully articulated to Lake. My priority was to get Tork out and away from the urban area. After that, there was only one thing that could happen, assuming we didn't get caught.

"We head into the bush," I replied. "I know people there. They'll help us."

I stared at Lake, willing her not to mention names or locations. She didn't. Instead, she gave April an option.

"Look, you don't have to come with us into the bush. You only have to help us get Tork out. That's a couple of hours of your time at the most. Then you go to work as usual. No one will ever know."

April wasn't going to be that easily assured.

"Somebody might recognize me."

"They won't," I said. "You'll all be geared up like a proper prisoner escort with balaclavas covering your faces."

But before April could answer, Lake stepped in.

"Do you understand what happens in those labs? Can you even imagine it? You can't. I can't. None of us can because our brains can't let us. It's too much. Germs breeding in you, feeding on you. Every organ inside you destroyed. They already control every moment, every aspect of our lives—what we think, what we feel, what we're allowed to say, who we're allowed to say it to. We have nobody. There's nobody on our side. We only have them, and they don't care about us. They make us, and when they want more of us, they make more. When they don't, they decide who lives and who doesn't. We have nothing. We don't even own our own bodies. We are nothing. Look at you. Is this all there is to you? To Tork? Or Faze? Or Clover? Are we all just containers for their evil shit?

And why are they carrying out these experiments? It's not to make our lives better."

April looked utterly stunned. I had to rescue her.

"OK, Lake. I think she gets the point. We won't be doing this in daylight. The plan is to go into the Holding Center an hour and a half before dawn. That'll give us the element of surprise and an element of urgency. I have a plan to get the guards to hand Tork over to us with no questions asked."

"How?"

I wasn't prepared to reveal how until I was sure she would join us.

"You'll have to trust me on that. Going in that early gives us time to get Tork out and all of you back to the urban zone in time to report for duty as normal."

April stared at us. We stared back, hardly daring to breathe.

"What do you want me to do?" she asked.

Yes! We had her.

✦

Security at Reyn's and Peak quarters on the Computer Science and Technology campus also relied on cameras with blind spots that were easy to find and exploit. Again, I let Lake take the lead. Reyn and Peak also kept glancing at me suspiciously as if I were engineering some kind of trap. But they trusted Lake, like the other members of their unit, and they'd liked Tork. They believed Lake when she told them what had become of Clover and agreed that they'd known about the relationship between Clover and Salt. I didn't need to ask why they had kept this from me. Where Lake engendered trust, I engendered fear. She was right. I was the enemy. But not now. I explained my plan to them and asked for their help. Their hesitation consisted of a brief look at each other, then a nod. I explained my plan in detail to them as I had done with April and gave them the chance to back down if they had any concerns. They didn't. They were in.

We tracked down Nea and Adar at the Physics, Chemistry, and Math campus accommodation. Lake continued to prove her powers of persuasion as she got their support. We explained that we had the numbers to make up the bogus escort team and free Tork, but we needed their help to get Lake and the others back to the urban zone before someone missed them while Tork and I went on alone into the bush. That meant they would have to drive my Lightweight in the early hours of the morning and wait at an arranged location until the rest of us arrived in an All-Terrain Utility Vehicle with Tork safely on board. They barely hesitated before agreeing.

✦

Now I had to procure an ATU. I drove Lake to my quarters and left her there while I went on foot to Military HQ. There was just one Op on duty as it was now past midnight. I flashed my MI ID and requested an All-Terrain Utility vehicle and two submachine guns. As a guard, April had her own, so two more, along with our regulation handguns, would be enough to make us look convincing. I knew I was signing my own death warrant when I signed the requisition forms.

I drove the ATU back to my quarters, parked it around the side out of sight, and re-joined Lake. So far, so good. Next, I checked that Tork was still at the Holding Center. He was. I would check again before we set out. I needed to figure out where Zac would be now. I resisted the urge to use my MI ID to track him on my computer, as I had done when I needed to find Cale because if the authorities checked my computer, they would know where I'd taken Tork. Instead, I consulted my map and tried to estimate his location. It was almost three months since I'd visited him, which meant there were several possible routes he could have taken since then. Finding him would not be easy, even with my knowledge and experience of navigating the bush. Would Cale and the same Arc still be with him? What was her name? I couldn't remember. Lake did, though. It was Tern. We couldn't be sure how Tern would react if she knew what we'd done, but Lake thought Cale would be OK about it. I was sure Zac would be willing to help and would know what to do. And Ethan too.

There was something else I had to do, and it would be a matter of trial and error until I got it right. First, I retrieved an old email from Ferris showing his MI Commander ID and insignia. Then, using it as a template, I created a new, false email addressed to myself with a letter attached in his name and printed them both. They looked convincing.

And that's when what I was preparing to do hit me. I was about to betray everything I'd been taught to uphold. The plan that I had conceived depended on me revealing my identity at the Holding Center. Once my crime was discovered, as it inevitably would be, I would be a fugitive for the rest of my probably short life. The realization made me stop and think about what I was asking of Lake and the others. I had to say something.

"Lake, are you sure you want to get involved in this? I've no right to ask you and the others to take such a risk. If we're caught . . ."

She interrupted me.

"I'm capable of making up my own mind, and so are they, so don't be so condescending. OK?"

I could see why she hadn't been a favorite of her Military Cadet Training School instructors.

I had only one more thing to do. I emailed Sig and told him that Military Intelligence required me to absent myself from regular Pol Com duties for a few days and asked him to cover for me. He would get my message when he woke up. He probably wouldn't care since he didn't interact much with me. I doubted he would put himself out to cover for me, but if I could get a day, half a day even before he reported my absence, that would be enough.

That was it. It was 03.30 A.M. We had an hour to wait before picking up the others. Now was my chance to tell Lake about the boy in the photo.

"I've found out who Ferris is."

"Who?"

"My Military Intelligence Commander."

She stared at me in disbelief.

"That makes no sense," she said. "Why would your Commander commission you to find himself?"

"I think he's hoping to find his mother."

"What did he say?" she asked.

"When?"

"When you told him."

"I haven't told him. I don't know where he is."

"You spend all that time looking for him, and when you find him, he disappears?"

"I think I may know how to track his mother. Not that it matters now."

"Because of what you're doing for Tork?"

I couldn't answer her. I couldn't bear to say out loud that my life and career were now in ruins. I did what she would've done, I shrugged.

"How were you going to track her?" she asked.

"Through the Psychoscience Training Unit archives."

"Which is part of the Medical Training Center. That's why you got me sent there."

"I didn't tell you because I didn't want you taking any risks. I wanted to wait until you knew your way around and then ask you to explain their systems to me. I'd have figured out a way for me to get into the archive myself then. I wouldn't have asked you to do it."

"What were you expecting to find?"

I explained that I had discovered that some Psychoscience researchers had access to the files on the Natural Birth Experiment and that it was possible that those files still existed in their system. She accepted this without asking how I'd found out, so I didn't have to reveal anything about Ethan and his role as a Psychoscientist.

"So, all the mothers, including Zac's, could be listed in that archive?"

"Yes," I agreed.

"Why is everything always hidden from us?"

The question was rhetorical. We both knew why. There were no methods of conveying unauthorized information to The Citizenship. All we got were the daily public broadcasts exhorting us to uphold The Moral Code, do our physical exercise, and take our vitamins. That was all the information we were allowed.

There was no more to be said. We had to keep our minds clear and concentrate on the task ahead.

"I need to go back to my quarters to pick up my kit," said Lake.

"OK. Full combats, balaclava, pistol. And be back here for 04.30."

"I know," she replied and left.

I checked that the submachine guns were loaded, made sure I had my fake orders print-out and my MI ID, as well as my Pol Com ID, went over the plan in my head again, and waited for Lake to return.

She arrived back at 04.30 A.M. on the dot. I drove the ATU, and Lake followed in my Lightweight to our rendezvous with Nea and Adar. Nea and Adar took over the Lightweight and drove off to the ex-urban location where we would later meet up so they could drive everyone, except Tork and I, safely back to the urban zone.

Lake and I then picked up April, Reyn, and Peak. Like Lake, they were in combats as I'd instructed while I had replaced my Pol Com insignia with my Military Intelligence insignia, though I kept the former in my pocket just in case. There was no point in me hiding my identity as I depended on it to get us in and out of the Holding Center, but the others were wearing their balaclavas. I issued the submachine guns to Lake and Reyn, who joined April in the rear of the ATU while I sat up front with Peak, now our driver.

✦

We got through security at the Holding Center's outer gates and drove straight to the inner reception block without any difficulty. Lake, April, Reyn, and I disembarked and marched through to the Guard Room. I didn't envy Peak's task as he had to wait in the ATU until whatever time we re-emerged with Tork. If we ever did.

There were three guards on duty and a bank of screens, all but one showing the innards of the Center. The exception showed our ATU parked outside and the vague shape of Peak sitting in the driving seat. It was all down to me now. I produced my MI ID and held it up to the senior guard.

"I have orders to collect Prisoner Op5932189."

The senior tapped his computer screen, bringing it to life. Lake, April, and Reyn stood erect in a semi-circle behind me, cradling their submachine guns. Their balaclavas showed only their eyes.

The senior spoke, "I have no instructions on that."

I took my fake MI letter from my pocket, gave it to him, and watched him read it.

Department of Security
Military Intelligence Command
Military Headquarters

TOP SECRET
21.10.2221
19:20
To: MI Senior Op 4279344
You are hereby instructed to collect Prisoner Op5932189 from Political
Commissariat Holding Center, and escort said prisoner to MI HQ Special
Interrogation Unit.
By order of
MI Commanding Op 2411228

At last, the senior guard looked up.

"That's you, is it? Op 4279344?"

I held up my MI ID again so he could check. The other two guards
glared at me. Nobody likes their authority undermined. Behind me, my
pretend escort stood perfectly still. The senior picked up a phone and
keyed a number.

"Bring Prisoner 5932189 to the Guard Room."

There was a pause while the other person responded.

The senior set his phone down, scanned my letter into his computer,
and tapped a few keys. Then we waited.

The computer pinged as a message came through.

The senior glanced at his screen and spoke to whoever was on the
other end of the phone.

"I don't know how they think they can get away with it."

My stomach jolted violently and almost emptied itself. We'd had it.
They were on to us. I had to force myself to stand still. Nobody else had
moved. Not the other two guards. Not my escort.

The senior was looking at me, but he was still speaking into his phone.

"Bloody Intel . . . Yeah. Bring him over."

He set the phone down and turned to watch one of the screens before
I could say anything. As if I was going to say anything. It was OK. They
were bringing Prisoner 5932189 to the Guard Room. We all watched the
screen, and, in a few moments, Tork appeared flanked by two soldiers.

His hands were in cuffs, and he kept his head down as they hurried him along a corridor somewhere in the bowels of the building.

Even when he finally appeared in the Guard Room, he didn't raise his head. I motioned to April and Reyn to take over from the accompanying soldiers. I stamped my thumbprint on the electronic signature pad that the senior guard placed in front of me and collected the handcuff keys from one of the soldiers. Then I led my team out. If Tork recognized me, he gave no indication.

Outside, I watched April and Reyn shove our prisoner into the back of the ATU and get in themselves, followed by Lake. Peak already had the engine fired up as I climbed in beside him. We drove up to the outer gates. They opened automatically at our approach. We drove through, not daring to speak. They closed behind us. We kept going, only gradually increasing our speed until we were sure we weren't being followed. We weren't. We'd done it. We were out, clear, free. We'd done it because no one had ever dared do something like this before. Nobody ever would've expected that anybody would pull such a move.

It wasn't until we'd safely cleared the urban area that I heard the cheer go up from behind me. I turned and saw Lake, April and Reyn pull off their balaclavas. Tork looked shocked—bewildered even. I tossed the handcuff keys to Lake, and she freed his hands. I left it to her to explain to him what was going to happen next. That was when she discovered he'd had no idea that he'd been destined for an After Lab. She said later that he'd shook for several minutes when she'd told him.

◆

When we arrived at the rallying point with Nea and Adar, the look of surprise on their faces brought the enormity of the risk we'd taken home to me. But we weren't safe yet.

"Right," I said. "Lake, April, Reyn, and Peak, you go back to the urban zone with Nea and Adar. Tork and I need to keep going."

"No," Lake said. "I'm coming with you."

Always the troublemaker. I'd half expected this from her. But not from any of the others.

"We've come this far. We can't stop now," said April.

"Yes, you can," I said. "You can go back to your lives. No one will ever know."

"How many other people have been disappeared into the labs?" asked Reyn.

"Who knows," said Lake. "Hundreds? Depends on how long it's been going on."

"The Citizenship needs to know this," said Nea.

She was right. That was exactly what Zac and Ethan were planning. I could give them some hope.

"Some people have found a way of escaping," I said. "There's a group of them hiding out in the bush. And some other people are planning to organize them into a force to expose the labs. It's already starting to happen."

"We could help," said Lake.

"I meant you don't need to," I said. "It's being done."

"I know what you meant. And I know who you're talking about, and I'm coming with you."

"Me too," said April.

"We've nothing to go back to except a life of slavery," said Peak. "Always having to do what we're told without knowing the reason why."

"And if we ask, we could be the ones being hauled off to the torture labs," said Adar.

"Right," said April. "That's it settled. We're all coming with you."

"I'm not going," said Tork.

We all glared at him.

Lake was first to break the silence.

"We've just risked our asses for you."

"I'm not going without Faze."

"Faze is safe," said Lake.

"What they were going to do to me they'll do to Faze now in revenge," Tork said.

I should've known he'd react like that. I should've got her out too. But his situation was urgent. He was my priority. I'd known what was going to happen to him, so I'd had to act fast. I hadn't been thinking in terms of retaliation. My mind doesn't think such things. Why would it?

Until very recently, I'd believed everything was the way it was for our good and that nothing bad would ever happen to us if we worked hard and followed the rules. But I didn't know what was really going on. I still don't. I only know this one little bit. The bit that shows we are nothing to those in charge. We are bred only to be used in any way they decide regardless of the harm, pain, suffering, or whatever they inflict on us.

"They won't," I said. "I'll get her out. I promise. But right now, you are a liability."

I explained to Tork that we needed to get him safely out of range before the Holding Center discovered they'd made a massive mistake in letting him go to a bogus MI unit. Otherwise, he would be putting everyone at risk. I reckoned that allowed us two hours at the most. Since there were now eight of us and two vehicles, we could split into two teams. Lake would take the ATU and lead one team with Tork into the bush, and I would take April, Peak, and Reyn in the Lightweight and somehow liberate Faze from her close supervision. We consulted our maps and chose a rendezvous point in an old quarry well hidden in an area of what experience told me would now be an overgrown tangle of upland forest.

With that agreed, we were about to head off in our two separate teams when Tork held his hand up towards me, palm facing outward as if he was signaling stop. I knew he wasn't. And I knew what to do. I held my hand up towards him, and together we reached forward until our palms touched. He didn't need to say anything. I understood. Then he turned and made the same gesture to everyone present. And each responded as I had done. We instinctively knew that we couldn't part without some acknowledgment of what we'd just been through together. It was the right thing to do. I couldn't have initiated it, but I supposed Tork was more accustomed to being tactile, given his relationship with Faze. It reminded me of how much I had wanted to reach out and touch Lake's hand. Now I was doing it—reaching out to her, touching her— and it wasn't scary. It felt good. So good that, for a moment, we locked our fingers together.

I was connected to these people now. They were risking their lives, not just for Tork or me, but for each other. We had created a bond that had nothing to do with the so-called Citizenship or The Future or The Moral Code. All those things were false. They were inventions to make us believe we belonged to something greater than ourselves when in fact, their real purpose was to keep us silently in our place as worthless cogs in a gigantic, unknowable wheel. Well, we weren't worthless. We cared about each other. We cared about ourselves. And it felt good. It felt right. We could look at each other in the eye and say, "I know you. I know you because you are like me." I'd never felt that before.

I watched Lake and her team drive off, and I wanted her and them to be safe. I wanted to see her again. Unharmed. Scathing. Sarcastic as ever.

"What's the plan?" asked April.

I didn't know. I'd said I would do it on the spur of the moment because I wanted to do it. It needed doing. I had no idea how. But at least I knew how to get to Faze's location.

"Can't we do it the same way we got Tork out?" asked Reyn.

"No. They'll be on the alert for something like that," said April.

"They might not. It depends how quickly the guards at the Holding Center realize their mistake in handing Tork over to us and how quickly they're prepared to reveal it outside their remit," I said, with more bravado than confidence. "But we have to act fast. Faze won't be under too close a guard until the news gets out."

"So, we can just go in and get her?" asked Nea.

"Maybe," I said, thinking aloud. "Faze works on a building project. It's a huge site. People are moving about all the time—people working on the dome structures, vehicles delivering building materials, constant comings and goings."

"Isn't that perfect cover for us?" asked Peak.

"We don't actually need cover," I replied. "We need a plausible story. She may not be under armed guard like a prisoner, but her site supervisor has been ordered to keep her under close watch."

"OK. What's the story?" asked April.

"Get in the vehicle. I'll work it out on the way."

16

Work was just beginning for the day when we reached the dome building site. We drove straight through to the site admin office, April in the
passenger seat beside me, Peak and Reyn in the back. I instructed them
to stay in their places while I went into the office. There was only one site
supervisor behind the desk. I produced my MI ID.

"I'm here to follow up on a case. I need to speak to Op5877891. I
interviewed her before a few months back."

I flicked through my cell phone and showed her the diary entry for
my previous visit. She scrolled through her computer's records to confirm.

"Yeah. Got you. Why do you need to see her again?"

"Military Intel business."

"You know she's in a spot of bother?"

"I heard—nothing to do with me, though. I'm only interested in
a kid that's supposed to have killed himself. She knew him in Cadet
School. I just need to ask her a few more questions about him. We don't
like loose ends. Especially when it involves crazies, if you know what I
mean?"

Could she know what I meant when even I didn't know what I
meant? I was talking crap. But it was the sort of crap that appealed to a
person with an inflated sense of their importance. I knew that because I
used to be that person.

"I'll get somebody to bring her down," she said, reaching for her
phone.

"No need," I said. "Point me in the right direction, and I'll find her.
Element of surprise, you know?"

She smirked then. She was on my side against these stupid, insub-
ordinate kids who didn't know how to conduct themselves. These silly

emotional types who needed to be taught a sharp lesson. Suicidal types who were a nuisance to people like her and me who were just doing our jobs. She accompanied me to the door of the office and directed me where to find Faze.

I drove the Lightweight right to her and again instructed the others to stay inside before I got out and called her over.

"Remember me?" I asked.

She looked at me then shook her head. I didn't blame her. If she did remember me, I was the enemy. If she didn't, I could still be her enemy.

"Tork's free. We got him out early this morning."

She appeared to be searching my face for evidence of the awful trick she was sure I was playing on her. Then she spoke.

"Tork's dead."

"No," I said. "He's not. I promise you. He's safe."

"You came here before to ask us about Salt?"

"Yes. A lot has happened since then. Tork wants you to get out of here."

"They told me he's dead."

"They lied."

I saw the hope flicker in her eyes.

"Do you want to go to him? We can take you. But it's up to you . . ."

"Yes. But how? They watch me all the time."

"Are they watching now?"

She looked around.

"I can't tell."

I looked around too. I couldn't tell either. Nobody appeared to be paying us any attention.

"OK," I said. "We have one chance, and this is it. But you have to be sure. You can't come back from this."

"I'm sure."

I took another glance around as I opened the Lightweight's rear door.

"Get in," I ordered.

Quick as a flash, she was inside. I saw Reyn and Peak grab her and push her down onto the floor. I shut the door and looked around again. No one was even glancing in our direction. I deliberately stood there, at the back of the Lightweight, for ten, twenty, even thirty seconds. Nobody looked at me. Nobody approached me. I strolled to the driver's door, opened it, and got in. Even then, I waited. Nothing. I started the engine. I moved off. Slowly. Then gathering speed. Not too fast. Just enough. Past the piles of struts and blocks, past foundations, past machinery, past people working, people minding their own business. On towards the open gates. Through the gates. Out on to the road. Everybody in the Lightweight dead silent, like we were all holding our breaths. Along the road. Faster now. Driving further and further away. A murmuring of voices from the back. Reyn and Peak helping Faze to sit up. April staring straight ahead through the windshield. Me checking the rearview. Nothing. Empty road behind. Nobody following. Had we done it? Keep going. Too soon to tell. Still, nobody following. Faster. This is crazy. Keep going. Don't speak. Don't jinx it. Don't say a word. Drive. Just keep driving. Five K, eight, ten, twenty. Get off the road. Into the bush. Bouncing. Crashing through undergrowth. Shouts from the back. Slow down. Slow down. And then, at last, the cheer. From me this time. We did it. We actually did it! Keep going—no time to lose. Get to the quarry. April on the map. This way. Through the bush. Dodge the trees. Weave. Keep weaving just in case.

But there was no sign of the others at the quarry. No ATU. I drove right up to the edge of the drop and stopped. I could see the weed-choked lake that filled the basin below.

"Where is he?"

That was Faze asking about Tork. Yeah. Where is he? Where's Lake? And Nea and Adar? No movement. All silent. I got out and went around to the rear of the Lightweight and opened the door. Reyn and Peak stumbled out, stiff and sore from the drive. I heard April get out of the front passenger seat. Faze got out the back.

And there he was. Tork. Running out of the bush, running towards Faze. Her face. Shock. Disbelief. Crumpling into tears. Into joy as he lifted her in his arms. Lake, Nea, and Adar appeared from out the bush too. We stared—all of us—at Faze and Tork. They were oblivious to us. He set her down and grabbed her face in both his hands. Faze laughing and crying at the same time. Tork too. She took his face in her hands, mirroring him. They stared into each other's eyes. Then they kissed, pulling each other closer and closer as if they would never let go. I'd never seen such a display before. Should I be looking? Intruding? How could I not? I felt a hand on my shoulder. Lake. She didn't speak. She didn't even look at me. But I knew. I also knew we didn't have the time for this.

"Where's the ATU?"

"Back there," Lake said. "I hid it, in case you were followed."

"OK, everybody," I shouted. "Listen up."

They all turned to look at me. I heard my voice speaking as if it were someone else's. Like my listeners, I had no idea what the next word would be, or the next, or the next. But I had to keep talking. I had to pull this together and get us all to safety as soon as possible.

"I want everybody to get behind the Lightweight. I'm going to release the handbrake. Then, on my signal, everybody push."

They did it. I reached in, freed the brake, jumped back, and yelled. They heaved the Lightweight over the quarry edge. We heard the giant splash as it hit the lake below, and we watched it sink.

There were nine of us now. We all piled into the ATU. Me as the driver; Lake beside me as navigator, map and compass on her lap; and the rest in the back. Plenty of room for everybody.

Our aim now was to track down Zac and join forces with him to expose what was happening in the After Labs. His team would have moved on from the house, but at least we knew in which zone they would be operating.

"Due North," said Lake.

"You sure?"

"Yes."

She pointed out the windshield.

"That way."

If those satellites were still up there, they were no good to us. All that twenty-first-century technology was useless since The Wipe Out. In place of computer-designed models for experiments and testing of new products and ideas, we were the guinea pigs because, as I now realized, our only purpose was as fodder for the powerholders' ambitions.

I swung the ATU in the direction Lake pointed and gunned the throttle.

✦

That first day was a long one. Our only aim was to get far away from the urban zone in the least time while maintaining a course roughly in the direction of where I thought Zac was most likely to be. But we only had an estimate of his coordinates, so there was always a lingering fear in the back of my mind that we might never find him. I didn't reveal any of my thoughts to the others. Not even to Lake, but she was no fool.

We each had enough personal nutrient supplies to last at least a week since everyone carried more than they needed as a matter of course—all part of being a responsible Citizen prepared for any eventuality. However, breaking a prisoner out of a Pol Com Holding Center and going on the run was not one of the eventualities the authorities had in mind. They'd have been anticipating another disease outbreak and the potential need for Ops to seek shelter wherever they could. The ATU had an emergency supply for up to twelve crew for similar reasons. We had fuel in the tank and in the reserve cans to keep us driving for several days, but that was no guarantee we had enough. Progress was slow in this sort of terrain and would only get slower. We couldn't take the risk of going to one of the re-fuelling nodes that I had used previously as an Earth History driver because I would have to use my military Driver Op code to access it.

✦

Soon we were deep into the bush. Being the more experienced navigator, Lake left the passenger seat and took up position on the roof. I could hear a constant stream of chatter from the others in the rear of the vehicle. Not excited or fearful, but calm, earnest conversation. At least they didn't seem to be regretting going AWOL.

Then a shout from the roof from Lake.

"Stop! Stop!"

I stopped. She stuck her head in my side window.

"Looks like a swamp up ahead. It's not shown on the map."

That wasn't unusual. The maps were from when airplanes flew over the land, taking aerial photographs or from satellite imaging. Where we now were was once farmland. Thousands of acres of pasture and crops. When the farmers became sick, they abandoned the land and poured into the towns seeking help. But the towns were lethal with disease. Hospitals couldn't cope. People died in the streets. Farmland returned to nature. Nothing was now the same as it had been. I knew this from old photographs my various Arcs had shown me. They meant little to me because this rampant wilderness was all I had ever known—this and the urban underground building programs replacing the pre-Wipe Out cities.

Everybody in the rear took the opportunity to get out and stretch their legs while I joined Lake on the roof and worked out a route around the swamp.

That night we set up camp for our first time. It reminded me of field trips during my Cadet School days when there had been so many people milling around and so much chatting going on. How did they find so much to talk about? I felt just as uncomfortable and out of place now as I had done then. And, like then, nobody talked much to me. Well, I guessed that was a good thing. I was the leader, after all. There needed to be some distance between them and me. I left them to it and went for a walk.

You don't walk too far on your own in the bush at night if you've any sense. I just went a little way away and found a fallen tree to sit on. So, was this it? Me still the outsider? The one who doesn't belong? No. That wasn't entirely true. I didn't feel like an outsider with Lake. And I certainly didn't with Zac. We understood each other, Zac and I. I missed his company. I felt safe around him.

A rustle from behind startled me. It was Lake.

"You OK?" she asked.

"Sure."

She sat down beside me.

"They can get on your nerves, can't they?" she said.

"What?"

"Junior soldiers."

"Isn't that what you are?"

"I've been places, seen things, done things. I nearly got killed. Remember? All your fault."

She was right.

"I'm joking," she said. "You know what a joke is, don't you?" She shook her head in apparent exasperation and continued, "OK. You don't. Look. I've got something for you."

I looked. She was holding a computer pen drive towards me.

"What's on it?" I asked as I took it from her.

"Remember before we set off this morning, I said I had to go back to my quarters to pick up my kit? Yeah? Well, that wasn't the only place I went. I went to the Medical Training Center and broke into the Psychoscience Training Unit."

"You what?"

She shrugged.

"I know, yeah. The last thing they'd expect anyone to do because no one would have any reason to do it, so no proper security except a couple of locked doors. Easy. Anyway, just listen. You said you needed access to their archived files, so I stole the supervisor's access card from her desk—they all keep their cards in their desks because they're afraid of losing them if they take them out of the building. I didn't know what exactly you were looking for, so I copied the lot onto that."

"If you'd been caught . . ."

"I'm probably on some security video. But so what? I knew I'd be going with you and not coming back."

"You knew more than I did."

"I usually do, which is why you need me. Now, come on. We'd better get back to the others before they start thinking you're some sort of an oddball. I mean, you are an oddball, I know that, but we don't want everybody to know."

I put the pen drive safely in my pocket and followed her. It was so frustrating to think that the identities of Ferris' mother, aka Weird Smiley Woman, and Zac's mother could be on this little device, and possibly their fathers too, and I had no way of accessing it out here.

The others didn't seem to have noticed that I'd been gone. I sat down amongst them and listened to the conversation as it moved around the group. It wasn't so much its content that surprised me because it mainly consisted of examples of the process of threats and humiliations that their military school and even their nursery and junior schools had employed to keep them obedient and subservient. I had been through that myself and understood their need to express themselves finally. It was the animation of their conversation that was the surprise. I'd never heard any group talk with such enthusiasm, everybody eager to say their piece, some even talking over the top of others in their keenness to have their view heard. It was new, and heady, and liberating. And very, very subversive.

I caught Lake's eye. She was smiling at me. OK, I was an oddball, but even I knew this was good. I smiled back at her. I also knew that even if we got caught, this, right now, would always be good.

17

By our third day crossing through heavily wooded hillsides and the intervening weed-choked valleys, I became desperate. We'd not come across any sign of Zac or any other form of life, apart from a few animal shrieks at night. At least we weren't being followed, as far as I could tell. I didn't know if Pol Com would send out their forces to look for us or if they would leave it to the Special Search Units that were already in here somewhere looking for the Re-Cos and, therefore, more familiar with the bush. The Re-Cos were also a considerable risk to us. They wouldn't know we were on their side, so they would shoot on sight as I now accepted they had probably done with Salt.

A bigger worry was the effect our futile roaming was having on the rest of the crew. They had gone past the euphoric phase of our breakout and were now becoming anxious and unsettled. I didn't blame them. I felt that way myself, but I couldn't show it. I wasn't even much good at keeping up their morale. I left that to Lake. She kept them going with her mixture of sarcasm, wit, and common sense. Only Tork and Faze remained relatively unconcerned. They were just happy to have the freedom to be together. I found myself envying their ability to transcend the reality of their situation.

We were settled in on our fourth night when it all kicked off. Nea and Adar were on the second watch on the roof. The rest of us had snuggled into our makeshift beds in the rear. First, I heard the shouting. Loud. Indecipherable. I had just about registered it as human, several humans, when a volley of shots from right above my head nearly burst my eardrums. I yanked open the overhead hatch as the others leaped out of their beds and grabbed their firearms. That's when they, whoever they were, returned fire. I grabbed our nearest lookout and pulled him, or her, I couldn't tell which in the dark, down through the hatch. The bullets were still hammering off our ATU as I went back up for the other one. Too late. The roof was empty. April was right behind me with her submachine gun, ready to climb through. I kicked her back down, and at that moment, the ATU started up and jolted forward, sending me falling on top of her. We scrabbled to regain our balance as bullets continued to pound the sides of our now speeding, bouncing, jolting vehicle. I knew we hadn't a chance. I knew they'd have their own ATU. They'd catch up with us. They'd rocket us. Even if, somehow, we managed not to crash in this mad flight in the dark, they'd blow us out of existence. I should've been the one behind the wheel. That should've been my first instinct. It would've been what the old me would've done—self-preservation. But I couldn't have driven off while I still had two look-outs on the roof. I had to get them to safety. Whoever was driving had known that, had waited until I'd made my failed attempt to bring down the second look-out before taking off. That second lookout was now gone. Shot. Probably dead. Who was it? I looked around at the figures crouched around me, clinging to whatever they could to counter the tossing and swaying. There were two I couldn't see.

"Lake!"

Nobody answered me. But Lake hadn't been on the lookout.

"Nea!"

Seven pairs of wide eyes stared back at me. Nea had been on the roof with Adar. Adar was still here. Nea wasn't.

The pounding of bullets stopped. Had we outrun them? Unlikely. They'd found us, and they wouldn't give up on us now. They'd keep after us until they got us. That was their job. They couldn't go back without us.

Our ATU reared and swung and whined as it made an arcing turn. Was our driver mad? It had to be Lake. I staggered to my feet and made my way into the cab.

"What are you doing?" I yelled at her. "You're heading us back into them."

"Hold on," she yelled as she heaved the ATU into another wide swing of a turn.

"Lake! You can't possibly see where you're going."

"Can't risk the lights," she shouted.

That was true. It would be another hour before dawn, and right now, we were plunging around in darkness with only a half-moon intermittently offering some light from behind the clouds.

"There's another swampland around here somewhere," she continued, still shouting above the noise of our straining engine.

"So, get away from it," I shouted back.

She ignored that.

"I saw it yesterday when I was on the roof, and you were driving before we stopped for the night. Look."

She tossed a map to me as she continued.

"It's not really a swamp. It just looks like one because it's so overgrown."

This was crazy. I didn't even bother looking at the map. She read my thoughts.

"I'm the navigator on this trip. Right? It's my job to know the terrain. I read the map every day. I read the geology, the contours, everything. I study it until I can see it in my head. I know there's what seems to be another swamp up ahead. But it isn't. We can go right through it. They won't know that. They'll see it, and they'll shit themselves."

"We'll be the ones shitting ourselves when we're drowning in it."

"We won't. It only looks like a swamp. It's not. It's an old reservoir. There's a submerged road through it. If we can find it, we can drive it."

"A roadway out here in the middle of nowhere?"

"It wasn't always the middle of nowhere."

OK. She was right about that.

"How are we going to find it?" I yelled above the straining engine noise.

"We're not if you're doing the map reading. We have to swap places."

She had already raised her ass off the driving seat while keeping her foot on the throttle.

"Slide under me," she ordered.

"Hey! Watch it," yelled somebody from the back as the ATU almost bucked out of control.

I slid under Lake, got my foot on the throttle, and grabbed the steering wheel as Lake swung herself into the passenger seat. She got out her mini-torch and shone it on the map.

I flicked my eyes to my rearview and checked the lights of the pursuing ATU. They had fallen way behind us and were now at right angles to us, so they hadn't yet spotted our change of direction. I swerved to avoid a tree, then another, and another.

"Keep going," said Lake. "We'll be in a clearing soon."

I wanted to ask who made her the leader, but it would keep. Anyway, she was right. The trees gradually began to thin out.

And then we were almost in it. From a distance, and with the half-moon glistening across its dark, reed-choked water, it definitely looked like a vast, treacherous swamp. I slowed and turned the ATU to drive along the edge of it. I couldn't see its full extent, but Lake knew from her previous sighting that it was a large, rectangular shape and that we were now on its southern edge.

"OK. Where's the road?"

Lake looked up from the map.

"Yeah, keep going."

"Going where?"

"It's there. We'll find it."

I continued driving along the swamp edge until Lake told me to stop. I still couldn't see any road, but she insisted it was there. She had calculated where the road would be, and it would continue in a straight line to the other side just under a kilometer away.

"How do you know it's still intact?" I asked.

"It was built on hard rock."

April stuck her head into the cab.

"Do you know how deep reservoirs can be?" she asked Lake.

"Very. When they're properly damned," replied Lake. "But I saw the overflow yesterday. The dam's a ruin now. The water level's only just above the roadbed."

The remaining crew all piled up at the entrance to the cab.

"How can you tell?" asked Tork.

"Look," said Lake as she shone her mini torch on the map. "See the contours running down all around the valley? They're tight. Right? Then, when they get to here, they widen out. That's because the steep sides change into gentle slopes here. Where they reach the bottom of the valley, they disappear because the bottom is a flat surface. We're here, and the water that we're looking at is less than a meter deep."

"How much less?" I asked.

"Maybe just over a half a meter, point seven-five at the most. We can drive through point seven-five, can't we?"

"Maybe. But we've got to find the road first," I told her. "And quick."

She got out while I kept the engine ticking over. I kept an eye on my rearview while the others watched Lake walk the shoreline. The other vehicle's lights were nowhere in sight. But that could simply mean they were on to us and had switched them off now that dawn was approaching and the darkness fading.

Lake climbed in again.

"I've got it. Keep going."

Either I trusted her skills and went with her, or I ordered everybody out to take our chances on foot in the bush. I decided to go with her.

After a few minutes of slow driving along the edge, Lake instructed me to face the ATU into the swamp.

"You sure?" I asked her.

"Positive. I could see traces of the road from the shore. It's covered by vegetation, so if you weren't looking for it, you'd never know it was there."

"But if I can't see it below the water, how can I steer us across it?" I asked. "You say this isn't a swamp, but the bottom will be full of sediment. If we miss the road at any point, we'll sink into it and get stuck."

"I'll walk in front of you," offered Tork.

"We both will," said Faze.

I agreed because I needed all the help I could get.

Tork and Faze pulled a couple of branches off a tree and stripped them to make poles. Then they both ventured into the water, using their poles to locate the road and its sides. Soon they were in up to their knees and signaling me to follow. The dark grey of the dawn sky was changing into a pattern of pale orange and blue overlain with streaks of pink cloud as I eased the ATU into what still looked like a swamp to me. I hoped that Lake's map reading skills were as good as she claimed.

Lake kept up a stream of words of reassurance while I steered the ATU behind Tork and Faze as they walked either side of the submerged road to show me its width.

We were well over halfway across when Faze lost her balance and disappeared down into the water. A cry of alarm went up from the crew. I stopped and ordered the crew to stay on board. Then both Lake and I jumped out into the now thigh-deep water. But Tork had already found Faze and grabbed her back up onto the roadbed. We could see that some of the road had broken up and had gotten washed away. That was what had caused her to lose her footing. It could also cause the wheels on that side of the ATU to lose traction. But there was no way we could turn around. We had to keep going forward. I ordered Faze into the rear of the ATU. Lake took up position on the road along with Tork while the rest of us climbed back on board.

The going had to be much slower now as Tork and Lake took extra care to locate what remained of the road. They prodded and poked with their poles before each step. Sometimes one or the other lost their footing, but they were prepared for stumbles now. It was heart-in-the-mouth stuff. The ATU rocked and swayed. Some of the wheels rode solid ground while other wheels spun uselessly in empty water. There were no complaints from the crew in the back now. We all knew this was our only chance.

But we did it. We emerged safely on the other side, four of us soaked to the skin, and all of us weak with the tension we'd endured. There was no sign of our pursuers. Even if they tracked us to the apparent swamp, I was confident they wouldn't chance driving headlong into it as we had done. I certainly wouldn't have without Lake's insistence that it was possible. At worst, they might drive around the swampland and hope to pick up our trail on the other side. That would take them several hours. I didn't say it, but I was also aware that there was no guarantee that they didn't have as dedicated and skilled a navigator as we had. So, no time for complacency.

✦

It was mid-afternoon by the time I risked a stop. Lake had wanted me to stop earlier to allow the crew to vent their feelings about the loss of Nea, but I'd re-asserted myself and kept going because we needed to be sure no one was following us before we could risk it. Now we were tucked behind the trees on the edge of an area of upland forest, and Lake was doing her best to assure Adar that he and Nea had done the right thing when they'd opened fire on our ambushers. I was on the edge of the group as usual. Adar kept glancing at me as Lake was talking to him. It wasn't until Lake also glanced back at me that I realized I needed to say something. I moved in and sat in the middle of the group.

"Lake's right, Adar," I said. "If it hadn't been for you and Nea, we would all be on our way back to the Holding Center now as prisoners. That's if they hadn't shot us all on the spot."

"Do you think they're still after us?" asked Peak.

"They'll not give up that easily," I said. "But we've given them the slip for now."

"What if Nea is still alive?" asked Reyn.

"Is that likely?" I asked Adar.

"No. They got her for sure," he replied.

It was then that I saw the blood on his sleeve.

"You're hit?"

"No."

He wiped his hand down his sleeve. His hand came away sticky red.

"It's Nea's," he said as he stared at it.

I couldn't find any words. April, who was sitting beside Adar, put her arm around him and pulled him close. I nodded to Lake to come with me, and we moved a little away from the group.

"Where exactly are we?" I asked her.

She went to the ATU, pulled out the map, spread it on the bonnet, and showed me.

"We're here. Zac's probable location is over there. We're about thirty kilometers off from where we need to be."

As I followed her index finger on the map, something caught my eye.

"Look."

"What?"

"Caves."

"Yeah?"

"I think I know this area."

"There are loads of caves all across the map."

"Yes. But only these are in Zac's zone."

"So?"

"Zac took me to some caves. They ran underground like tunnels and led to some sort of building."

"This just says caves. It doesn't show tunnels or a building."

"I know it's a longshot," I said. "But we're heading that direction anyway. We can take a look. Maybe hide out in one of them for a night."

Lake shrugged, "Sure."

✦

The caves were a lot harder to find than the map suggested. Undergrowth choked the whole area—bushes, brambles, trees—and made it entirely unrecognizable. I didn't see anything that looked remotely like the area that Zac had walked me through to meet Ethan. Even if these were Ethan's caves, what exactly did I expect from Ethan if I found him? Not much. But he could at least contact Zac on my behalf or maybe give me an indication of where to find him.

After an hour driving into and out of the forest, circling what I assumed was the location of the caves, I had to accept that I'd indulged myself long enough. I'd checked my cell phone several times, but I had no signal. No surprise out here. By now, the crew was voicing their anxiety that we were lost. It was time to call a halt. I could've told them that we'd been lost from the start. The minute you enter the bush, you are inevitably lost in a strange, alien, and potentially perilous world. Either you go with it and rely on your natural instincts to survive, or you fight against it and risk perishing out here where nobody will ever care about you again. Instead, I parked up in the cover of some trees and gathered them around the map and explained that we were exactly where we should be and assured them that it would be only a matter of time until I found my contact and we could begin planning how we would fight back against the After Labs. But, as I looked around at my eager but very inexperienced crew, the realization that there was little we could do against the whole, unknowable system hit me. Like them, I had been so fired up by the excitement of outwitting the guards and getting Tork out and then sneaking Faze out from under the noses of her supervisors that I thought I could do anything. Now here we were adrift and vulnerable, and we'd lost one of our own. Somehow, I had to pull this together. I called Lake to one side.

"I need you to supervise setting up camp for the night."

Her response was predictable.

"Why?"

"Because I want to do some more exploring on foot while there's still some daylight left."

"And what about them?" she asked, indicating the crew who were now sitting around looking dejected.

"Set them to work," I said. "They need to be busy."

"No. They need you to tell them you know what you're doing because I don't know what you're doing."

"I just did."

"No, you didn't. You spun them a line. And they know it. They've put their trust in you. Now you have to trust them. Why have we stopped here? What's the big thing about caves?"

I braced myself, turned back towards the crew still gathered around the map, and pointed to the caves shown on the map.

"One of my contacts is located in this area. If these caves are the ones I think they are, we have a good chance of finding him. But I need to do this alone. If he sees a group of soldiers in his territory, it'll scare him off. He'll not know who we are, so he'll think we've come to arrest him."

I was aware of Lake staring at me. This notion of a contact hiding out in the caves was news to her. I was grateful that she refrained from asking me any questions. I broke eye contact with her and continued talking.

"There's a couple of hours of daylight left. I'm going to search on foot. If I find what I'm looking for, I won't be back for some time."

"I'll come with you," Lake offered.

"No. I need you to stay here and take charge."

"What if you get lost in the caves?" she asked.

It was a fair question. But by now, I had convinced myself that I was right about the caves being the entrance to Ethan's hideout. I had to check it out.

"I won't. I'll be back before morning at the latest."

✦

It was almost dark when I found what I figured should be the entrance to the caves. Thick, dense brambles spread across the whole area. That was good because I remembered Ethan pushing them back to let us through. I'd gotten scratched by them. Then, when we were inside, he'd checked that the brambles had swung back into place. But which brambles? This place was a mass of them. There was no way I could identify the ones we'd previously entered. And there was no way of knowing if I was even looking in the right place. But this had to be the right place. I just needed to look harder.

And then I saw it. Down low and well hidden. Not a cave entrance, but a clump of grey fur—a dead rabbit—caught in a wire snare. It had to have been set by Ethan. This was his food. He would have to come to collect it soon. All I had to do was wait. But not out in the open in case I scared him off. I moved across to some bushes and settled in out of sight.

There wasn't a sound or a movement anywhere. The night animals hadn't come out yet, and the day ones were staying well away. Somewhere less than a kilometer away, my crew was deciding the watch rota for the night. Somewhere else, hopefully much, much further away, our pursuit crew were doing something similar after their long day of searching for us. The gang of Re-Cos was out there too, also being tracked down. We were all animals now—prey and predators. The bush is vast, with plenty of space for everyone to hide and never be found. Even the Earth History project can only cover a tiny fraction of the rural territories.

"That was some stunt you pulled yesterday."

I rolled onto my back and yanked out my gun.

"Too late," the voice said. "You'd be dead meat now if I'd wanted."

Ethan stepped into my hiding place in the bushes.

"I was expecting you to come along soon," I said. "I wasn't expecting you to kill me."

I replaced my gun.

"What've you done?" he asked.

"What do you mean?" I countered.

He held up the binoculars that were hanging from a strap around his neck.

"Saw it all."

"I need your help," I said.

"Again?"

✦

After he retrieved his rabbit, I walked with him to the brambles and watched as he seemed to disappear into them. Yes, I remembered this, but clearly, I hadn't paid enough attention the first time. A gap opened up as he held several strands back to allow me through. He pulled the strands back into place, and we made our way through the cave system and up into his hideout.

I told him everything that had happened since I last saw him. He admitted that, although he'd watched our escape from the pursuing ATU, he'd had no idea who we were. He'd even watched us approaching the area of the caves and had seen us park up among the trees. Then he'd watched me coming on foot, but it wasn't until I'd hidden in the bushes that he'd chanced getting close enough to be able to recognize me through his binoculars. I was sure I detected a note of admiration in his tone, but I kept that to myself.

"Do you know where Zac is?" I asked.

"Maybe."

OK. I could've been wrong about the admiration.

"I have seven soldiers with me who want to help expose the After Labs."

"Oh, yeah? Where'd you get them?" he asked.

"They were cadets along with Salt in military training school."

"Seven rookies, you mean."

"They know the risks. They're ready to do what has to be done."

"That wasn't the plan."

"OK. How many Re-Cos have you got on board?" I asked.

It was a cheap shot, and I immediately regretted it.

"Look, I know that even if you could track them down, you can't just walk into a group of escapees and expect them to, firstly, not kill you on sight, and secondly, to agree to go along with you. These kids are our best hope."

"They're a liability," he said.

"They're smart. They're courageous. One of them nearly ended up in an After Lab himself. They're a tight unit. You should see them . . ."

"Whoa! What's come over you? You off the chems? You been bonding?"

"I know you have a way of contacting Zac. Tell him I need to see him."

"Have you told your little bondees about me?"

"Oh, don't worry. I didn't really expect any help from you, so I've told them nothing about you. I said I had a contact who was of the same mind as they are about exposing the After Labs. I meant Zac. Not you."

"I don't think he'll appreciate all of you turning up out of the blue."

"Shouldn't you let him decide that?"

"Just giving you the heads up."

"So, you'll contact him?"

"I thought I'd seen the last of you."

"Sorry to disappoint."

"Not at all. You liven up my dull life."

He was doing it again, confusing me. But this was the sort of thing Lake would say to me. She wouldn't mean any harm. It was sarcasm—a joke. He was already heading out the door. He stopped and called back in.

"Want a drink or something?"

I remembered the last time he'd offered one of his concoctions.

"No, thanks."

✦

Twenty-five minutes passed before he returned. I didn't know what sort of radio comms he and Zac had set up, so I wasn't surprised that it took that long. But he still kept me in suspense as he deliberately took his time pouring himself a drink before telling me what I wanted to hear.

"Zac will meet you at your ATU at first light."

"Thank you."

"My pleasure."

"There's something else I want you to do," I said.

"Isn't there always?" he replied.

I ignored that too and produced the pen drive that Lake had given me.

"I need to see what's on this."

He took it from me.

"Yeah. Should have enough battery for that."

He switched on his computer and inserted the pen drive. The heading 'Psychoscience Training Unit: Archived Material' appeared on the screen.

"Shit!" exclaimed Ethan. "How did you get that?"

"One of the 'rookies' got it for me," I said.

He grinned.

"OK. Let's see what we've got here."

"Hopefully, we've got the names of everyone who took part in the Natural Births Experiment," I said.

Now he was impressed.

CHAPTER
18

Zac appeared at dawn. I'd returned to my crew, and even though we were expecting him, we held our guns at the ready as we watched his ATU approaching through the bushes. I waited until I could see his face through his windscreen before giving the order to stand easy. Tern and Cale were with him. If he trusted them, then so must we. Tern stayed in the background, but Cale was delighted to reconnect with his old classmates.

I'd been looking forward to meeting up with Zac again, but I was disappointed to find him brusque. Maybe Ethan had been right about him being less than pleased that I'd brought so many strangers with me. The introductions were brief. Zac asked no questions. Ethan had already told him why we were here. He was mainly concerned with getting us off the hillside and into proper cover. I agreed to follow him to his secret house where my crew and I could hide up in relative safety. Ethan did not appear at any stage, though that was no surprise.

This time getting us out of sight took priority, so there was no backtracking or route doubling designed to disorientate us. Zac drove straight to our destination in less than an hour, proving that when he took me to meet Ethan, he'd been fudging the route as it must have taken us over two hours to arrive at Ethan's caves.

✦

As we settled into the house, I sensed a growing excitement among my crew. They'd been anticipating this meeting with Zac and his crew ever since we entered the bush. Now here we were at what they regarded as our revolutionary HQ. This was where things would start happening. I, too, felt that we were at the beginning of something big, life-changing. But that was not how Zac saw it. He motioned to me to go outside with him.

We sat on the remains of an old wall near the house.

"I never thought you'd do something like that," he said.

"Neither did I," I said.

"They can't stay hidden here forever. They'll be searching all over the place now. We won't be able to move for them."

"I didn't know where else to take them."

He didn't respond.

"Look, I know I wasn't keen to get involved before," I explained. "But I didn't understand back then. I mean . . . I didn't want to think about it . . . about what goes on. I couldn't see what I could do. I had my own job, my own plans. But now I know there are things I can do, that we all can do. We've proved that."

He stayed silent.

I kept going.

"They've just given up everything to save Tork and Faze. They want to do more. They want to do what you want. They want to close the labs forever. That's why they're here. I can't send them back now. They'll end up in the labs themselves."

Ethan had been right. Zac didn't want us here. We were putting him and his team at risk. I should've thought it through. I should've insisted that everyone except Tork, who was the only one who had been actually in danger, go back to their posts. I should've refused to get Faze out.

Zac turned to me.

"Right. You're here now, so let's try and figure this out."

He stood up and strode back towards the house. I followed.

The proper introductions that we'd previously postponed out of the need to get everyone to safety now became in-depth interviews as Zac quizzed each of my crew in turn. Each asserted their determination to help end the suffering of their fellow human beings. Tern also declared that she'd had enough of a system deliberately designed to keep people uninformed and alienated from each other. At first, I wondered what was behind her statement. I doubted that any of my Arcs would've been willing to take such a stand. But then I barely knew them. All we ever talked about was what was necessary to complete our work. I didn't have Zac's ability to reach beyond the surface to the person within. Then I realized that Tern kept glancing at Zac as she spoke. Even I could figure out why.

With Zac satisfied with my team's sincerity, the discussion turned to what our options might be. I knew Ethan had computer and filming equipment supplied illegally by Zac and stashed at his hideout. I also knew the layout of the general reception area of the Bio-Med Research Center. Lake knew the Before Labs layout, and Ethan would be familiar with the layout of the After Labs. But how would we ever get through the very high and rigorous security regimes that would be in place?

"What if we had Bio-Haz suits?" suggested Lake.

"Yeah. Great," I said. "How would we get them?"

"Steal them," said Peak.

"From who?" asked April.

"Overcome the guards," said Reyn.

"What if you were to call in this house?" Lake asked Zac.

Zac, like the rest of us, waited for her to elaborate.

"Say that you've just found it. They'll think it's contaminated . . ."

I knew where this was going. She knew my old house story.

"And they'll send out a Bio-Haz team?" I asked.

"Yes," she agreed. "We ambush them, take their suits."

"How many would they send?" asked April.

This was getting ridiculous.

"Too many," I said.

"What about the gang of escapees?" Lake asked.

"What escapees?" asked April.

I hadn't deliberately not told my crew about the Re-Cos. There'd been so many other things on my mind. I hadn't made time to sit down with them and go through everything I knew about the bush. Now I let Zac tell them.

"Could they fight?" asked Peak when Zac had finished. "I mean, wouldn't they be too sick?"

"The sick ones will have died by now," answered Zac. "The ones still out there are the survivors."

"But we don't know where they are," I said.

"And if you did, what would you expect from them?" April asked.

Everybody was looking at me, waiting for me to lay it all out as I'd always done before. But I couldn't. I had to face facts. How could a bunch of mentally and physically scarred fugitives possibly help us storm the most heavily guarded, most impenetrable place I'd ever seen? Would they even be prepared to consider going back there?

"Even with the Re-Cos, there wouldn't be enough of us to invade the labs," I said. "We would be shot on sight. Nothing would change, and no one would ever get to know what goes on inside. Zac has a better plan for using the Re-Cos."

Zac took over and explained that we'd both come up with the idea of persuading some of the Re-Cos to allow themselves to be filmed talking about what they'd gone through in the labs and broadcasting it through the public information system. It wasn't the sort of plan that elicited cheers of enthusiasm. I had to keep the momentum going before we lost everyone's support.

"Our immediate challenge is to make contact with the Re-Cos," I said.

"Ethan picked up some radio signals from an SSU a week ago, so we know where the Search Unit thinks they are," said Zac. "But it's no longer as simple as we thought."

I got that. Not only were the Re-Cos being hunted by the Special Search Units, now there was the added risk to them from the team out hunting for my crew and me. Even if we could track them down, they would always be on their guard, so we had to assume they would have no hesitation opening fire on us.

"Can you show me the area on the map?" I asked.

"What are you thinking?" Zac asked me.

"I'm thinking that if I go in alone, there's less chance of them being spooked."

"Oh, yeah," Lake butted in. "They shot Salt, didn't they? And he was alone."

"We can't be sure they did," I said.

"They saw his uniform and thought he was from an SSU. That's what you said," she continued.

My crew looked at me like I was crazy. I hadn't revealed to them that I now believed that someone had shot Salt.

"That's just a theory," I said.

And so, the discussion continued. Lake and the others were already poring over the map, trying to figure out where a group on the run might find shelter. I knew that venturing into an area where the SSUs were searching was madness. But we'd already ventured into madness when we'd freed Tork and Faze, and we'd survived. Could we do it again?

Zac came and sat beside me.

"It doesn't have to be you," he said. "I couldn't do it before because of Tern and Cale. I had a duty to keep them safe. But they know everything now, and they'll be safe here. I know the terrain. I was the one who got you into this. You'd never have taken all the risks you did if I hadn't put ideas into your head. I can get you and your team away from here to safety. Somewhere beyond the Earth History zones. Beyond all known zones. You could build a new life there."

"The Sick Lands?"

"That's just a name to stop us going there. We don't know what it's really like out in the blanked-off areas."

"No. I was the one who decided to save Tork. I promised him and the rest of them that we would be the ones to start changing things. They don't want to run off into hiding and do nothing. They want their chance to fight back. We've already lost Nea. I owe it to her to see this through."

"Then, we'll take the risk together."

The old Zac was back.

"I know who Ferris is," I told him.

He stared at me.

"And I know the numerals for all the mothers from the Experiment."

I showed him the pen drive.

"They're all on this."

He took the pen drive from me and held it in the palm of his hand.

"My mother's in that?"

"Yes."

"You can find her?"

"Maybe. It depends. If I can somehow get into the personnel files for all the Disciplines, I'll be able to track them down."

"Not much chance of that now."

I knew what he meant. He handed the pen drive back to me. Without access to the personnel files, it was valueless. He didn't even bother asking who Ferris now was. I let it go.

"OK," I said. "We'll go together. But not all of us. Not Tork and Faze."

"And not Tern and Cale," he agreed.

✦

Using the coordinates that Ethan had been able to supply from his eavesdropping, we worked out a route to the Re-Cos' most likely location. We planned to persuade them to return with us to Zac's house to carry out the filming. But our plan depended on us being able to find them. We agreed that if we didn't find any trace of them within four days, we would give up, and I would take Zac's advice and lead my crew to The Sick Lands, where we would take our chances on what dangers might await us there.

✦

We opted to travel in Zac's ATU, so we emptied three of his ATU's reserve cans into my ATU in case those left behind might need it. They all could drive, but none of them had any experience driving an ATU, so I set Tern up in my driving seat and took her for a quick, intensive lesson. I didn't know where they could go if anything went wrong, but Zac told me not to worry: Tern knew what to do.

Zac had already figured out a fuelling node on our route where he could refill his tank and his reserve cans as if he were on regular recce duties. April, Adar, Reyn, and Peak piled into the rear of the ATU, Lake took up her usual position on the roof, and I climbed into the passenger seat. I looked across at the driver's side mirror and saw the reflection of Zac and Tern deep in a hushed conversation. I watched as Tern reached her hand out to Zac. Zac touched his hand to hers, as Tork and I had done, and as Lake and I had done. Then he pulled her into an embrace. I looked away because I knew what this was about, and it was none of my business. If anything, I envied them, and I realized I also envied Tork and Faze. A moment later, Zac climbed into the driving seat beside me.

I kept my eyes peeled while Zac drove. I knew that Lake would be doing the same on the roof. None of us spoke much. We were too aware of the danger we were facing. Even if we managed to avoid the search teams and find the Re-Cos, how would we convince them we were friendly? All we had come up with was to park the ATU when we calculated we were close and continue on foot. Then one of us would approach them in the open. It wasn't much of a plan since it left us vulnerable and exposed, but we hoped it would show how non-threatening we were.

I don't believe in anything that I can't perceive with my own five senses. At least that's what I tell myself. But sometimes, it's hard to shake off the irrational when something you can't put your finger on keeps niggling at you. It wasn't that I'd heard or seen anything, and Zac didn't seem concerned, but I had a feeling that something wasn't right. I said nothing, and by the end of the second day, we reached the fuelling node without any apparent cause for concern.

But I should've said something. If I had, we might have been more alert. We might have stopped before the node and taken time to reassess things. We might even have turned back.

Instead, while Zac was filling the tank and April and I were lining up the empty reserve cans, the trees on our left suddenly appeared to come to life as a line of soldiers emerged from them and moved towards us, guns aimed straight at us. It was too late to do anything. They had us surrounded. No time to reach for my firearm. No time to run for cover. I raised my arms immediately. Zac saw them too and calmly replaced the fuel pump in the node and raised his arms also. They'd already captured our look-outs—Adar, Reyn, and Peak—who were no match for their stalking skills. Lake had been absorbed in the map, so was the last to see them. They didn't bother asking us who we were or what we were doing. They already knew.

The leader demanded to know where the others were, meaning Tork and Faze. Zac asked what others and tried to pretend we were just a regular Earth History unit. It didn't work. They ordered Adar, Reyn, and Peak into the rear of their ATU and shoved Zac, April, Lake, and I into the back of Zac's ATU. Four soldiers climbed in after us. I heard two more— a driver and a navigator—take over in the front, and, as our engine fired up and we moved off, I heard the other ATU growl into life to follow us.

We drove several hours in silence. No questions were asked by them or by us. None were needed. They had achieved their mission, and we had failed ours before we'd properly started. No idle talk among themselves either. They were too disciplined for that. I spent the time mentally beating myself up for not having had the wit to keep watch myself instead of leaving it up to three rookies. I'd no idea what was going through Zac's head, but I could guess at the horrors in Lake's. I also worried about those we'd left behind at Zac's house. In a few more days, it would be evident to them that we weren't coming back. Would they have the courage to leave as Zac wanted them to do? Or would they hang around too long waiting and risk being discovered? The one thing I hoped they wouldn't do was to try to find us. Tork and Faze would be instantly arrested if they re-entered the urban zone. They would all end up in an After Lab, even Tern and Cale. There would be no mercy for any of them, just as there would be none for us.

CHAPTER
19

"Where are they hiding?"

The voice was calm. Her expression was . . . what? Neutral? Like it didn't matter if I answered or not. I answered anyway. The same answer to every question she asked me.

"I am Military Intelligence Operative 4279344. I am engaged in an undercover operation. I demand to speak to my Commanding Officer, Military Intelligence Operative 2411228."

She sighed. She wasn't neutral. She was bored.

"How long are you going to keep this up?"

"I am Military Intelligence Operative 4279344. I am engaged . . ."

"There is no evidence anywhere to support your claim of being engaged in an undercover operation."

We were in a cell somewhere. Not anywhere urban. I could tell from the length of time it had taken to get here. Any minute now, a Truth Team would arrive with their drugs and hypnosis. And then I remembered.

"There is," I said. "Two people know I'm on a Military Intel mission."

I told her about my encounter with the female MI Commander, who had taken over from Ferris, and how I had informed her that I was engaged in confidential duties. And I told her about the email I had sent to my Pol Com colleague, Sig, advising him that Military Intelligence required me to absent myself from my regular Pol Com duties. Both had been bluffs, but there was just a chance they would pay off now. My interrogator stared at me. I held her gaze. Seven lives were at stake here—Zac's, Lake's, April's, Adar's, Reyn's, Peak's, and mine. She hadn't mentioned any of them. She wouldn't. Not yet. Not until they'd been doped with truth drugs and started talking. I had to go all the way.

"When you contact my Commander, tell him I've identified both subjects in the photo."

"What photo?" she asked.

"I can only report to my Commanding Officer, Military Intelligence Operative 2411228," I replied.

She sighed more deeply this time, gathered up her notes, and left.

I was confident she would check out everything I'd told her. I'd have to be patient. It would take time. First, she'd have to report what I'd said to her boss. He, or she, mightn't believe me, but they couldn't dismiss anything that involved a Military Intelligence Commander. They would know that if what I said was true, they would be in deep shit for ignoring it. But they would also know that if I were lying, they'd be in equally deep shit for wasting MIHQ's and also the Political Commissariat's time. MIHQ would treat them as fools, but they probably wouldn't receive any repercussions beyond a humiliating verbal reprimand.

On the other hand, Pol Com could have them removed from their posts and demoted to menial work. They were probably discussing all this right now, weighing up the pros and cons. What would I do in their position? I couldn't allow myself to dwell on that. I had to stay positive. I stretched myself out on the cell bunk and settled in for a long wait.

✦

The boots came in the middle of the night—heavy, rhythmic, marching. I knew they were coming for me. I heard the bolts in my cell door slamming open. I barely had time to stand up before my cell filled with the hulking shapes of a Pol Com escort team. Sig! Could it be? I couldn't tell. All were wearing balaclavas. I could only see eyes. And all were heavily armed. But it had to be him. My interrogator had followed through. Someone had contacted him. He'd confirmed what I'd said. Now he'd come to collect me. But why so many guns? He'd know I wasn't a threat. I wanted to speak to him to confirm that it was him. But which one was he?

"Sig?"

That was all I got to say. It was as if I'd issued a signal. Two of them grabbed an arm and pinned both arms behind my back while a third handcuffed me. One of them, probably the one who'd cuffed me, shoved me out the cell door. The other two marched me down the corridor with two of the remaining escort in front and two behind. I now knew, despite their balaclavas, that Sig was not one of them. I also knew which option my interrogator and her boss had chosen—the one I hadn't even allowed myself to consider though I'd been aware of it. They had chosen to do nothing and send the problem up the line to the Pol Com interrogators because that's what you do with traitors. And traitors end up in an After Lab. I couldn't let that happen. I had to get free. But how?

We left the inner corridor and marched up another one towards daylight. I guessed the escort team's armored truck would be waiting at the end. If I were going to try to free myself, I would have to do it as soon as we emerged into the open air. OK, my arms were useless, but I could kick. The element of surprise might gain me a second or two to get out of their grasp and run. I wouldn't get far, but if I could force them to fire at me, to kill me, I would escape the After Labs' torture. But what about Lake, and Zac, and the others? Could I really abandon them?

We were at the end of the corridor. I could smell the fresh air. I could see the truck waiting with its rear doors open. I told myself, "Now! Do it now."

I glanced down at the legs on either side of me. Kick now. Do it. Kick! Now! I couldn't. I didn't want to die. Not here. Not now. Not yet. Because as long as I was alive, there was still a chance to expose what was going on. I should've told them everything during my interrogation, but I'd been trying to protect my Commander. But not anymore. I owed him nothing. I owed Zac, and Lake, and my crew. I owed my Arc. I owed the mothers. And above all, I owed the people who were being tortured in the After Labs. I had to stay alive as long as possible for their sake. I let the escort team shove me into the truck. The usual pattern. Four in the back with me and two upfront.

I could see nothing within the enclosed rear as we moved off, but I knew we must be driving towards the guarded exit gates since this was a military compound. I felt us slow down as we approached them. We stopped. I heard a muffled conversation between our driver and a guard. We waited. What was wrong? Why hadn't we been allowed to go? Still, we waited. Two minutes. Three. Five. I lost count. The rear door was yanked open from the outside. I saw a figure silhouetted against the light.

"Out," he commanded.

Who? Me? Yes, me. None of my four escorts helped as I lurched to my feet and crouched my way to the open door. The figure took hold of my upper arm and pulled. I jumped out onto the ground. Four of the gate guards stood aiming their rifles at me. Another guard was still talking to our driver through the truck's open window. He moved back, and the truck took off. I watched the gates close behind it as it sped off. So, I wasn't going to the Pol Com Holding Center. At least not yet. The guard who had ordered me out of the truck now ordered me back into the corridor and marched alongside me as I retraced my steps back to the cells with the other four armed guards following. When we reached my cell, he removed my handcuffs, ordered me inside, and bolted the door. I stood listening now to his retreating boots and wondered what had just happened.

Nobody came to explain anything or even to check that I was still alive. It was the same the next day. And the next. It didn't matter that I yelled until my throat was raw and that I kicked and battered at my cell door. The cell had its own water and nutrients supply. Nobody needed to come.

On the third day, I heard the boots again. Two sets this time. Walking fast, but not marching. Not urgent. I heard the bolts slide across. The door opened. And there he was. At last. My MI Commander.

The guard who had shown him to my cell closed the door and retreated. The Commander got straight to the point.

"What have you found out?"

"You're the reason I'm in here. Get me out."

"Tell me what you know."

"Your name is Ferris. You were born in the Natural Births Experiment, and you're looking for your mother."

"Have you found her?"

"I have access to her records—to all the Natural Birth mothers' records—but you have to get us out of here first."

"Us?"

"Zac and the others."

"Who? What others?"

"They were arrested with me. Zac knows you. He was born in the Experiment too. He told me all the stuff you didn't. I wouldn't have found out anything without him."

"And the others?"

"They've been helping too."

"What do they know?"

"Everything I know."

That wasn't true. I had only revealed what I knew about the Natural Births Experiment to Zac and Lake. The others knew nothing. Ferris would be aware I could be bluffing, but I hoped he couldn't afford to take the chance.

✦

They released all seven of us half an hour later. We collected our personal belongings as Ferris signed our release forms. I made a point of checking my gun, phone, and my mini-torch. The beam wasn't working. I opened up the battery compartment and looked in. I already knew why it wasn't working—I had removed a battery and hidden the pen drive in its place before I'd set out. My captors had had no reason to look inside. The pen drive was safe. I left it where it was and closed the compartment. Nobody noticed anything unusual. I was just a soldier checking my equipment. Zac kept glancing at Ferris, but Ferris avoided eye contact with him. Zac reluctantly got the message. I stayed in the background with the others while Ferris and Zac went through the procedures required to retrieve Zac's ATU. And then we were free.

Ferris and I traveled in his Lightweight while Zac and the others followed in Zac's ATU. I'd been right about the compound being somewhere remote, but Ferris seemed to know exactly where he was going. Why wouldn't he? He was a senior military Commander. He probably knew every military installation there was. Previously I'd always felt ill at ease with him, intimidated by his high rank, but this was different. I felt awkward, embarrassed even. I'd never felt that before with anybody, except maybe when I witnessed Tork and Faze kissing. Until then, I'd never felt so exposed to someone's vulnerabilities. Now I understood that it wasn't fear of being seen acting subversively that had prevented Ferris from telling me the truth about the woman and boy in the photo. It was his fear of being seen to be weak and needy. That's why he'd used me to search for them. I could understand that. That's how I would feel. That's why Zac's openness about feeling the loss of his mother had made me so angry. But I hadn't thought of Zac as being vulnerable. I'd thought he was foolish to admit so much, but I also thought he was brave as I'd gotten to know him better. Now I realized that this man sitting beside me in the driver's seat was just like me. His outward appearance of power and control, while real enough, took a lot of effort to maintain. Inside, we were both struggling to make sense of who we were. Knowing that released me from my awe of him.

"Where are we going?" I asked.

"To a safe house," he replied.

✦

The safe house stood high in the hills southeast of Urb One. Ferris explained it had been designed specially by Military Intelligence architects to be safe from all types of surveillance, including long-range spying devices and biologically fortified with an air filtration system to filter out all airborne viruses. It was a concrete construction, built underground and fitted to meet up to twelve people's needs. Each bedroom and living area and the central meeting space had its own computer and a separate, wall-mounted monitor to receive public information broadcasts.

"Is this where you live?" I asked.

"Sometimes."

"Who else stays here?"

"Only those whom I invite."

"It's a war office," said Zac, who had been wandering around, opening doors and gazing at the rooms beyond while Lake and the others stood quietly in the background.

"Each of the Disciplines has a number of these houses," said Ferris. "This is one of the Military Intel ones."

"So, you're a man of importance now," said Zac.

"I'm sorry," said Ferris.

"Why?" Zac asked before Ferris could continue. "Because I'm not? Because I'm nobody? Because I held out as long as I could against them?"

I thought Lake's eyes were about to pop out of her head. Nobody speaks to such a high-ranking officer like that. But Ferris was unperturbed.

"What good did it do?" he asked Zac.

"No damn good at all," Zac agreed.

Ferris turned to me.

"You said you know where they are?"

I took the pen drive out of my mini-torch, inserted it in the nearest computer, and opened it. The heading 'Psychoscience Training Unit: Archived Material' appeared on screen as it had when Ethan had accessed it for me on the computer in his hideout. I went through the processes Ethan had shown me and opened up the Natural Births files. There was silence as Ferris and Zac watched me bring up the thirty mothers' ID numericals and the matching thirty babies' numericals. Lake moved in closer so she could see too. The others stayed back, as I hoped they would. I didn't want them asking any questions.

Zac was the first to speak.

"2411215, that's me. Engineering Operative 1382766, that's her— my mother."

Ferris remained silent, so Zac prompted him.

"Where are you?"

Ferris pointed to his number.

Zac stared at it on the screen.

"And 1321542 is your mother," he said as if Ferris couldn't see it for himself.

"1321542," said Ferris. "I tried hard to remember that. I couldn't."

"We had to forget to survive," said Zac.

"Did you remember?"

"Not her ID number," said Zac. "Only her name. Tora."

Ferris said nothing.

"What was yours called?" asked Zac.

"Amel."

We waited for him to continue. He didn't.

"Is there more?" asked Zac, turning back to the screen to deflect attention from Ferris.

I knew there was. The videos that Ethan had seen when he was in training were on the pen drive. Ethan and I had started to look at some of them, but he couldn't continue. I couldn't then either. I'd have felt like a voyeur if I'd kept going. I'd have been tempted to look for Zac and Ferris, and that would've felt like going behind their backs. They were both here now, but could I tell them? Could I let them watch themselves as little boys being deliberately confused and terrified into submission?

Ferris was leaning over me, scrolling for more. I had to prepare them.

"Do you remember what happened after you were taken from your mothers?"

"The brainwashing?" asked Zac.

"They filmed it all," I said. "It's all on here."

"The other children?" asked Ferris.

"Yes."

I thought he was asking if they were all on film. But that wasn't it. I realized he was seeking a diversion as he continued.

"Is there any information on where they are now?"

"Not on this, but we should be able to find them in the personnel files."

"Print out the numbers and use one of the other computers."

I saw him look at my young crew and knew what he was thinking.

"Is it OK if they get some rest?" I asked.

He agreed. I took Lake to one side and ordered her to supervise the room allocations to get them out of the way. I also asked her to tell them what she knew about the Natural Births Experiment. Then I made the printout and went off to find another computer. I knew Ferris and Zac would view the videos as soon as they were alone. We had to allow them that. I had no way of contacting Tern to let her and the others back at Zac's house know we were safe, but I trusted that Zac had made sure she would know what to do when we didn't return.

✦

I tried each of The Nine Disciplines in turn—Computer Science and Technology, Engineering and Architecture, Archaeology and Anthropology, Biology and Medicine, Education, Mathematics and Physics, Agricultural Sciences, Security, and The Political Commissariat but I couldn't find any of the mothers' ID numbers in their personnel files. I tried to convince myself there could be any number of reasons why, not least, their involvement in a highly sensitive, top-secret experiment. But that only reinforced my fears. How could I tell this to Zac and Ferris? Zac would immediately know what it could mean. Ferris wouldn't. We hadn't yet told him anything about the After Labs. He knew we'd been arrested for having freed Tork and Faze, but he didn't yet know why we'd freed them, and he knew nothing of what we'd been planning to do before we'd got arrested. He had been focusing all his attention on finding out what I knew about his mother, and I had played on that to get us free. How could I now tell him his mother had been disappeared?

I put that thought out of my mind and set about searching for the Natural Births children in the files. I found them easily. In addition to Zac and Ferris, four other children were now Military Ops. Five were in Computer Science and Technology, three in Engineering and Architecture, one in Archaeology and Anthropology, five in Biology and Medicine, two in Education, three in Math and Physics, three in Agricultural Sciences, and one in the Political Commissariat. That made twenty-eight. One other, who had worked in Education had died at the age of twenty-two. Another who had worked in Archaeology and Anthropology had died at thirty-seven. There were no records of the causes of the deaths. Most of their careers to date were unremarkable except for Ferris and one other. That one other was very remarkable indeed. Somehow, despite her early trauma, she had risen through the ranks of Biology and Medicine and was now a Grand Controller. This woman could be our most powerful ally. I had to tell Ferris and Zac.

✦

They weren't in the room where I'd left them. I eventually found them outside, sitting together, close but not talking, just staring into space. Something had changed between them. They became aware of me, and, as they looked in my direction, it was as if I was seeing them for the first time. It wasn't that they seemed like strangers to me. Instead, I had a sense that they were more real than they had ever been before.

We returned to the house, and I told them about finding a Grand Controller among the Natural Births children. Zac was elated. Like me, he realized this could be the contact we needed to get the labs shut down. It was time to reveal everything to Ferris.

20

Ferris wouldn't believe Zac and me. He knew the labs carried out grue-some experiments. He'd even guessed that was why Lake didn't want to go back there. But he was convinced they only experimented on animals and that if they used human subjects, they had to be willing volunteers. He hadn't made any connection between the labs and me, though. He'd no idea I had any interest in them. He certainly had no interest in them, no curiosity about what went on in them. What was wrong with him? It was time to ask Lake and the others to join us, so, between them, they and Zac could tell him everything they knew.

He listened, but even then, he wouldn't believe it. I was so angry I couldn't speak.

Zac was incensed.

"You must know about the escapees?"

"Of course," Ferris said. "Gutless lab staff who couldn't cope with the nature of the work."

"No, they're not staff," said Zac. "They're regular Citizens who've been put through unimaginable torture."

"Some of them even set diseased apes free," said Ferris.

"You're not listening," said Zac. "The Bio-Medical Research Center is experimenting on human subjects. Not just apes. Not anymore. It's too time-consuming. Using apes is not effective enough. They only use apes and other animals for training. I'm telling you, they are experimenting on humans—men, women, children, even newborn babies, and nobody is doing anything to stop them because nobody outside the After Labs knows."

"You're not going to give up on this, are you?" said Ferris.

He opened up his laptop, brought up the Bio-Med Research Center, and entered his biometric ID. The home page came up along with a list of menu options. He clicked on Current Laboratory Research and immediately got a list of animal-based research studies.

"Type 'human subjects' into the search window," suggested Zac.

Ferris did so, but nothing appeared on the screen.

"Try 'human studies,'" said Lake.

Ferris sighed and typed it in. 'Access Denied' appeared on the screen.

"There!" yelled Lake. "They're hiding it."

Ferris opened his email account and began rapidly typing. Zac, Lake, and I moved in to watch as he composed an email to the Bio-Med Research Center Director, asking that the Director allow him access to all the After Lab files. He signed with his full MI Commander credentials and hit send. For now, there was nothing more to discuss, so we settled back to wait for the reply.

I felt that, at last, we were getting somewhere. When Ferris realized the truth, he would have to help us. If the mothers had been disappeared into the labs, we would find them in the lab files. Ferris would demand the closure of the labs, and no one else would have to suffer.

We heard the ping of an incoming email and rushed to join Ferris at the laptop. He opened it, and we all read the words: 'Access to all Human Studies files is restricted to authorized Bio-Med Research staff only.'

I waited for Ferris to speak. He didn't.

"This proves it," I said. "They do carry out experiments on humans."

"It may not mean that," said Ferris.

"What else could it mean" asked Zac.

But Ferris still wasn't convinced.

"If they do use a few humans, they would select only those already terminally ill—the non-viables."

"No," said Zac. "They use healthy humans and deliberately infect them so they can study the progress of a disease close up."

"How do you know this?

"You'll have to trust me on that," said Zac. "All I can tell you is I was informed of this by a very senior former lab worker who was in a position to know."

"All right, maybe they use criminals, outcasts who are a danger to The Citizenship," said Ferris.

"Like our mothers?" asked Zac.

"What do you mean?" Ferris snapped.

I couldn't stay quiet any longer. I had to spell it out for him.

"There are no records to show what became of the mothers after the Natural Births Experiment ended. We don't know where they are, but when a person goes missing from the system, it can mean they've been sent to a lab to take part in experiments."

"She means to be forcibly experimented upon," said Zac.

"I know what she means."

"And you know it's possible. You've seen the videos. You know what they're capable of."

"They wouldn't do that to healthy, fertile women. We need women like that."

Could he be so naïve? Although I hadn't watched the Natural Births children's brainwashing videos, I could guess what they depicted after hearing Ethan talk about them. And I'd witnessed the effect that viewing them had had on both Ferris and Zac. Now Ferris denied what he'd seen, what he'd been through as a child. Ethan said the brainwashing would do that. I had to butt in.

"That kid I rescued—you know what his crime was?"

"Treason."

"No! Tork has feelings for a girl. He loves her. That's all. I don't know what they did to you when you were a child, but I know you loved your mother. That's why you wanted me to find her. Tork isn't sick. He's not a criminal."

"In the eyes of the law, he is."

Lake couldn't contain herself any longer.

"The law that tortures people? Is that the law you believe in?" she asked him.

He ignored her and addressed himself to me.

"There has to be other records on the mothers. The Disciplines keep records of all their experiments."

"Where?" I asked.

"The Bio-Med Training Center's files."

"That's where the pen drive data came from," said Lake. "I down-loaded the whole archive. There's nothing more."

Now he acknowledged her.

"No. You downloaded from the Psychoscience Training Unit—a small, niche branch of Bio-Med. There has to be other files somewhere within Bio-Med—the ones that recorded everything from when we were conceived until we were separated. I've been looking for those files for years, but I don't have the clearance. Those are the ones we have to find."

OK. He didn't care about what was happening in the After Labs. All he cared about was himself and his loss. But Zac and I cared, and we could turn Ferris' self-interest to our advantage.

"We can," I said.

"How?"

"The Grand Controller who was born in the Natural Births Experiment the same as you and Zac. She would have the authority to get into any files she wanted."

He got it before I'd finished talking and was already dialing Grand Control headquarters. When someone picked up, he introduced himself as Commander 2411228, Military Intelligence, and asked to speak to Grand Controller 2411200. His call was diverted three times, and each time his rank got him through to the next level until we heard him say, "Thank you for taking my call, Grand Controller."

It was that easy. His rank commanded so much respect that he could gain access to a Grand Controller within minutes, but his status meant nothing regarding the Natural Births Experiment and the Bio-Med Research Labs. There all doors were closed.

We listened as he set up a meeting with the Grand Controller in her office in one of the admin buildings in Urb One the next day. He agreed that Zac and I should go with him.

✦

I was nervous as we waited outside the Grand Controller's office. Before my adventures with Zac, I'd regarded members of the higher tiers of governance as unknowable superior beings of great power, intelligence, and dignity who worked tirelessly for the good of The Citizenship and The Future. Now I wasn't so sure. The authorization for what went on in the Bio-Med Research labs, and the ratification of the Moral Code laws that could send any hapless offender to them, had to come from people such as the one we were about to meet with face-to-face.

We were finally ushered in by an armed guard. I took my lead from Zac and stood to attention as Ferris introduced us. The Grand Controller took no notice of Zac and me. She indicated to Ferris to sit. Zac and I remained standing to attention.

She informed Ferris that she was swamped with work and ordered him to hurry up and say whatever it was he'd come to say. As soon as he began speaking, I could tell she'd riled him.

"You are Grand Controller 2411200, also known as Kit. You were born in the Natural Births Experiment forty-three years ago."

The Grand Controller looked like she was about to explode.

"What is this nonsense?"

Ferris continued unperturbed.

"I know this because I was born in the same Experiment, as was this man, Military Operative 2411215. He would've been known to you as Zac."

"Yes, I remember you," said Zac before she had time to respond.

She glared at Zac, then stood up.

"Get out."

She meant all of us. Zac relaxed out of his attention stance. I did likewise. We weren't going anywhere.

Ferris turned to me.

"Show her the video."

I took the pen drive from my pocket and moved towards the laptop on her desk.

She stepped in and blocked me.

"I'll call security."

"Do," said Ferris. "And I'll have you arrested for obstructing a Military Intelligence investigation."

Could he do that? Probably not, but he had unsettled her. I could see her controlling her breathing before she responded.

"I have no knowledge of a Natural Births Experiment. I don't know you or this man, and I have no interest in whatever it is you think you are investigating."

"Well done," said Zac. "You have become a perfect Citizen."

"This meeting is over," she said.

By now, I had inserted the pen drive and found the videos. I looked at Ferris. He nodded. I clicked on 2411200, and the video came to life with the sound of a child crying.

A woman's voice came in over the crying.

"You have to stop that now. Kit? Kit? Do you hear me? You have to be brave."

The child—a little girl—came into view. She was sitting on a couch and sobbing so much that her voice came in gasps when she spoke.

"I want to go home."

The Grand Controller sank into her chair.

The woman in the video said, "This is your home now."

"No! No! I want mummy."

"You're too big for a mummy. You have to be brave. Can you do that for me? Can you be a big, brave girl?"

The little girl held out her arms to the woman. The woman pushed them away.

"No. I told you. None of that."

Zac moved away and sat on one of the chairs that lined the far wall where he didn't have to see the screen. Ferris sat stock still, steeling himself to keep watching. The Grand Controller was now experiencing the same as what they'd both been through when they'd viewed their videos.

I looked at the Grand Controller. A blotch of red was spreading up from her neck and across her cheeks. Her eyes were fixed on the screen, watching her ten-year-old self.

The woman on the screen was still talking.

"You have to forget about your mother. She's gone. You won't ever see her again."

The little girl curled into a ball in the corner of the couch.

The screen went blank, then cut to another scene.

The same little girl was now standing with her back against a wall. The woman was busy working at her desk, but she was still speaking.

"Everybody hates a cry baby. Cry babies are no good. I hope you're not a cry baby. Are you? Are you a horrible, nasty little cry baby?"

The little girl turned her face to the wall.

The woman continued, "Because if you are, we will have to take you back to the punishment room."

The little girl turned and shouted at the woman.

"I'm not! I'm not a cry baby."

The woman looked up from her pretend work and smiled.

"Good! I knew you weren't. I knew you were a good, sensible Citizen."

The screen cut to a new scene. Now the little girl was sitting on a bare floor in the corner of an empty room. The walls and ceiling were grey, and there was only a dull light from the single bulb hanging from the ceiling. The little girl was sobbing quietly. A door opened and the same woman as before entered. The little girl cowered further into the corner. The woman came and stood over her.

"Do you want to stay locked in here forever? I can do that. I can keep you here on your own for the rest of your life."

A man came in. He was smiling.

"Now, now," he said. "There's no need for that. Kit's a good little girl. And she's going to be very brave."

He crouched down in front of the child.

"Aren't you, Kit?"

The Grand Controller slammed her laptop shut.

"Enough."

"We've been through it too," Ferris said, more gently than I'd ever before heard him speak.

I could only guess what the three of them and the other Natural Births children had been through, and I didn't want to see it either.

The Grand Controller moved away from her desk and as far away from her computer as she could get. I almost expected her to sink to the floor in a corner. She didn't, of course. She was a grown woman now. But at that moment, I could see the small, frightened ten-year-old Kit still inside her.

She turned and faced Ferris.

"Why are you here? What do you want?"

Ferris looked at me.

"You tell her."

I told her how I had tracked down the mothers' identities and how I'd been able to match the children to the mothers. Also, that we knew where all the children were, but we needed to find out what had become of the mothers.

"Why?" she asked.

The question stumped me. Ferris had gone to so much trouble to try and find his mother, and Zac was equally desperate to find his. If there were any point in even trying, I would want to know everything possible about my mother too. Why didn't Kit feel the same? The Psychoscience Researchers had put the Natural Births children through a particularly cruel form of aversion therapy. I understood that from what Ethan had told me and from the little bits of video I'd seen. Had this caused Kit to blank out all feelings for her mother? Or had it made her hate her mother so much that she now denied all knowledge of her? Maybe she hadn't been as mentally strong as Zac or Ferris. Denying everything, no matter how futile that was in the face of the video evidence, was better than admitting that the brainwashing had broken her.

"We suspect . . ." I began, then changed as I remembered this was my tactical bluff, not Ferris'. "I mean, I suspect they may have been disappeared into the Bio-Med Research Center Labs."

She addressed herself to Ferris. I was way too lowly to deserve her attention.

"What has this to do with me?"

Ferris ignored her and let me answer.

"You were a medical biologist. You came up through the ranks. You are one of the Bio-Med Discipline's representatives on The Grand Controllers. You greatly outrank the Bio-Med Research Center's Director. You have the authority to gain access to all the records on the Natural Births Experiment. You can find out where your mother is, where all the mothers are."

"They'll be old women now," she said.

At last, an acknowledgment.

"Not that old," said Zac.

"They are aged between fifty-nine and sixty-five. Your mother would be sixty-three now. She gave birth to you when she was twenty. Her ID is 1354711," I informed her.

She sat down one chair away from Zac. I could see him wanting to reach out to her. He held back, though. She wasn't the type to appreciate physical contact, no matter how well-intentioned.

"There's every chance she could still be alive," he said.

She shook her head.

"No. She doesn't exist. I don't have a mother. Nobody has a mother."

Zac looked at me in exasperation.

"She was also a biologist; in Agriculture Sciences," I said. "She worked in Urb Two before she joined the Experiment. You lived with her for ten years in the same compound as all the other mothers and their children, just like Zac and Ferris did. You must be like her. You chose to be a biologist too. You probably even look like her. There'll be photographs on file. You could find them."

"What would that achieve?" she snapped at me.

Again, I was puzzled by her lack of curiosity. But that wasn't it.

"If they're dead," she continued.

That was it.

"Is that what you want to believe?" asked Zac. "Would that make it easier than believing she didn't want you? That she abandoned you? That's what they made us believe, isn't it? That's how they tried to make us hate our mothers. We wanted them dead. We needed them to be dead so that we could survive."

"And that's the way it should be left," she said. "Why rake it all up again now?"

I had to say something, or we were going to lose her.

"I don't know for certain if your mother, or any of the mothers, ended up in the Research Center labs, but people are in them now. Human beings are being used for experiments. That's what we should be talking about."

Kit turned to Ferris.

"What does she mean?"

But Zac was already on his feet.

"She doesn't care," he said. "She's their greatest success—a completely numb machine only capable of repeating the same actions, the same thoughts, over and over again."

"I don't believe that," I said.

They all looked at me, even Kit. I had to keep going if we were to salvage something from this meeting.

"Maybe on the surface, she seems like that. Maybe that's the only way she knows, but it's not the way she wants to be. It's how the system forces us to be. It's how we protect ourselves. You can't let anybody see how you really feel. You can't show any weakness. You have to be strong. Independent. You have to survive."

"Yes. She's got it," said Kit. "Listen to her. Survival—that's what's important. We have to do whatever it takes to survive. For the sake of The Future. For the sake of The Citizenship."

"That's not what I mean," I said. "They don't allow us to think for ourselves. If we step even the least bit out of line, they take us away for re-programming. They turn us into robots. And those they can't turn, they send to the laboratories to be tortured."

"I really don't know what you're talking about. Nobody is being tortured. The research labs only use animals."

"I've seen the orders. A boy I know, nineteen years old, healthy, would be in one now deliberately being made to suffer greater agonies than any one of us here can ever imagine if we hadn't rescued him."

I shouldn't have said that. I'd made an accomplice out of Ferris, who'd helped me escape charges by going along with my claim that I'd been working undercover for him. Would Kit know about that? Probably not. Why would she?

"The work that goes on in the labs is necessary for our continued existence. It does not involve any human subjects," she insisted.

"Have you actually seen what goes on in them," asked Zac.

"I don't need to."

"I think you do," he said. "I think the whole of The Citizenship needs to see what's being done in their name."

"The Citizenship will accept that animals have to suffer so that humans can survive. Cures are being found. Vaccines developed. Our susceptibility to disease is being eradicated."

"No. Humans are suffering as well as animals. Viruses are being manufactured and stockpiled. More than enough to destroy us all. Why?"

"We must be prepared to defend ourselves."

"Against who?" I asked. "There's nobody left. There's only us."

She didn't answer.

"Isn't there?" I asked.

"Earth is a vast planet," said Zac.

Did they know something I didn't?

"What are you saying?"

"There may have been other survivors."

Ferris joined in.

"With access to better technology than ours, better resources, depending on where they are. We don't know. But if they do exist, they could be a very serious threat."

"If they've got all that, why would they want to attack us?"

"We can't afford not to be prepared," said Ferris. "We have to be ready to defend ourselves."

"And this is the justification for torturing people in the After Labs?"

"We do not use human subjects," sighed Kit.

"OK," said Zac. "Forget about that for a minute. What about our mothers? Will you help us find them?"

"They are the past. They're no longer relevant. To rake all that up now would be a treasonable offense."

"You'd rather charge us with treason than acknowledge your mother?" I asked.

She ignored me and addressed herself to Ferris.

"I have more important work to do, and so have you, Commander. I suggest you get on with it."

And that was that. She wasn't going to be of any help to us in either finding the Natural Birth mothers or in shutting down the labs. There was nothing more to be said.

Ferris stood up.

"Thank you for your time," he said and walked out the door.

Zac and I followed him.

✦

We drove away from Urb One in silence. I felt guilty about blurting stuff out about rescuing Tork. I was fairly certain Kit wouldn't have noticed in the circumstances, nor would she have cared. I assumed Zac's silence was a sign of his despair. We had utterly failed to make an impact on the Grand Controller.

When we got back to Ferris' safe house, there was no discussion about how the meeting had gone or what we should do next. Instead, Ferris and Zac went off to their separate rooms. I rounded up Lake and the crew and advised them to prepare for heading back to the bush the next day.

"You mean we're giving up?" asked Lake.

"No. I mean, we've reached a dead end."

I was as disappointed as they were.

"What's going to happen now?" asked Peak.

"There's nothing more we can do," I said.

"I mean to us. What are we going to do? Where can we go?"

It was a fair question. I could think of only one reasonable answer.

"I'll ask the Commander to get you all re-instated in your old jobs with no repercussions."

"What about Tork and Faze?" asked April.

"I don't see why Faze wouldn't be accepted back on the dome building project in Urb Six."

"And Tork can go back to the Holding Center?" asked Lake. "Then we can all forget about him? It'll be like nothing ever happened. We just had a little adventure, that's all. But it's all over now. As you were, soldiers."

"And Nea died for nothing," said Adar.

How do you raise someone's morale when your own is at rock bottom?

"Think of what we achieved," I said. "We saved Tork's life. You did that."

"Going to look for the Re-Cos was a stupid idea," said Reyn.

I knew he was right. I'd always thought it was a bit risky. I couldn't say it back then because I didn't have anything better to offer. I couldn't admit it now either because if I did, they'd never trust my judgment ever again.

"They would've provided the proof we needed," I said.

I didn't hear his response because a sudden thought came to me. Oh, shit! The pen drive. I'd left it in the Grand Controller's computer.

"There's something I have to do. Tell the Commander I've borrowed the Lightweight."

"Where are you going?" Lake asked.

"I won't be gone long."

"I'll come with you."

"No. Wait here."

I left before she could say anymore.

✦

I didn't bother telling Zac either. I'd be back before he, or Ferris, realized I'd gone. The Grand Controller wouldn't be there at this time of night, and I trusted my MI ID would get me past security. No need to make up a story. I would simply explain that I needed to pick up something that I'd left behind earlier.

✦

As I expected, after checking that I had indeed met with the Grand Controller earlier, the guard on duty at reception walked me to the Grand Controller's office door. We were both surprised to find the door unlocked and the Grand Controller inside sitting at her computer. The guard mumbled his apologies for disturbing her and left. I think I only got to stay because she was too distressed to be able to think straight. I could tell she'd been crying. That wasn't something I'd often seen, but I recognized the signs since I'd had some recent experience of it myself. I assumed she'd been watching the part of the video that she couldn't watch earlier.

She closed her screen.

"What do you want?"

"The pen drive," I mumbled. "I forgot to take it back."

"I'll keep it," she said.

"Of course. Make a copy of it."

She made no move to do so. I could understand why.

"I'm sorry," I said.

"What for?"

"What they did to you."

She looked away. It was a long time before she answered.

"It was for the best."

"Was it?"

This time she didn't answer, so I kept on talking.

"Zac doesn't think so. It's harder to tell with Ferris. He doesn't show stuff on the outside."

"He was always like that," she said.

"You do remember him!"

"Always very serious. Never showed his true feelings."

"I used to be like that," I said.

She wasn't in the least interested in how I used to be, but I had to keep trying. I wasn't sure why.

"I was very good at it. So good that I ended up not being able to feel anything. Actually, that's not true. I could feel anger—a lot of anger. I still do sometimes. And fear. Not of the things that everybody fears, like being attacked by a bear or a wolf in the bush at night. I mean fear of being alone. I know we're all alone. We're meant to be alone. Isn't that what we're taught? But it's hard. You have to pretend you don't care. And that makes you hard. I mean me. It makes me hard."

I was babbling again. And Kit was just sitting there, not even looking at me.

"I remember Zac too," she said.

"What was he like back then?

"Gentle. Kind."

"He still is."

Now she turned to me.

"Have you watched these?" she asked me.

"Not all of them."

"Mine?"

"Yes. Only because Ferris arranged the meeting with you, I felt I should get to know you."

Tears appeared in her eyes again. She got up and walked around the room. I kept quiet and waited. When she finally spoke, it was to the walls, the ceiling, the empty corners of the room.

"I let them do this to me."

I struggled to find a response. She was a Grand Controller. I was nobody. But she was also Kit, the little girl whose life they had destroyed. Surely no amount of status could compensate for what they'd done to her?

"You were a child," I said. "You had no choice."

She faced me.

"Oh, but I had. I knew they were wrong. I knew what they were doing was wrong. I should've known my mother wouldn't have abandoned me the way they said, but I let them convince me she did."

"They had all the power. They took yours and used it against you," I said.

That was the best way I could think of to characterize what I'd seen in her video. Two people had worked on her—the woman and the man—adults so much older than her and with what must have seemed so much daunting authority. The woman was the mean one, whereas the man appeared to be kindly. It was an act, but a child wouldn't have understood that.

"I knew I'd never see my mother again, and they made me not care. I gave in to them. I went along with everything they said. Everything they wanted."

"You had to. That was your survival instinct."

"I never allowed myself to get close to anyone after that."

I'd grown up never knowing what being close to someone was like, never wanting to either. They designed me that way. It was how all of us from the Factory Births and later the Ex-Vivo Programs had been designed. We had no experience of closeness; therefore, we didn't know how to be close. That's what our leaders, our manipulators, intended. But it didn't always turn out that way. I knew that because, despite all their efforts, I felt close to Lake, to Zac, and even, in a weird way, to Kit.

"They told me that I'd only imagined that I'd had a mother. That all those years I'd spent with her were an illusion—that they never really happened. They tried to make me believe that I'd been born in a factory, like everybody else, and that I'd been sick and that my memories of having a mother were just fever dreams."

"That's what they do," I said. "They destroy your real memories and replace them with false ones they implant into your consciousness."

"I believed them. It was years before I began to doubt. But it was too late then. I'd already become the person they'd groomed me to be. I had status and power. I was somebody important. I knew they could take all that away if I were to challenge the narrative they'd given me. So, I said nothing. Anyway, it didn't matter by then because my mother abandoned me; however, you look at it. I couldn't forgive that. I grew to hate her so much I didn't care what had become of her. I put her out of my mind again as if she'd never existed."

"You could find her now."

"She knew all along she was taking part in a time-limited experiment. She knew she would be giving me up, and she went along with it."

"Maybe she had to. Maybe they gave her no choice. Or maybe she wanted a child of her own so much that she was willing to go through anything to have you even for just a little while."

She stared at me. I got the feeling this was the first time she'd allowed herself to consider this possibility.

"Maybe she didn't believe they would take you away from her," I continued. "I mean not forever. Maybe she thought she would see you again. Maybe she still thinks that. Wherever she is, maybe she's still hoping that someday she'll find you, or you'll find her."

She still didn't answer.

I almost had her. If only I could set off the right spark. I tried again.

"If we could find her . . ."

"What's it to you?"

What? Nothing. It's nothing to me. Why should I care? OK, I do feel what I guess must be sympathy for Kit. And Zac. And even Ferris to a degree. I mean, I'm willing to help them with their searches. I've gone to great lengths to help Ferris when I didn't even know what I was looking for or why. All the trouble I've gotten into since has been because I followed Ferris's orders in the belief that he was sending me on a genuine Military Intelligence mission. So, no. The identities of the mothers are nothing to me. I won't be any better off if we track them down. I still won't know who my mother is.

"I'm sorry," I said. "I didn't mean to cause you all this distress."

She spoke her next words so low that I barely caught them.

"I've seen the files."

"What?"

"I have access to all the Bio-Med Training Center's top-secret files. I searched after you left. I've found the complete record of the Natural Births Experiment."

CHAPTER

21

I stared at the list of numbers on the screen. This was what she'd been looking at before I'd arrived. One column showed the thirty mothers' ID numbers. Another showed the ages at which they gave birth. The ages ranged from sixteen to twenty-two. A third matched each mother with their respective children's ID numbers. The fourth recorded the dates of their children's births, and the fifth recorded gender. All thirty children had been successfully delivered full-term.

I scrolled to the next page. Details were brief and to the point, but it was clear there had been no volunteers. On the contrary, before selection, each woman had been found guilty of a serious crime. Eight of them had engaged in inappropriate relationships; four had been found guilty of theft; six incited rebellion; four sabotage; three of serious assault on other citizens. Two were accused of false recording, and three were guilty of already being pregnant. They were all given the option of participating in the Experiment or being punished as traitors to The Citizenship and The Future.

The pages that followed gave details of the progress of the pregnancies and the pre-separation years. I quickly skimmed through the antenatal check-ups, blood pressure readings, diet supplements—all diligently recorded. Then details of the birth, the aftercare, and everything regarding the mother and child's health and well-being until the separation. Notes about a few minor illnesses, a few bumps and scrapes, and one broken arm. Nothing unusual. It was the accompanying photographs that got me. There were Zac and Tora, Kit and her mother, Cia, and the photo I knew so well of Ferris and his mother, Amel. And all the other mothers and their children. All smiling and happy. Also, photographs of the children at varying ages as they grew. There were no records of how the separations were achieved, at least not in this file.

I found what I'd been looking for—the page titled Mothers' Post-Separation Destinations. I looked around for Kit. After scrolling to the start of the file for me, she'd retreated to the background. And that's where she'd stayed. She already knew what I was about to find.

The page was laid out in two columns—the first listed the mothers' ID numbers. The second showed where they'd been sent after their children had been removed from them. There were only three possible destinations—the Bio-Med Labs, death, or something recorded as TSL. I checked the identities of the dead first. There were six. An unusually high number, I thought. Five of them meant nothing to me. But one sent a shock wave right through me. It couldn't be. Even though I was mentally prepared for her to disappear into the labs as a human test subject, I still hoped that it wasn't true. It was an argument that I'd deliberately used to force a reaction from Ferris and Kit, but I didn't really think that the labs would have been using humans thirty years ago. They'd have had enough animals back then.

I stared at her entry, unwilling to let it be true. There were no personal names here, only numbers. Maybe I'd read her number wrong. I hadn't. Perhaps it had been recorded wrong. Very unlikely. I didn't need to scroll back to the photographs. She and her son were embedded in my mind's eye—Weird Smiley Woman and Boy. How could I tell Ferris that the mother he'd spent so long searching for was dead? I'd been sure I'd find her here. I'd imagined going to him with the good news. I'd thought that wherever she was, he and I would find her. That no matter what it took, they would be reunited. But that would never happen. A brief footnote told me that after Ferris had been taken from her, she had been demoted and sent to work on a building project. Within a year, she had died in an on-site accident. I checked the other deaths. They, too, were recorded as accidental and had occurred within a year of their separation from their children.

I re-checked what crimes the six dead had committed. Each had been found guilty of the same thing—inciting rebellion. Was this a coincidence? Or was it a ten-year delay of their death penalties? A case of once a subversive, always perceived as a threat? Or had they been the most difficult to handle after the separations? Had they been causing trouble? Had they been demanding to see their children? Had they refused to be intimidated into submission?

I read the numbers of those whose destination was listed as the Bio-Med Labs. There were five. Was this the proof that humans were being experimented on back then? I still hadn't come to Kit's and Zac's mothers, so I pushed that thought to the back of my mind and read through the remaining group of nineteen whose destinations were all noted as TSL. That's where I found them. I turned to Kit. This time she was watching me.

"What does TSL mean?" I asked.

"It means they're probably dead too," she replied.

"Why?"

"TSL is an acronym for The Sick Lands."

I didn't know what to say. The very thought of The Sick Lands was enough to fill anyone with dread, which is why they were very rarely mentioned. It was inconceivable that anyone sent there could survive. This was grim reading.

I went back over the five who had been sent to the Bio-Med Labs. Four of them had been found guilty of inappropriate relationships and one of theft. Were they now dead too? I asked Kit what she thought. She didn't know, and I got the impression she didn't care. The files provided nothing but bad news. Any hope she, or Zac or Ferris, might have had was now shattered. Why should she care what happened to other people's mothers? She'd been forced to bury the memories of those early friendships. Had Zac been right when he told her she was a numb machine incapable of caring about anyone? Maybe, but I couldn't get the image of the terrified little girl that was Kit out of my mind.

"Why do you think some were sent to the labs?" I asked her.

She shook her head. She didn't know.

"To be used for human experiments?"

She still didn't reply. I had the advantage, so I kept pushing her.

"That's what they do. If you no longer fit their needs, they destroy you. Physically like in the labs, or emotionally and psychologically like they did to you."

She elbowed me out of the way and sat down at her computer. I watched her bring up the Bio-Med Research Center and search for the lab files. Several files opened up as she keyed in her access code. But not the one she wanted.

"The Commander tried that," I said. "'Restricted to authorized staff only' kept coming up on the screen."

"We'll see about that."

She returned to the Mothers' Post-Separation Destinations pages and set a printout in motion. Then she stuffed the printout into her pocket and strode to the door.

"I'll drive you," I offered as I hurried after her.

✦

The sun was coming up as we passed through the checks at the Bio-Med Research Center's security gates and parked. Kit's status as a Grand Controller allowed us to sail through the following sets of security checks until finally, a guard led us into the very same office where I'd first met Lake. The most senior security operative on duty entered and apologetically informed us that the Director, whom Kit had demanded to speak to, wasn't on the premises and assured us that he would be here as quickly as he could. We resigned ourselves to wait. I didn't feel as spooked as I had on my first visit, maybe because it was early morning and therefore quiet or, more likely, because I was in the company of a Grand Controller. But then I thought of the suffering that even now must be going on somewhere within this compound. Even if it was confined to animals, it was still sickening.

After about twenty minutes, a tall, slightly disheveled man entered

"Grand Controller, what can I do for you?"

Kit produced the printout from her pocket and thrust it at him.

"These women—the ones listed as being sent here—I want to see all files you hold on them."

The Director glanced down the page.

"This was before my time. I don't know anything . . ."

"You don't need to know. Get me the files."

"Certainly, Grand Controller."

He hurried out. Kit paced the floor, and I sat in a chair and waited.

It was another thirty minutes before the Director returned. By this time, Kit had worked herself into a fury. The Director, however, seemed to have grown in confidence.

"I'm sorry, Grand Controller, but I've been unable to find any reference to these women on our systems."

"That's nonsense. Have you gone through all the personnel files?"

"It was the personnel files that I checked."

"Then check the After Labs subjects' files."

"Lab subjects? You mean the animals? I don't understand."

"You do use human subjects in your laboratories, don't you?"

"Absolutely not."

"You never conduct any kind of trials on humans?"

"This is a first-line research Center, not a hospital."

"But you do use human subjects."

She said it as a statement. Not a question.

"It is beyond my remit," he began, then he stopped and corrected himself. "I have no knowledge of any experiments carried out on humans in this facility."

I decided to butt in.

"Can you show us the After Labs?" I asked.

"I'm afraid that's completely out of the question. The risk of contamination would be too great."

"We could wear Bio-Haz suits," I offered.

"No. That wouldn't be possible."

"Why not?"

"I mean, I would have to clear it first."

"With who? I asked. "A Grand Controller, maybe?"

He turned and smiled at Kit.

"I'm sure you understand. I could arrange a visit in a couple of days if you wish?"

"That won't be necessary," said Kit.

He followed after her as she walked away.

"It would be no trouble. Once I get clearance, I'll show you around myself."

She ignored him.

To me, she muttered, "Lying bastard."

We were both too fired up to go back to her office. Instead, I drove us to Ferris' safe house.

✦

Ferris displayed no emotion when I told him that his mother had died. Even when Kit showed him the print-out, he only glanced at it before passing it to Zac. Zac read it all carefully then read aloud the entry about Ferris' mother. For a moment, I thought he was unnecessarily insensitive until I realized that maybe Ferris needed more than a deliberately quick look at words on a page to be able to accept the truth.

Kit had been keeping her anger in check since leaving the Bio-Med Research Center. Now she had a plan of action.

"I want you to organize a raid on the Bio-Med laboratories," she said to Ferris.

"On what grounds?" he asked.

"Breach of The Moral Code."

"What breach?"

"Tenet number nine. 'No Citizen may physically or mentally harm another Citizen on penalty of death.'"

"I would need more than a presumption to justify such an action."

"I have reason to believe Citizens are being harmed in the laboratories, and I demand an investigation, Commander."

I could hear the gasps from Lake and the crew as Kit continued speaking.

"That's my duty and my right as a Grand Controller. And it is your duty to obey my orders. I want that place swamped and the Director, and anyone else who gets in your way, arrested for obstruction."

"Yes, Grand Controller."

"Make sure your soldiers are fully protected. Do you have access to Bio-Hazard suits?

"Yes, Grand Controller."

"Don't let anyone enter the labs unless they're wearing them."

"Yes, Grand Controller."

"Take a camera," I said. "Film everything."

"Yes," agreed Kit. "I want everything in that place recorded. And confiscate all their computers. Leave only what they need to ensure the subjects' health and safety—animal or human."

"Yes, Grand Controller," Ferris said.

She indicated Zac and Lake and my crew, who were by now barely able to contain their excitement.

"Take them with you and get on with it."

Ferris drew himself to attention, saluted Kit, and gave the order to prepare to leave immediately. I moved to take charge of my crew, but Kit called me back.

"No, you stay with me. I need you as my driver."

Ferris got on his phone and began barking instructions and organizing his forces. By the time he'd finished, Zac, Lake, and the crew had geared up and were ready to go. As they left in Zac's ATU, I could hear Kit on her phone, ordering someone to have a team prepared to move at a moment's notice. When she hung up, she explained that she'd been talking to the Medical Director of the hospital closest to the labs. As soon as Ferris and his soldiers secured entry into the labs, a highly trained team of doctors and medics, appropriately protected in Bio-Haz suits, would take over the human subjects' care.

"That's if there really are human subjects in there," she added.

CHAPTER

22

It took Ferris less than an hour to get his team of raiders assembled. When Kit received his phone call, she and I set out in the Lightweight to meet up with him at the entrance to the Center.

We arrived first and watched as twenty ATUs approached the main gates in single file. The first ATU, bearing the Military Intelligence HQ insignia and so presumably carrying Ferris, bulled on through the gates, knocking them off their hinges and smashing them into the ground as it drove over them. Stunned guards, who were also soldiers and, therefore, subordinate to Military Intelligence, watched helplessly as the other nineteen ATUs trundled through. The pattern repeated at each subsequent gate. If the guards didn't open the gates quickly enough, the ATUs smashed through and kept going.

At Kit's instructions, I maneuvered the Lightweight to the front of the convoy and drew up alongside the first ATU, which had now come to a halt in the courtyard outside the Reception block. Ferris and his team disembarked, and Ferris gave the signal for the remaining nineteen ATUs also to disembark. About half took up guarding positions to prevent anyone entering or leaving, and the rest, including a group carrying Bio-Haz suits, charged into the main building. I couldn't see Zac or any of my crew, but I knew they were there somewhere. Ferris, Kit, and I followed the charging soldiers inside. A raiding party soldier tossed a Bio-Haz suit to Ferris as he ran to take up a position at the front of the raiders.

✦

The noise was deafening as the raiding party thudded through the narrow corridors, flinging open doors, shouting at everyone to get out, grabbing, and frog-marching those who didn't move quickly enough.

Several times Kit and I had to flatten ourselves against a wall to let them rush past.

Then the labs. Maximum security. No Admittance notices on the outer doors. Bio-Hazard warning signs all over the place. Keep Out. Skull and Crossbones. Authorized Personnel Only.

Soldiers in front of me. Behind me. The raiding party soldiers, pushing and shoving, shouting, "Stand back! Stand back!"

The Center Director appeared out of nowhere.

"Stop! Stop! You can't go in there!"

Soldiers grab him, rip off his door access card, toss it to a Bio-Haz-suited man. It's Ferris. He holds the card to the door sensor. The door opens. All the Bio-Haz suits go through. More soldiers go through too. Kit and I follow them. This is not the germ zone. Not yet. Here is only the beginning. I see the signs: Lab One, Lab Two, Lab Three. These are the labs where Lake worked—where the animals are held and fed before they go into the animal experimentation labs. A soldier in a Bio-Haz suit pushes past me, her camera positioned on her shoulder, filming everything she sees. Up ahead, someone opens a lab door, and suddenly the screams are deafening. The animals—terrified. No one is harming them, but they scream because they know humans mean pain, and now they're surrounded by more humans than they've ever seen before.

I want to go in. But I can't face it. Where's Kit? Has she turned back? Lake appears.

"Come on."

I run with her. She takes me to a storeroom. Bio-Haz suits hang on the walls.

"Hurry up."

She grabs two sets of surgical scrubs from a shelf and tosses one to me. We strip off completely and put on the scrubs. We enter a blue-lit room. I do everything she does—I pull on rubber gloves, pick up a Bio-Haz suit and step into it, pulling it up to my neck. I pull one of the helmets over my head. We help each other seal ourselves from head to toe. We go through another door into another tiny room and out into a corridor. This is the corridor that leads to the After Labs.

Ferris and his suited team are here ahead of us. They move slowly. Not because of their suits, but because they are looking in the windows that line the corridors. I look too. I don't understand what I see. Or rather, I see so much that I can't separate it into distinct, recognizable shapes. I stop to try and make sense of it. A Bio-Haz-suited soldier knocks against me. I'm disrupting the flow. I move on and follow the soldier into a room. It's a room like a hospital ward. There are ten glass, or possibly Perspex, cubicles inside—five down one side and five on the opposite side. Each cubicle is completely enclosed and has what looks like a smaller cubicle at the front to provide an access tunnel. Outside each, there is a metal cabinet from which a thick tube runs into the cubicle, and on the walls, there are banks of machines and monitors. There is a bed inside each cubicle. I can't see if the beds are occupied. I move closer to the nearest cubicle. Yes, there is something in the bed. A person? A human? I'm afraid to look. But I have to. I have to see if it's true. I see a shape under a blue disposable sheet. I see a nose, cheekbones, a mouth, closed eyes. I can't look anymore. I move on to the next cubicle. Another shape under a blue sheet. Too much. I move on more quickly to the next cubicle and the next. More shapes. More faces. Some with oxygen masks. I can't tell if they're male or female, young or old. I see intravenous lines, feeding tubes, tubes taking blood out of arms and into machines and tubes bringing blood back in, tubes sprouting from under sheets, and into collection bags. ECG monitors above the beds. All sorts of other monitors to the side. I take my time now. I stop at each cubicle and look properly. Some faces display what looks like severe, deep red bruising. Others are white and mark-free. All subjects are comatose. And all are very definitely human.

I followed the Bio-Haz-suits into another lab. It's the same here—more cubicles, more machines and monitors, more human subjects. Two lab staff in Bio-Haz suits stand back and watch us, not knowing what else to do. One of our team orders them out, and they shuffle into the corridor, where guards have already lined up four of their colleagues.

There are four After Labs in all. The last one I enter is the most harrowing. One end looks like an Ex-Vivo nursery with its rows of glass boxes. Each box contains a tiny baby. I can't bear to look too closely, but I see the tubes, the contusions. The other end of this lab houses more of the bigger cubicles that I saw in the other labs. They have similar machines and monitors, and their occupants are similarly tubed up. But these occupants are children from maybe two or three years old to around ten years and, like the adult subjects and the babies, they are unconscious and motionless. The staff has already gone from here. The only sounds are the continuous beeping from the various machines. As we file out, the new team of doctors and medics from the nearby hospital move in.

I meet up with Lake in the corridor. We can't speak. We can only clutch each other's arms in acknowledgment of the horrors we've just seen.

✦

After we'd changed out of our Bio-Haz-suits, Lake insisted on looking for Clover among the staff held in the courtyard outside the Reception block. All the staff was in regular clothes now. Ferris' interrogators would take them to a Holding Center for debriefing. I had no idea what Clover looked like, and I didn't expect to find her, but I understood Lake's need to look for her. To my surprise, she was there. Lake recognized her immediately.

Clover showed no sign that she recognized Lake. It soon became clear why. She was among the ancillary staff from Lab Four, where the babies and children were experimented upon, and was no longer the person that Lake remembered. I could only guess what she'd been through, what she'd needed to do, the brainwashing she'd experienced. How could anyone stay sane in that environment? Lake asked her about her baby, but she appeared not to remember anything about a baby or being pregnant. Even Salt's name seemed to mean nothing to her. The other lab medics and ancillaries nearby paid us no attention. They showed no curiosity about what was going on. I couldn't tell if the raid frightened them or made them angry or if they were relieved to be free from their awful jobs. Probably none of those things. They were past feeling anything.

What about the five Natural Births mothers? Were they here? I couldn't tell. A few women fitted the age range but now was not the time to ask them. Ferris had instructed his soldiers to seize all computers from the Center, so hopefully, their details would be somewhere in the files. There was nothing more we could do. Lake went off to catch up with April and the rest of the crew, and I went back into the Center to look for Kit.

I found her in the Director's office watching everything on the bank of monitors that covered the entire Center inside and out, including the After Labs.

"Where've you been?" she barked. "I need you to drive me to my office."

✦

I barely took in what Kit was saying as we drove. My head was still full of what I'd just seen. Ethan had told me. So had Zac. But seeing it for myself was something else. Images in my mind that I knew I would never shake. I desperately needed to be alone. I needed to think. Or maybe I needed not to think. But how? How could I stop myself? I needed to make myself a blank, go back to the bush, and get away from everybody. But I couldn't. I was here. I was in the middle of it. I was part of it. But what was it? What just happened today? OK, we'd proven what Ethan had already known. But who else knew and didn't care? Who else knew and thought it was the right thing? We'd stopped it for now. But when would it start up again?

I heard Kit say, "I'm calling an emergency meeting of the Grand Controllers."

I had to pull myself together. I knew she was on our side. I had to trust that she would do everything she could. But would she be able to convince the other Grand Controllers that using our own Citizens for medical experimentation was indeed a breach of The Moral Code? Would they care?

After I dropped Kit at her office, I drove up into the hillside above Ferris' house. I wasn't ready to join in the inevitable discussion about what we had all witnessed in the labs. I felt a strong urge to talk to Ethan. No, not talk. I wanted to confront him. I wanted to ask him why he had allowed himself to be used in the way he had when he knew where it would lead. That was my illogical brain speaking. I knew why. And, worse, I knew that in the same circumstances, I might have done the same. I would've done the same. I'd have gone along with everything they'd told me because they'd have made me believe it was the right thing to do. No. That's not why. At least not all of it. I'd have done it to keep myself safe. I'd have sacrificed anything and anybody to maintain my safety and status. I could've been a human experimenter too.

I felt cold sweat running down my back, my mouth filling with salvia. I got out of the Lightweight. I needed air. A feeling of nausea and lightheadedness came over me, and I stumbled and fell. I lay there on the damp ground on my front. I couldn't get up. I didn't want to get up. I wanted to stay there. All night. Forever. Never to go back. Not to Zac. Not to Ferris. Not even to Lake. They didn't know who I really was. What I was capable of.

"What the fuck are you doing?"

I covered my head with my hands and pushed my face down into the earth.

"Hazel! For fuck's sake. Get up."

I knew it was Lake. But I couldn't get up. I couldn't turn around. I couldn't face her like this. I felt her hands grabbing my shoulders. I couldn't even resist as she pulled me half up and knelt beside me. I couldn't open my eyes. I couldn't look at her. She pulled me tight into her and held me.

"I saw the Lightweight going up here. I knew it was you."

I couldn't speak.

"Ferris and Zac haven't come back yet. The others are at the house. They're exhausted. Come on. We need to get back to them."

She hauled me to my feet and shoved me into the passenger seat of the Lightweight. I hadn't the energy to resist.

Peak, Adar, Reyn, and April lay sprawled across armchairs and sofas at the safe house. Nobody was in any mood for discussions.

"You need to sleep," Lake said to me. "And so do they. Proper sleep."

I watched her urge each of them off to their rooms.

"Thank you," I began, but she cut me off.

"Go."

I went.

✦

I don't think I slept at all that night. Sometime towards dawn, I heard Zac returning in his ATU. I got up to hear his news and found that Lake was already up, having not slept much either. My crew remained dead to the world, so I let them sleep.

Zac told us that they had arrested the lab Director, two doctors, twelve nurses, and ten ancillary staff in the human labs. Also, six ancillaries from the animal lab and two admin staff were being held for questioning. None of the soldiers who had guarded the labs had been arrested because they had not been aware of what went on inside.

"What'll happen to Clover?" Lake asked.

"She's too disorientated for questioning, so she's been moved to the hospital. She'll get proper care and treatment there."

"And the other five mothers? I asked. "Have you been able to find out anything about them?"

"No."

"Do you think they could've been used for experiments?"

"We've checked the records. Only animals were used back then. They'd have been given jobs looking after monkeys, rats, whatever."

"So, they could still be there, among those being held?"

"Possibly," he agreed. "If they're among the After Labs staff, they may be severely mentally damaged."

"Like Clover," said Lake.

Or psychologically manipulated by Ethan into believing that what they were doing was right, I thought.

"What about the children of those mothers?" I asked. "I have all their IDs and current locations. I can find them."

"And tell them what? That their mother is dead or insane?" said Zac.

I shut up. Maybe he was right. Perhaps I should leave things as they were. With six mothers dead, nineteen exiled to The Sick Lands and probably dead by now, and five others either dead, missing, or brainwashed into insanity, there wouldn't be any good news for anybody.

"What happens now?" asked Lake.

"Ferris says we can return to normal duties."

"What does that mean?"

We listened as Zac outlined the futures Ferris had planned for us. Zac was to return to the Earth History project and continue his work as before. Peak, Adar, Reyn, April, and Lake had the option of either returning to their previous posts or, if they wished, Ferris could arrange new postings for them as junior military operatives at Command Headquarters. There would be no further repercussions regarding our springing Tork from the Pol Com Holding Center because, in effect, we had rescued him from an immoral and soon to be illegal punishment. Instead, Tork and Faze would be sent to separate facilities to be re-educated in good citizenship.

"Brainwashed, you mean," Lake said.

"What about me?" I asked.

"Kit likes you," Zac said. "She wants you as her driver and personal assistant."

I didn't know how to respond. I knew that Zac was keen to return to Tern and his Earth History post. However, the rest of us enjoyed the freedom to think for ourselves, plan our own actions, and experience our own emotional responses to the people and events around us. We couldn't close all that back down now. But what was the alternative? I needed time to think. And I needed to talk to April, Adar, Peak, and Ryan so they could make their own decisions about what they wanted to do.

✦

Ferris and Kit arrived together. Both looked worn out. Ferris had spent the night supervising the interrogation of the prisoners and gave us a brief update on how it was progressing. As expected, those capable of coherent answers maintained they followed orders and had no other options. The Director had also claimed to have been acting under orders, but he couldn't, or wouldn't, say who was issuing them. Others, like Clover, were too traumatized to provide any useful information. Ferris also had a team of analysts searching the computers taken from the lab for evidence of communications between the Director and any external entity. So far, all they had found were records relating only to the number and types of experiments that had been carried out.

"This might be interesting," he said as he tossed a pen drive in my direction.

"What's on it?" I asked.

"Probably nothing much, but have a look when you get a chance."

Zac asked Kit how she intended to ensure that there would be no further experiments on humans. That was what I wanted to know too. The pen drive could wait.

Kit explained that she had been attending emergency meetings with The Grand Controllers and The Implementors and showed them the films taken during the raid. All the Controllers and Implementors had denied any knowledge of what was going on in the labs, and all agreed that it must never happen again.

Zac wasn't convinced. Neither was I. Someone had to have authorized it to provide the resources. The Director couldn't have done it all on his own. Why would he? What would he have had to gain? It had to have been part of a political strategy decided and approved at the highest levels.

"What can we do?" asked Lake.

"Release the raid video to the public," said Zac.

"That would risk causing widespread panic," said Ferris.

"That's what's needed to shock people out of dumb obedience," Zac said. "We need anger and outrage. People have been used and manipulated long enough. We need a revolution."

"What if the Citizens don't panic?" asked Kit. "What if they're not shocked? Look what we've already accepted—euthanasia, state-controlled birth programs, egg harvesting from teenage girls. We're a Citizenship of manufactured orphans. We're created to have no relationship to each other, no emotional or cultural connections, no traceable blood ties, at least not traceable by us, no loyalties, nothing to bind us to each other. We've been designed not to care, not to have feelings."

"But we do," I said. "We've proved that. You've proved it."

"We were only able to do what we did because I went out on a limb and took the law into my own hands. There will be no reward for what we've done. We won't be thanked by a grateful Citizenship because The Citizenship would rather not know what goes on behind closed doors. There is no 'Citizenship.' It doesn't exist. Out there is a collection of individuals who care only about themselves. But don't worry. I'll make sure it's understood that Ferris was acting on my instructions—the instructions of a Grand Controller. That's his defense. The rest of you were acting on his orders—the orders of a high-ranking Military Commander. That's your defense."

"What's yours?" asked Zac.

"Simple humanity."

None of us said a word. Her speech about The Citizenship proved she knew that acting out of humanity was no defense at all.

Zac was the first to break the silence, "What do you think we should do?"

"We need the Supreme Council to say publicly that experimenting on human subjects is morally wrong," Kit answered. "The Grand Controllers and The Implementors have made a joint request asking them to insert an additional tenet into the Moral Code, specifically stating that humans are not to be used for any type of laboratory experiments or testing."

"You mean you've actually met The Supreme Council and discussed this?" asked Lake.

"No. We're only allowed to use digital communication with them."

"Isn't that the problem," said Zac. "You can make any demands you like, but they don't have to listen to you. You so-called Grand Controllers and Implementors have no power. You're puppets. You do what you're told. You're governed by a fake Moral Code designed only to keep people frightened and subservient instead of your consciences."

"We have to work within the system because there are too few of us to do this any other way."

"The Supreme Council is only six individuals, and you and I, and the entire Citizenship are allowing them complete control over everything," said Zac. "But you're right—there is no Citizenship, and you've just listed all the ways we're prevented from being a Citizenship, all the ways we're kept alienated from each other. Citizens need to be allowed to show that they do care. We gave you that opportunity. From ten years old, you were brainwashed into thinking you didn't care. How long did it take you to realize you did? A day? Two days at the most? If you have it in you to care after what was done to you, you have to give the Citizens a chance to show that they can care too. Forget about trying to influence The Supreme Council. They're not going to change anything because they have no reason to change. The only people with a vested interest in change are the Citizens. You just have to show them how. Show them they are the ones with the real power."

"I'm only one person," said Kit.

"You said the Grand Controllers and The Implementors were in agreement about making sure that human experiments would never happen again," I reminded her.

"Yes, but I don't know how far they would be prepared to go beyond that because it's true—they are puppets."

"Then ask them," said Zac.

"You need to be careful," said Ferris.

"I'm past being careful," said Kit.

There was complete silence in the Lightweight as I drove Kit back to her office. I couldn't tell if she was too exhausted for conversation or worried about what would happen next. Probably both. If things went wrong, she would be the one to pay. She'd already suffered so much. We couldn't let her sacrifice herself now for something we'd all wanted. There had to be other people who felt like us—people who cared about each other and would work together to help each other. Lake had taught me that. The Re-Cos were doing exactly that somewhere in the bush. My crew had proved they cared about each other. Other young cadets would care if only they were given a chance before the system swallowed them up and turned them into the sort of automaton I had almost become. Kit cared because we'd helped her remember the cruelty that had been inflicted on her. Zac and Ferris cared for the same reason. Despite what Zac had said, I still believed that the other, now adult, children from the Natural Births Experiment would also care. At the very least, they deserved to know what had happened to their mothers.

I asked Kit if I could come with her into her office to look again at the top-secret Bio-Med Training Center file containing the mothers' and children's ID numbers that she had previously accessed. It was obvious she'd barely registered what I'd asked when she agreed without question.

I had just activated Kit's computer when I remembered the pen drive that Ferris had given me. But where did I put it? I couldn't remember. I searched all my trousers and tunic pockets, but it wasn't there. Had I been so careless that I'd set it done somewhere and forgotten it? No. Not like me. I'd have put it somewhere safe. I searched my pockets again and eventually found it tucked away in a zippered pocket inside my tunic. I inserted it into a port and was just about to open it up when it occurred to me that this might be my last chance to view the secret Bio-Med file that I'd asked to see, so I opened it up instead. I scrolled to the information that matched the Natural Births mothers with their children and copied it to the pen drive I'd already inserted. At that exact moment, a male voice boomed loudly from the public broadcast monitor, making Kit and I nearly jump out of our skins.

"Citizens, I call on you to stop what you're doing and pay attention."

We stared at the screen.

A man in a black balaclava stared back at us, his eyes glittering through the cut-out holes and his lips obscenely red and wet in the mouth slit. His words were clear.

"You are living in an experiment. Since the day you were created, you have been controlled, abused, manipulated to do the bidding of an unknown master. You have been told that you have no choice but to obey. That is not true. You have a choice. You have power. We have power, and we are going to use it."

The man held up a small container.

"We are going to fight them with their own weapons. If I were to open this jar, we would all be dead within weeks. Do you know what it contains? I'll tell you. In here is the deadliest virus you've never heard of. A virus far worse than the one that caused The Wipe Out. Oh, The Wipe Out! We're all so scared of The Wipe Out."

He held the jar out towards the camera. There was something familiar about his voice—that sarcasm.

"Do you know where this came from? Of course, you don't. But our leaders do. And the special ones. The ones who've been trained to kill you with it."

Ethan.

He laughed. Ethan gone mad.

"And where are they trained? You know the answer to this one. The Bio-Medical Research Center. Where else? You think it's only animals they experiment on and kill. You don't care. Nobody cares what they do to monkeys, dogs, cats, mice. But it's not animals. Not since they killed them all. Now it's humans. But you don't care about that either. You've been designed not to care. You do know that, don't you? Is it working? Has it ever been put to the test? Well, I'm putting it to the test now."

Yes. Definitely Ethan. He'd done it. He'd hacked into the public broadcasts system. Every Citizen was hearing this right now.

"Unless all human subjects in the Bio-Med Research labs are removed to proper medical care, and the labs shut down and decommissioned, I will release the contents of this jar. You think you have no power? I'm going to show you what you have. Leave your accommodation blocks. Leave your work units. Take control. Get out on the streets, go to the Bio-Med Research Center. Demand that they stop the experiments. Don't leave until the torture of your fellow Citizens is stopped."

He leaned in close to the camera.

"If you don't, I will wipe you all out. Do you understand what I'm saying? I will wipe you out because if you don't act now to save your fellow Citizens, you are not worth keeping alive."

He sat back. Confident.

"I will be watching. I have eyes everywhere."

"We've already done it!" I shouted at the screen.

The screen went blank. I kept on shouting at it. I couldn't help myself. "We've already done it! There's no need."

"Who is he?" asked Kit.

"He doesn't know we've done it."

"Who? Hazel, who is he?"

"He's . . ." I hesitated.

"Hazel, if you know who he is, you must tell me. He must be stopped."

"He's a madman."

Kit's phone rang. She grabbed it and immediately somebody began shouting at the other end. I had to get out. I had to get back to Zac. I had to get this stopped. I whipped the pen drive out of Kit's computer and ran out of the office and back to the Lightweight.

There were already people out on the streets. Dozens of them. Young citizens in military uniform. Older ones dressed according to their professions. All uncertain, bewildered, not knowing whether to believe the threat, not knowing what to do. None of them had ever experienced such a broadcast before. I had to get back to the safe house before Security troops arrived and blocked all exits from Urb One.

✦

When I arrived, Ferris was on his phone, demanding to know who would have the capability to do this? Why isn't there intelligence on this? Who would put the entire Citizenship in such danger? Who are the likely suspects?

Zac, Lake, Peak, Adar, Reyn, and April stood watching him. When they saw me, they started up a babble of questions. Had I seen the broadcast? Who was that man? Why is he doing this? Zac, in contrast, stayed calm. I told them I'd seen it but revealed nothing else.

Just as Ferris ended his call, the broadcast monitor on the wall lit up, and a very composed-looking woman began reading from a document.

"This is a statement from The Supreme Council. Everything is under control. There is no reason to panic. A hacker has infiltrated our central information system. He aims to create fear and mayhem amongst The Citizenship. Do not listen to him. He is an enemy and a traitor and will be hunted down and dealt with severely. Please return to your accommodation units or your workplaces. Do not remain out in the open. I repeat, do not remain out in the open. The Future depends upon you. You are The Future."

Was that it? Was that all they could think to say? No reason to panic yet, don't remain out in the open? No reassurance in that.

"Broadcast the raid videos," Lake urged Ferris. "We can prove the labs have been shut down. It's what he wants. It's the only way to stop him."

Ferris' phone rang again before he could answer her.

I grabbed Zac's arm and shoved him towards the door. Lake made to follow us, but I told her to stay with the others and listen for what Ferris planned.

I waited until we were outside and out of earshot before I confronted Zac.

"I know that was Ethan."

"He won't do anything. He's bluffing," Zac said.

How could he be sure? Was Zac in on this? He wouldn't have known back then that we would go on to raid the labs. All any of us knew was that we were trying to find the Re-Cos. Tern and the others would have assumed we'd been captured or killed when we didn't return—had Zac told her how to contact Ethan? Had she gone to him for help? Did they concoct this together? And the others—Tork, Faze, and Cale—are they in on it? They're so young. So eager. So idealistic. Ethan would have had no trouble convincing them this was the right thing to do.

"Did you know he was going to do this?" I asked. "Is this what you and Tern were whispering about before we left?"

"What?"

"I saw you. I know you were planning something."

"Not this."

"What then?"

He stared at me, and I could tell he was trying to find the right words for something. Finally, he spoke.

"In another few weeks, Tern is due to be replaced by another Arc in the swap over. We can't let that happen. Do you understand what I mean?"

I nodded. Of course, I did. I'd seen them together. I knew they had feelings for each other.

"We'd already planned to go on the run before you arrived with your crew. We just hadn't figured out what to do about Cale. What you saw was me telling her where to go to wait for me if we didn't come back when I said we would."

"You didn't tell her to go to Ethan?"

"Is that what you think of me?"

No. I didn't think Zac could be behind something like this.

"Listen," he continued. "This is as big a shock to me as it is to you. All I want is to get back to Tern and get as far away as possible."

"To The Sick Lands?"

"It can't be any worse than here. This is the real sick land."

"Does Ethan really have viruses in that container?" I asked.

"I don't know. It's possible he took samples with him when he went AWOL from the labs."

"Who do you think the eyes are that he said were here and watching?"

"There are no eyes."

"Could it be the Re-Cos?"

"He wouldn't risk approaching the Re-Cos even if he could find them on his own. He's hiding from them as much as he's hiding from the Special Search Units. The Re-Cos know who he is and what he's done. They'd kill him on sight."

"And you're absolutely sure he's bluffing?"

"He has no accomplices working with him, so he has no 'eyes,' and he wouldn't chance coming here, the Center of all government and security, on his own. Remember what he looks like—his hair, his clothes. He'd be spotted instantly. So yes, I'm certain of it."

"What can we do?"

"Nothing. He's set something in motion that's now out of his, and our, control. Ferris' analysts will trace his computer. They'll pinpoint his hideout and send a search team to capture him. But he knows that. He'll not hang around."

"So, even if Ferris broadcasts the video now, Ethan won't see it?"

"No. But everyone else will. The entire Citizenship will see it."

"And that, combined with Ethan's broadcast, will create the anger and outrage you wanted."

"I wanted controlled anger and outrage, not fear and panic."

"What do you think we should do?"

"We have to tell Ferris."

✦

I was grateful that Lake and the others kept quiet as we told Ferris everything we knew about Ethan. It was all news to them, too, and I didn't want them asking questions and stirring up more trouble than we could deal with for now. Zac explained his belief that Ethan was bluffing about releasing the viruses, but he admitted that he couldn't be sure.

"In that case, we can't afford to take chances," said Ferris.

"You have to release the raid videos," Lake insisted again.

"I agree," Ferris said. "We need to show the Citizenship that what the hacker has demanded has been done, and his threat has been averted."

His phone rang again. He answered, listened for a few moments, thanked the caller, and hung up.

"They've traced the location of his computer," he informed us. "There's a Special Search Unit currently in that area, and they now have the coordinates."

Zac and I both knew they wouldn't find Ethan there, but we said nothing.

The public broadcast monitor flared into life again, and the same female announcer appeared and began speaking.

"*This is an order from The Supreme Council. All Citizens are hereby instructed to return to their accommodation units or their workplaces. This order will be enforced by our Specialist Bio-Security Units.*"

At this point, images of soldiers leaping out of trucks—all heavily armed and wearing full-face respirator masks—came on screen.

The announcer continued as a voiceover to visuals showing the Bio-Security soldiers taking up positions in the streets of Urb One.

"*Every Citizen is required to cooperate with this order. Those who do not comply will be forcibly removed and taken to a place of detention for their own safety.*"

We watched as the screen showed a Bio-Security patrol advancing along a street towards a large group of Citizens. As the patrol got closer, the Citizens scattered and ran, and the patrol gave chase. One of the patrol soldiers raised his rifle to his shoulder. The screen switched back to the head and shoulders of the announcer.

"*Our Specialist Bio-Security Units will open fire where it is deemed necessary to maintain law and order in our streets. You have been warned. The Future depends upon you. You are The Future.*"

The screen cut to black to signal the end of the announcement. We stopped staring at it and stared at each other.

"They wouldn't really open fire, would they?" asked April.

Ferris's phone rang. It was Kit taking control, issuing instructions. We listened as Ferris responded with, "I think you're right . . . Yes, I have everything I need. I can mobilize instantly . . . Yes, Grand Controller. I can certainly do that."

He finished the call and turned to Zac.

"You come with me. The rest of you stay here."

"What's happening?" I asked.

"When you need to know, I'll tell you. In the meantime, I want you to stay here and remain on standby. Understood?"

"Yes, Commander."

✦

There wasn't much for the rest of us to do after Ferris and Zac left in the Lightweight. Lake, April, Adar, Peak, and Reyn each had a theory about where Ferris and Zac had gone and why. I wasn't in the mood for speculation. I needed to be busy. And so did they. I ordered them to check their ammunition stocks, prepare their weapons, and check the ATU to be ready to go at the first word from Ferris. After reviewing my own ammunition supply and weapons, I asked Lake to inform the crew about Ferris' proposals for their futures. Then I went off to access a computer somewhere private.

As I expected, the pen drive contained a download from one of the After Labs computers. I assumed Ferris had given it to me because he hoped I would be able to find something relating to the five Natural Births mothers who had been sent to the Bio-Med labs. I started in the personnel files where all staff details were recorded and scrolled through the lists of medics, technicians, or ancillaries who were working, or had at any time, worked in the labs. I soon realized it was pointless. Lake had told me that all staff sent to work in the After Labs were given new ID numbers meaning they were redesignated in the same way all the human experiments subjects were redesignated. If the mothers were among the staff, there was no way I would recognize them. There was also no way of identifying who on the outside had input to the labs. There were no records of meetings, no emails, no records of any sort of correspondence.

But there must've been some reason why Ferris thought this would interest me. I kept looking and found the list of human lab subjects. Each subject was described as a patient and had a separate file that detailed what experiments had been carried out upon him or her. It was clear that the experiments had been going on for the past seven years. That was not long enough for the five mothers to have been sent there as subjects. The rest of the download contained data relating to the experiments but only experienced bio-medical experts could decipher it.

I scrolled through hundreds of ID numericals tagged with the word 'Completed' before I realized this was the death list. Only forty remained alive—thirty adults, five children, and five babies—the ones I had seen and barely recognized as human, the ones now being cared for by the medical team ordered in by Kit. How many of them would survive?

Eighteen further patients were listed as 'Aborted.' At first, I thought these were embryos, but when I read the number and type of experiments performed on them, I realized they had to have been adults. There was one undeniable connection between the nineteen—they were all aborted on the same date. Then it struck me. Aborted didn't mean life terminated. It meant the experiment terminated. These were the ones who had escaped—the Re-Cos. The lucky ones. Or were they? I gave up at that point. The mothers had been either dispersed or disappeared into the system, and there was no way I was ever going to find them.

The wall-mounted public broadcast monitor lit up, and the same woman as before began babbling the same announcement as before: *"This is an order from The Supreme Council. All Citizens are hereby instructed to return to their accommodation units or their workplaces. This order will be enforced by our Specialist Bio-Security Units . . ."*

I didn't listen. I couldn't. That old lonesome feeling had come over me again. The one where I know something is missing within me, and I feel it like a physical thing in my stomach, in my whole being. In the past, I hadn't known what it was. Now I did. Because now I knew what it was like to feel bonded to another person, to care about another person. To love another person and want to be with them. Tork and Faze knew how that felt. Zac and Tern knew. Even Salt and Clover. Did Lake? I remembered how she'd been unable to take her eyes off the woman and boy in the photo when I'd first shown her a copy and how I'd told her she could keep it. At the time, I hadn't known why. Now I did. I wouldn't have been able to name it back then, but there was love in that photo. It radiated out from it. It helped you feel less alone in the world, yet at the same time, it made you feel even more isolated.

I would probably never know who gave it to Salt, though it most likely was Arc371. She would've had access to such images during her training, although she wouldn't have known where it originated. I could understand why he'd kept it and why it was the last thing he'd been looking at before he died. Now it seemed Arc371 was dead too.

Lake entered the room.

"This is where you are! I've been looking for you."

"Do you ever wonder who you really are?" I asked her.

"You spend too much time in your own head," she answered.

"I mean, we have no history because our history has been destroyed. We have no connections to each other because we don't know who our mothers, fathers, brothers, sisters are, and we have no way of finding out because all that is redacted from our records. Who does that? Why do they do it? We're not even allowed to be friends with each other, and we're definitely not allowed to care about each other."

I wanted to say so much more. I wanted to tell her how much I cared about her, but I couldn't form the words. She must've sensed that because she held her hand out towards me. As we touched palm to palm, I again experienced the warm, soft sensation of my skin melting into hers.

"We do care," she said. "I care about you. And I know you care about me."

Did she mean what I hardly dared hope she meant? I couldn't be sure. And I couldn't risk making a complete fool of myself by asking her. I broke contact.

"Why were you looking for me," I asked. "Did you want something?"

"No. But you do have a habit of disappearing off on your own. I wanted to make sure you're all right. What are you doing?"

I showed her everything I'd found on the pen drive.

"Go back to the personnel files."

"Why?" I asked.

"To check if anyone from the staff disappeared off the system on the same date as the Re-Cos."

I scrolled through the personnel list again, focusing on the dates, and found five that matched the date that the nineteen Re-Cos had been 'Aborted.' Each of the five was marked 'Cancelled.' There was no further reference to them after that.

"Does that mean they were euthanized?" asked Lake.

"I don't know," I said. "Deaths are recorded as 'Deceased.'"

"Then this must be the five mothers. They're not dead, but they disappeared off the records on the exact same date as the Re-Cos escaped. They're out in the bush somewhere."

"Maybe."

Ethan had said that some lab workers had helped the Re-Cos escape. I hoped it was the five mothers. But I also knew it was too big a leap to make such an assumption

"Did you talk to the crew about what Ferris said?" I asked.

"No."

"Why not?"

"You should do it."

My phone rang. It was Ferris.

"Get going. I need you and your crew at the Info and Comms Center asap. Kit and Zac will meet you there."

"Yes, sir. We're on our way."

As Lake drove Zac's ATU towards Urb One, we could see that even more people had come out onto the streets. Most were pacing around in confusion, not knowing what to do, but some individuals seemed to be urging them into action. Was this the beginning of the mass panic that Ferris had feared when Zac had wanted him to broadcast the labs raid video? Something was definitely stirring. As we continued our journey, we saw more and more Citizens leave their work places or their accommodation blocks. By the time we reached the northwest exit that leads to the Bio-Med Research Center, a large group of Citizens, including regular soldiers in uniform, was gathered in front of a unit of Specialist Bio-Security forces lined up across the exit to prevent them getting through.

Lake slowed down for a closer look. This wasn't a bunch of random people in panic. This was a swiftly growing crowd of focussed and determined Citizens with a common aim to break through the Bio-Security line and go to the Bio-Med Research Center. Ethan's video had worked as he had intended. He had roused the Citizens out of their numbness and out onto the streets. Whether fear, anger, or a mixture of both, was driving them was irrelevant. They were taking the first steps in asserting themselves, and now they were feeding off each other's energy. They were shouting, pushing, and shoving against the line of Bio-Security soldiers.

✦

Military vehicles equipped with broadcast systems blasted out above the noise of the crowd.

"Clear the streets! We have orders to shoot. Clear the streets! This is your final warning. Clear the streets, or we will shoot."

But the crowd wasn't listening. Zac had been right. The Citizens had been waiting all their lives for this opportunity to unite and fight back. Their arousal wasn't just about the labs. It wasn't even about the threat of a virus. It was a people finally breaking free. We knew that. The Bio-Security soldiers knew that.

Lake skirted the ATU around the edge as the crowd surged forward and charged the blockade. The Bio-Security troops raised their rifles. The officer in charge ordered them to fire. The soldiers stood firm. The crowd kept coming. The soldiers stared at them down their rifle barrels. The officer roared at his soldiers to "Fire! Fire!"

The soldiers stood as if paralyzed. The front line of the crowd broke through. Some soldiers got knocked aside in the rush. But not one soldier opened fire. Instead, they raised their rifles to point harmlessly skyward and let the crowd pour through.

Nothing would stop the crowd now. Not guns and bullets, not orders from faceless dictators. Not even the threat of a deadly virus.

We arrived at the Info and Comms Center and parked up by the front entrance. Zac appeared and quickly ushered us inside.

"The Supreme Council has refused to condemn human experiments. Kit's been talking to all The Grand Controllers and all The Implementors. Most of them are too shit scared to do anything about it, but some of them have joined with her in a take-over bid."

"What?" I couldn't believe what he was saying.

"Seven Grand Controllers and four Implementors are upstairs with her now. They're going to broadcast the raid video publicly. If it all goes wrong, The Supreme Council will send a snatch squad here to arrest them. We need lookouts front and back and from upstairs. At the first hint of an arrest party coming, we will open fire to create a delay to let you get Kit and her team out of here. Kit knows where to go. Don't stop for anything. Got that?"

"Where's Ferris?"

"Don't worry about Ferris. He has his own orders. Place your lookouts and come upstairs."

"Reyn and I will stay here and cover the front," offered Peak.

"OK, Adar and I will cover the rear," said April.

Lake and I followed Zac upstairs to the Info and Comms suite where Kit and a bunch of stern men and women—the seven Grand Controllers and four Implementors—were waiting for us.

As soon as Kit saw me, she pointed to a camcorder already set up on a tripod at a front window with the best view over Urb One's streets and Center.

"Hazel, I want you to film everything that's happening on the streets below so we can live stream it to the public monitors. One of the technicians here will show you how."

"Yes, Grand Controller."

Zac took up a position at another front window, with a long view of the street leading from the Center of Urb One up to the Info and Comms building. Lake took a window overlooking the rear of the building.

A technician appeared and gave me a quick rundown on operating the camera. All I had to do was switch it on, point it, and zoom in on any interesting action. There wasn't much now that the crowd had forced their way through the Bio-Security blockade and was heading for the Bio-Med Research Center.

The technician then informed Kit that all was ready for her in the recording studio, and she and the rest of her group followed him out.

I looked around at Zac and Lake. A government takeover had never been part of our plan. We should be back with Tern and Cale and Tork and Faze by now. We should be on our way to a new life, free from the tyranny of The Supreme Council and their precious Moral Code. I knew that if Zac and Lake, and the rest of my crew, had to hold off an arrest party, I would be the only one with a chance of escape, along with Kit and her team. The rest would all be killed. But what was the alternative? We were soldiers. We couldn't back out now.

After a few minutes, the wall monitors flickered into life. I glanced towards my nearest one and saw the seven Grand Controllers and the four Implementors bunched around Kit, who sat in the middle and introduced each one by their title and ID numerical. Then, as the studio camera zoomed in on her, she began her public address to The Citizenship. I watched the still empty streets below through my camcorder lens as I listened to Kit speaking.

"Citizens, we have come together to offer you our assurances that all laboratory experiments on humans and animals have ended. I personally issued the order to stop them, and shut down the laboratories as soon as I became aware that such experiments were taking place. Military personnel, acting under my instructions, raided the Bio-Medical Research Center two days ago and arrested the Director and all staff working in the human experiment laboratories. All human subjects are now receiving proper care and treatment from fully trained medical experts. Such terrible suffering should never have been imposed on our people. All of us here today condemn it utterly and totally. We are now going to show you the film taken during that raid. I must warn you that it makes grim viewing, but you have the right to know what was being done to your fellow Citizens for your supposed good."

I glanced back from my camera and saw Kit's image replaced by the raid video showing Ferris' soldiers charging into the Bio-Med Center, and the horror of that place rushed back to me. Once again, I relived the raiding party barging through the animal labs. I heard the animals screaming in terror. I watched Ferris' Bio-Haz suited soldiers moving along the corridors and into the wards. I saw the cubicles, each with their array of beeping machines and monitors, the bruised, bandaged, unrecognizable human subjects hooked up to those machines. Again, I saw the lab director and staff's arrest and the new medics hurrying in to care for the human subjects. Although I'd been there and witnessed it live, seeing it on screen made it even more gruesome.

Kit's voice came in over the final scenes.

"As you know, an unknown individual has threatened to release a deadly virus on us. This individual is unaware that what he is demanding has already been achieved. I have reliable intelligence that he is not anywhere near Urb One—his broadcast has been traced to a remote location in the bush—nor does he have any accomplices within Urb One. We, therefore, believe that the threat posed by this man is non-existent.

We also want to make you aware that, a short time ago, several hundred of your fellow Citizens, acting on their own initiative, came out onto the streets of Urb One in protest at what had been going on in the laboratories. These Citizens are now making their way to the Bio-Med Research Center to make their feelings known. We fully support them in taking this action. However, now that the laboratories are no longer functioning, I would ask these Citizens to return to the Center of Urb One. And I am asking all of you watching this in your living quarters and in your workplaces to come out and join them here in the Center. If what you have just seen in the video frightens and sickens you, if you want to break free of this regime that dictates and controls every moment of your lives, come out onto the streets now."

Already, through my camera lens, I could see people coming out onto the streets below. I glanced around at the monitor. Yes! My film was live streaming. Everyone in their quarters or their workplaces was seeing the Center of Urb One filling up with protestors. Zac and Lake were also taking quick glances at the monitors. I caught Lake's eye, and she grinned and raised her fist in salute to me.

Kit's voice came in again over the images of the crowd building up outside.

"Go to the Center of Urb One now. Take it over. Make your feelings known. That is your right. You have the power to reclaim your own lives and create the future you want—a future where you are free to care for each other, help each other, and love each other. Go now. Let us leave fear behind. Fear is how they control us. Go, and others will join you."

Zac yelled from the background.

"Two armored trucks coming in from the eastern corner."

I swung the camcorder and zoomed in.

"Get them out now!" Zac shouted to me.

I ran to the studio and shouted, "We have to get out. Now! Come on!"

But Kit and the group were glued to the screen, which was still sending live pictures from my camcorder. Kit called to me.

"Look."

I looked and saw a crowd gather around the two trucks, blocking their progress.

"They're not letting them through," said Kit. "We can't leave now. We have to keep broadcasting."

"But if the soldiers in the trucks open fire . . ."

She interrupted me, "I don't believe they will. They've never before been ordered to fire indiscriminately into a crowd. They're not trained that way."

She was right, up to a point. Ordinary soldiers like Zac and me and Lake and my crew were trained as helpers and defenders, not attackers. We were drivers, construction workers, admin assistants, and, as with my job in Pol Com, investigators and security escorts. We weren't trained to mow people down. Even those guarding government buildings were there mainly to make the occupants appear important.

Other units were trained to be aggressors, like the Specialist Search ones operating in the bush. But I'd witnessed the Specialist Bio-Security soldiers refuse to fire on the crowd earlier. And I'd seen other soldiers in uniform taking part in the protests. Was there hope? Could Kit and the seven Grand Controllers and the four Implementors that had sided with her really pull off a takeover? Would the other Grand Controllers and Implementors sit back and let a takeover happen? The Supreme Council definitely wouldn't. The arrival of the armored trucks proved that.

Kit's phone rang. The rest of us concentrated on watching the crowd face down the armored trucks while she answered. The sound, as picked up by my camera mic, was distant and muffled, but we could still hear the crowd yelling at the trucks. Some were even thumping them with their fists.

Kit finished her conversation and signaled to the studio technician to restart filming as she turned to face the camera.

"Today, at fourteen hundred hours, The Supreme Council was disbanded. All six members have been taken into custody by our Military Intelligence forces and charged with treason against The Citizenship. I also have to inform you that nineteen Grand Controllers and eight Implementors have voluntarily resigned from their positions. I, and the remaining Grand Controllers and Implementors present here with me, will now form a new government. This new government, which will be known as The New Citizens' Congress, will be based on the principles of openness and transparency and on respect for the rights and freedom of each Citizen to live a full emotional and intellectual life free from tyranny and fear. All military units and institutions will be led by the Commander-in-Chief of Military Forces, who henceforth will be a member of The New Citizens Congress. We promise to do our utmost to make the transition from the previous cruel totalitarian regime as peaceful as possible. All we ask from you is your patience and co-operation. Together we are strong. Together we are free."

The monitor switched back to the scenes from my camera. The crowd had trebled in size. Many were cheering and punching their fists in the air, and more people were coming in from the side streets. The two armored trucks were now slowly and carefully reversing out of the way.

Kit made several more broadcasts confirming that the old regime was no more. The people out on the streets broke into cheering each time they heard her words. But there was little else for them to do. The retreat of the armored trucks proved that there would be no opposition to the take-over. Kit asked that all Citizens return to their regular duties in the morning to allow the New Citizens Congress time to formulate their program of reforms.

Ferris arrived and made a broadcast introducing himself as the new Commander-in-Chief of all military forces. He also announced that all political and administrative institutions and buildings had been taken over and were now in control of The New Citizens Congress. The take-over had succeeded without any bloodshed or destruction.

CHAPTER

25

I awoke some time mid-morning and felt the weight of Lake's sleeping body leaning against me. I stayed still so I wouldn't disturb her. We had both fallen asleep on a couch in Ferris' safe house. The rest of my crew were also asleep in various armchairs around the room. This would probably be the last time we would all be together. Zac would go back to find Tern. They would continue working together, and maybe someday soon, when the old laws became obsolete, they would be able to stay together. April, Adar, Reyn, and Peak would take up their new posts as junior military operatives at Command Headquarters.

Lake still hadn't said what she would choose. Would she join the others at Command HQ? It was a good offer. Or would she choose to return to the Medical Training Center in a better post? With her skills, she would do well in either posting.

I would do well, too, with Kit. Driver and Personal Assistant to a member of the new government would be a prestigious post. I'd be taking messages for her, making sure she got to meetings on time, maybe even attending meetings with her, taking notes, keeping her safe. I'd be bored out of my skull. I'd be right back at the start, this time without even an assistant for company.

I felt Lake shift beside me. She was awake. They were all awake. I'd been too deep in my thoughts and hadn't noticed.

"Where's Ferris?" asked Adar.

"We'd better start calling him Commander-in-Chief now that we're going to be working for him," said Reyn.

"I wouldn't worry," said April. "We won't get to see him. He never paid us any attention anyway."

"Maybe he'll make us his personal bodyguard," said Peak.

"Unlikely," said Adar. "We'll probably be stuck on guard duty somewhere."

"Hazel can put in a good word for us with The New Citizens Congress now that she's going to be hanging out with one of them," said Lake.

"Two," said Zac. "Don't forget Ferris is a Congressman as well."

"Yeah, Hazel. You've got it made now," said April.

I looked at Lake sitting beside me.

"What have you decided?" I asked her.

She shrugged, just like she used to when I first met her.

That's what did it for me. I knew then and there that I couldn't revert to being what I used to be, and I knew Zac couldn't either.

"You're not going back, are you?" I asked him.

"I have to go get Tern. I'll bring Cale and Tork and Faze back here," he answered.

"And then what?"

"I don't intend hanging around."

"I'm coming with you"

"You know where I'm heading?

"The Sick Lands."

✦

I borrowed Zac's ATU and tracked down Kit and Ferris at Kit's office. I needed to tell them why I wouldn't be taking up Ferris' offer—I owed them that much at least. They understood. Maybe if Ferris' mother were alive and in The Sick Lands, he would've come with us. Perhaps, if Kit were not now so involved in setting up The New Citizens' Congress, she would've come too. We knew her mother, like Zac's, was there somewhere. I promised Kit we would search for both mothers.

✦

When I arrived back at the safe house, Zac was waiting and ready to go.

And so was Lake, April, Adar, Reyn, and Peak.

"We talked about it after you left," Lake informed me. "We're coming with you."

"What about Cale and Tork and Faze?" I asked.

"If they want to come back here and accept the new posts that Ferris has offered them, they can take your ATU and drive themselves back. But why would they? Tork and Faze won't want to be separated. We'll have to wait and see what Cale wants. It's his choice."

Had I known they would do this? Had I dared even to hope? Yes. I had dared. I had hoped.

ACKNOWLEDGMENTS

My thanks to Witches With Wolves writing group, especially Mary Montague and Lesley Walsh, for their support. Also, to Giles Read of the Radio Society of Great Britain for his generous technical advice.

ABOUT THE AUTHOR

TERESA GODFREY lives in Co Fermanagh, Northern Ireland and writes poetry, short stories and screenplays. Her work has been published in various journals and anthologies in the UK and Ireland, including *The Honest Ulsterman, Boyne Berries, Crannog, Curlew, Blue Nib Chapbook V*, the Community Arts Partnership anthologies, and in *Her Other Language: Northern Irish Women Writers Address Domestic Violence and Abuse*. Her debut poetry collection, *This, Also, Is Mercy*, was published by Summer Palace Press in 2021.

Teresa has written five feature film scripts on commission and had two children's dramas—*Coolaboola* and *You Looking At Me?*—broadcast on Channel 4 television in the UK. Her feature film script, *The Redemption of Charlie Adams*, was shortlisted for the Orange/Pathe Prize and the Miramax Screenwriting Award and her screenplay adaptation of Ann Pilling's book, *Black Harvest*, won the 2005 European Union New Talent Award.

Made in the USA
Columbia, SC
24 March 2022

58036661R00143